Inn the Dead of Winter

by

Rhonda Blackhurst

The Spirit Lake Mysteries

Inn the Dead of Winter

COPYRIGHT © 2024 by Rhonda Blackhurst

Cover Art by *The Wild Rose Press, Inc.*

The Wild Rose Press, Inc.
PO Box 708
Adams Basin, NY 14410-0708
Visit us at www.thewildrosepress.com

Publishing History
First Edition, 2025
Trade Paperback ISBN 978-1-5092-6006-5
Digital ISBN 978-1-5092-6007-2

The Spirit Lake Mysteries
Published in the United States of America

Acknowledgments

The path to publication involves countless people, and I'm extremely grateful to every one of them. In particular, thank you to: Retired police chief and my husband, Clint, who advises me on procedure and is a good sport when I choose to deviate from what's real for the sake of story; My boys, Ben & Alex, who inspire me every day; My grandbabies, who stole my heart from day one and show me how important it is to take time out to play; My mom & dad, having always supported my passion for writing; Brenda and Sandy, my sisters by blood and choice—I love you; Sister writers Karen Whalen, Karen Docter, and Shawn McGuire who walk this path with me; Becky Sue Epstein for your help in making the book better; Sisters in Crime and Sisters in Crime-Colorado Chapter—I could never hope to find a more supportive, fun, group of writers; The Wild Rose Press—it's such an honor to be a chosen rose in their garden; My editor Ally Robertson—what a gem to work with; Cover artist RJ Morris, who works her magic to make the book visually enticing to readers; And to you, my readers—without you this journey would be lonely. Thank you for your support and faith in me.

Chapter 1

We were in the dead of winter in Spirit Lake, Minnesota, a town dubbed the paranormal capital of the nation. I gazed through the frosted windowpane at the ominous fog that hung low over Whisper Lake.

I crossed my arms in front of me, briskly rubbed my biceps, and shivered. It was a brutal cold that seeped deep into the bones and seemed to even send the inn's resident ghost into hibernation.

The library's gas fireplace clicked off by itself, the dancing flames disappearing. I guess I wasn't in the room alone after all. I shuddered and glanced down at my feet where Aspen, my red retriever emotional support animal, stretched lazily on his side, eyes half closed, unfazed.

Since the 1940s, guests of the Spirit Lake Inn, home to the famous apparition, have heard a woman's whispers on the lake, earning its name, Whisper Lake, the fireplace in the library turned off and on by itself, the espresso machine in the coffee bar hummed to life, and many other unexplainable incidents, all while no one else was present.

The old grandfather clock in the corner of the room ticked methodically as the pendulum swayed back and forth. When the clock's St. Michael chime announced the top of the hour—and fifteen minutes until teatime downstairs—Aspen rolled onto his stomach and pushed himself up onto all fours.

"Come on, boy," I said, ruffling the fur on his neck. "Snack time."

We checked in with Jade and Lily at the front desk, and when I headed toward the dining room, Aspen lay beside Jade.

I narrowed my eyes at him. "Traitor."

Jade snickered and reached inside the lower desk drawer and pulled out a bag. "I've got some peanut butter treats for him here."

"He can be bribed to do anything for peanut butter." I grinned as I watched Aspen gingerly take the treat from Jade's hand. "I'll be in the dining room giving it the once over."

"I wouldn't trust Tony, either."

I turned away and said over my shoulder, "You better be nice to him since he's the one who makes your meals when you're here."

I paused in front of the dining room's bank of windows, spotting an ice fisher fighting the wind and snow on the lake under the sky's dark ceiling. I shivered. Given how fast one could freeze to death in little time, it was no wonder it was called the dead of winter.

Apron tied around my waist, I arranged the dessert table just so and made sure the coffee pot and hot water for tea were ready.

"Andie Rose?"

Wiping my hands on the apron, I turned to face Marcie, the inn's maintenance worker. She was better equipped for the job than any man I knew.

"Yeah?"

"I'm going up on the roof. Snow needs scraping off again," she said. "That last snowfall is putting too much stress on it."

I grimaced. "That makes me so nervous with you up there, Marcie. It's icy. What if you fall and—"

"Andie Rose Kaczmarek," she scolded. "Would you be saying that if I were a man?"

Realizing my error, I said, "No. Absolutely not."

"Okay then. I've been doing it for years. Your grandpa and Honey knew better than to fuss about it."

"Noted."

Everyone knew my grandmother as Honey. Grandpop called her that all the time, and even I thought that was her real name until I was in my teens. Even then, I still called her Honey, along with everyone else in town.

"Is it okay to tell you to be careful?"

"Sure." She waved her hand as she turned to leave. "The only reason I told you at all is so you can advise the guests not to walk under the eve. They'll get buried by snow falling over the edge. Don't want a lawsuit."

She strode into the foyer and opened the door. A swirl of glistening flakes in an icy wind blew through the doorway as it closed behind her.

"All good?" Tony Valentino, the inn's chef, poked his head around the corner.

"Perfect." I took a step back and admired the beauty. "The dessert table, not you," I clarified, earning a hearty chuckle. Aspen, apparently done with his treat from Jade, wandered in and sat beside me.

"Aren't you just a hoot," he cracked.

"Lady Lucy paid me a visit up in the library," I said. "You're jealous, aren't you?"

He gave me the side eye while tilting his chin down. "Lady who?"

3

"The ghost. I named her Lady Lucy."

He rolled his eyes and shook his head. "Sir Archibald sounds more distinguished."

My stomach grumbled. "Maybe I should test one of these treats."

"From what I've heard, you can't stop at one."

I shot him a *watch-it* glare, and he sniggered. It was no secret to my staff that I was coming up on my seven-year anniversary in sobriety. From there I became a certified life coach and learned tricks of the trade to help others work through dysfunctional lives. Not that I was known for following the advice I gave to others.

I'd been lucky to find an AA sponsor, Sister Alice, to help keep me in line. She'd been sober for thirty years. "Traded one habit for another," she'd said. Sister Alice was sixty-five years old and moved back to Spirit Lake when she was thirty. Grandad and Honey gave her a room at the inn until she, in her words, "got her poop in a group."

If there's one word I'd use to describe Sister Alice, it would be... Well, it's impossible to sum her character up in one word. She was quirky, funny, spunky, feisty, and persistent. Sometimes in the most annoying ways. But underneath it all, her devotion to God was unbreakable, and she had a kind spirit. Sometimes one just had to try a little harder to see it. And how that woman loved her eyewear. *Uffda*. She owned more pairs of brightly colored frames (some with lipstick to match) than I had underwear. And I had a lot. It wasn't a surprise then that she and by-the-book Sister Ida, the house moderator and superior, clashed like cymbals. Sometimes it rose to a crescendo. Father Vincent had been called to mediate on more than one occasion.

"All right, then," Tony said. "I'm heading out. Izzy's starting dinner prep."

I gave him a thumbs up. "Have a good rest of your day. And behave."

"Right. What you don't know won't hurt you. And heads up, Izzy's a pain today."

I blew through pursed lips and shook my head. "Of course she is. What do you expect? She's seventeen." Izzy was Tony's sous-chef. She was a sixteen-year-old child genius when she came to work for us last fall and had just turned seventeen in December. "You're the one who talked me into hiring her."

"Well, even I make mistakes," he grumbled. I gave him *the* look. "I'm kidding. You know that."

I wandered toward the parlor, where giggles fluttered from across the room.

Three guests, Tina, Tootsie, and Carmen, huddled near the fireplace talking while their spouses stood by the window adjacent in silence. Four more guests drifted into the room, drawn toward the fireplace as if the flames were magnets.

"The dining room is open for afternoon tea, cucumber finger sandwiches, and scones," I announced.

"I hate to leave the warmth of the fireplace," Tootsie said. "The beauty of the snow is astounding, but I'd forgotten how cold it can get here." She tugged the sleeves of her white sweater over her hands, her long pink nails peeking out from beneath.

"Doesn't help that this is a brutally cold one," Sister Alice said from the doorway.

I turned toward her. "Perfect timing for tea. Or did you plan it that way?"

"Both." She said to Tootsie, "Nice to see you again,

dear."

"You too, Sister." Tootsie enveloped her in a hug that left Sister Alice breathless.

Once she broke free from Tootsie's grasp, she said, "I'll be back in a jiff." She turned to leave, encouraging Aspen to follow her.

Apparently, Tootsie and her husband, Simon, had been here before. And apparently Tootsie saw my quizzical expression.

"Third time here," she said. "We prefer the silence after the holiday craze. We have enough crazy at home over the holidays."

The inn was exceptionally busy during the summer, but even more so in September through the first week of January. The holidays drew a full house, not only because we decorated the inn and celebrated them in big fashion, but because the ghost was rumored to be more active and likely to be seen during the autumn months leading up to Halloween. "I take it ghost hunting isn't your thing?"

"Meh," she said with a wave of her hand.

Getting back to teatime, I said, "Get your refreshments and bring them back in here. Best of both worlds."

"Now that," Carmen held up a finger, "is the best idea ever."

It was Carmen's first time here. Her husband, Bobby, said he'd been here years ago with his first wife. Something Carmen didn't seem pleased with when he'd mentioned it to me.

"Nuh-uh," Tootsie said. "The hot tub tonight is the best idea ever." She turned toward me and grinned. "I've talked a few others into joining the winter hot tub experience tonight after dark. I can't believe I'm the only one who has done it."

Bobby gave her a disparaging smile. "You're crazy. Where's the fun in freezing to death?"

"I agree," Jerry said. "You wouldn't catch me out there in this cold for nothin'."

"Well, your wife disagrees. Don't you, Tina? The cold air is part of the magical beauty of it," Tootsie explained. "The heat of the hot water on a frosty night, the snow so pristine under the stars of a cloudless night. It's absolutely magical. Of course, it's extra cold this year, but that makes the hot tub better. They predicted clear skies after ten."

"Splendid." Amusement tugged at a corner of Jerry's lips, and he said to his wife, "You're crazy. I'll be right here, in front of the fireplace, waiting for you. Should take all of five minutes before you zip back in here." He chuckled.

"I'll be in here with Jerry," Bobby said. "Freezing to death isn't appealing. The stars are just as visible through the window."

"Chickens." Tootsie clucked, then guffawed. "Just you wait. You'll wish you had joined us. Live a little." She looked at me for obvious back up. "Tell them I'm right."

I admit I agreed with Tootsie on the issue. The experience was nothing less than exhilarating. But I held up a hand, shook my head, and chuckled. "I'm not getting involved. There are legitimate arguments for both sides."

Tootsie stood, touched Carmen and Tina's arms, and encouraged them to follow. "Let's go get some refreshments, shall we?" She glanced at Bobby, Jerry, and Simon. "Want us to get yours? Just in case it's too cold in there for you."

Tootsie's attitude hung between them, and I held my breath for a moment.

"Knock it off, Toots." Simon's voice was a low grumble.

"Knock what off?" She turned on him. "Showing the ladies how to live a little? That they're not only a mom and a wife, but they're also their own person?"

Simon grasped his wife's upper arm. "Toots," he warned. He turned his attention toward Bobby and Jerry. "You'll have to excuse my wife, gentlemen. She's become a bit too, shall we say, independent, as she gets older."

She released a heavy sigh. "Lighten up, Simon. You say that like it's a bad thing. I have always been independent. This isn't the dark ages. Women have every right to be independent of men."

Again, I agreed wholeheartedly with Tootsie, but swallowed my retort to Simon. A gift sobriety had given me. The ability to keep my mouth shut sometimes.

"Refreshments," I said merrily as I could to lift the cloud that levitated in the room. Two guests had been smart and skittered from the room unnoticed from all except me.

"Aspen's with Jade," Sister Alice said as she came through the door. She quirked a brow as she scanned the guests and touched the crucifix that hung around her neck. "Do I sense tension in the room? What did I miss?"

Tootsie took a deep breath and exhaled slowly. "My husband emerging from a cave."

Sister Alice quirked an eyebrow.

"Toots," Simon said again, this time with different

affect.

Bobby appeared indifferent, and Jerry's lips pressed tight beneath his full mustache.

Tootsie gave them a tight smile. "Sorry if I overstepped, gentlemen."

Simon snickered. "*If* you overstepped? Come now, love." He rested his hand on her lower back and steered her toward the dining room.

"No problem," Jerry said, but his tone said otherwise.

Bobby draped an arm loosely over Carmen's shoulder. "No harm, no foul, as the saying goes."

Jerry and Tina trailed behind them, and Jerry said quietly to his wife, "This cold weather is getting to me. Think I'll join you tonight. It'll be a good story for my colleagues, if nothing else."

Tina pecked his cheek. "They'll never believe it."

Sister Alice and I stood side-by-side, watching until they'd left the room.

"And that," Sister Alice pointed toward the doorway, "is why I am relieved to never marry."

"Pshaw," I said. "Like you have none of that drama at your house?"

"I don't share a bed, or even a room, with someone who's mad at me. Big difference."

****

After finishing a life coaching session with a woman from town, I walked her to the door, then went back to my office and stretched my arms high above my head. It was already seven-thirty. Keeping flexible hours helped grow my business, and I quickly procured four outside clients. I started offering guests a free session a month ago and got new clients, including Tootsie Timmons.

I meandered out to the reception desk where Aspen lay at Jade's feet. Lily had long ago left for the day and Jade, her shift up at eight, straightened the desk.

When I reached her, she said, "I swear it's like picking up after my kiddo here."

I smiled. It was the same thing Lily, decades older, said about Jade. Lily was in her sixties and had worked here for Grandad and Honey for most of her working years. Jade's language annoyed her. But I nipped that in the bud the first time I heard it. What she did away from the inn wasn't my business, but what's said at the inn, was. "First time guests don't need to think they're at some cheap, chintzy place," I'd told her. "And I can't imagine Grandpop and Honey allowed it either." She didn't dispute it. When I told her what my mother used to say, *Swearing is for illiterates, Andie Rose*, Jade had winced and said, "Ouch. That's harsh. No offense, but your mom sounds like a snob." I couldn't argue. While I wouldn't call my mother a snob, she wasn't exactly low maintenance.

I snickered as I thought about my mother's most recent phone call. Her vulgar language had shocked me. After the call, I'd half expected her to show up on my doorstep to put some distance between her and my dad who, in her words, "was driving her up the batsh*t crazy wall." As much as I wanted to sympathize with her predicament, I couldn't. Instead, it was my dad I sympathized with.

I observed Jade's growing belly. "Soon you'll have two little bambinos, and it won't be as easy." As if I knew anything about raising children.

"The expert that you are," she said, as if reading my mind.

"I love them as long as they are someone else's."

"You never want kids?"

I made a sound through closed lips, indicating *I don't know*. "My mother drops hints every time we talk, whining about when she'd finally become a Nana." I poked my pointer finger in the air. "Nana, not grandma," she said.

"What do you say when she goads you?" Jade asked.

"Nothing. I let it fall on empty ears. There was no winning with my mother."

Jade laid a hand on her belly. "I wish he'd come already. With my due date only five weeks away, Tom is driving me up the wall."

I hadn't liked her husband when I met him. But since that was shortly after he'd learned about his wife's affair, I had to cut the guy some slack. Jade's brief affair with the past chef at the inn had far-reaching consequences.

"Sounds like some guests are going to brave the hot tub tonight."

She snickered. "Suckers." She stood, and Aspen rose to a sitting position. "I did a polar plunge once. Never did that again."

I laughed. "This is hardly the same thing. With a hot tub, you're not jumping into freezing cold water. What charity did you do the polar plunge for?"

"None. It was on a dare when the lake was freezing over. I was young and stupid. As opposed to being old and stupid like these guys are tonight."

I took a step back and crossed my arms in front of me. "Excuse me? I grew up with a hot tub and we did that all the time."

"You mean they had hot tubs way back then?"

I gasped and turned toward Izzy in mock dismay.

"How rude." She snickered. "When you first started here, it was difficult to get two or more words from you, much less without attitude. What happened?" Although the attitude still lurked beneath the surface, it didn't show its head as much.

She grinned in reply.

"You done?" I asked.

"Yep. Getting ready to leave."

"That was fast."

"Yeah, I'm younger than you, so I move faster."

I scowled at her. "For your information, I'm not much older than Jade, and I don't hear you making cracks about her."

"'Cause she scares the crap out of me," Izzy said.

Now it was Jade who scowled. "You're an annoying little twerp. Go home."

A devilish smile played on her lips. "Mission accomplished." She looked at me. "By the time I'm your age, Kaz, I'm gonna own this inn."

She'd taken to giving me the nickname as a shortened version of my last name. Apparently, Andie Rose was too long. More likely because she was a typical teen.

"Not for sale." She'd made that same comment more than once before.

"Everything's for sale for the right price."

"Not the inn." While her goals impressed me, this wasn't just *any* inn. It was the love child of Grandpop and Honey. An extension of family. There was not enough money in the world to buy that.

My grandparents had owned two inns, one in Colorado and this one in Minnesota. When they died, they left both to my parents. My parents then gave me a choice of which I wanted—I chose to stay in Minnesota and they kept the one in Colorado.

I reached my hand down, rested it on Aspen's head, and gazed out the window, contemplating going into town to see Sister Alice, but the frosted windows and blowing snow gave me pause. A phone call to her, then curling up in my room with a good book, suddenly became more appealing.

After saying goodbye to Izzy and Jade and locking the front door, I walked past the windows toward my room. Several people lined the edges of the large hot tub. The steam rising furiously in the frosty air made it nearly impossible to see who they were. I watched for another minute, then slid my phone from my back pocket to call Sister Alice.

Chapter 2

Despite the brutal cold temperature of minus twenty-five degrees, I brought Aspen outside to do his business and then for a brief walk. After five minutes, Aspen didn't even put up a fuss when we turned back for the door; not even the you-never-let-me-walk-long-enough sad eyes he gave me when I didn't have him out at least half an hour. It was supposed to climb up to a whopping ten degrees this afternoon. Barely warm enough to take him out on the trail by Big Spirit Lake, but we'd give it a shot.

"Good thing I love you so much, boy," I slurred through stiff, frozen lips. I stomped the snow from my boots on the mat by the back entrance when I noticed the hot tub cover leaning against it. Proverbial dollar signs flew out the window as if watching a reel as I pictured the next electric bill. I stepped over to lift the cover onto the tub. Aspen stayed on the mat by the door. "Sissy," I grumbled playfully. I didn't blame him. It was so cold my nostrils were sticking together.

As soon as the door closed behind us, I slipped off my red wool mittens and rubbed my hands together vigorously. Indoor heat had just become the top of my morning gratitude list that Sister Alice, as my AA sponsor, insisted I start. "And don't be lazy and do it in your head," she'd ordered. "It needs to be a written list."

"Yes, Sergeant Alice," I'd said while saluting.

I shed my winter clothes in my upstairs studio apartment with a kitchenette and living area. Then I went downstairs with Aspen to the foyer where Lily was listening as Marcie complained about something. The giant desk dwarfed Lily's slight frame. I placed my palms gently on my cheeks, warming them.

"Hey, Marcie. What's up?" I asked.

"I don't know why it's so hard for people to pick up after themselves when they leave the hot tub." She shook her head.

My gaze darted around the room.

"Don't worry." She waved her hand in dismissal. "I wouldn't be talking about it if anyone was within hearing range. It's time for me to drain and clean it, I guess. Poor Lily had to listen to me vent my frustrations."

"Marcie's way of saying good morning," Lily teased.

"Well, I put the lid on already," I said. "Not that it's a big deal to take it back off." I couldn't imagine why Marcie was so worked up about it. She's not the one who paid the utility bills.

"All right. I'll work on cleaning the heating vents instead until it warms up some. Supposed to be a real heat wave this afternoon." She sniggered.

"Could one of you come up with a weather resistant sign to post by the hot tub? Maybe that'll help."

"I'm on it," Marcie said.

"Anyone seen Frank?" I asked. "His car is in the lot."

Both shook their heads.

"He sure is spending a lot of time here. More than I'd expect in the winter months. Is that usual for him?" Frank Flowers was our master gardener, managing our large yard, the flowers, and the potting shed. I'd only stepped foot in there a few times since I'd taken over the inn.

"I'm going to run out there and see what's keeping him so busy this winter."

"Like that?" Lily screeched. "Take my coat or you'll catch your death. It's on the coatrack." She pointed toward the side of the door.

I scoffed. "Your coat would never fit me. Besides, the shed is well-insulated and heated. Kind of. Okay, not so much. But I'm only gonna be a minute. And I've got Aspen to keep me warm." I tugged my sleeves down over my hands and wrapped my arms around my middle, preparing for a mad dash.

"You've plum lost your mind," Marcie said.

I chuckled. "You sound like Sister Alice."

"Don't make Aspen a victim of your crazy," Jade said. "Leave him in here."

As if agreeing, Aspen trotted over to Jade and slid into a lying position at her feet. I smiled. "Fine."

The door slammed behind me and, hitting a patch of ice, I nearly fell on my butt as I turned to run. I caught my balance right before I went down. "Holy wicked whiskey!"

Despite my fingers covered by my sweater, they quickly burned from the cold. I opened the door to the shed and kicked it shut behind me before I gagged at the smell, one I was all too familiar with from my youth. I bit the inside of my cheek. Surely, I had to be wrong. As far as I knew, Frank was the only one who came out here. We kept clay pots for decorating and potted plants in the greenhouse. And the humidity. *Uffda*. During the winter months, Minnesota's climate was drier, especially in these bitter cold snaps.

I blew into my cupped hands to warm them. "Frank? I think you can turn off the humidifier." He didn't answer, so I called his name louder. Still no answer. He hadn't been inside the inn, so if he wasn't here, then where was he?

Blowing warm air once more into my cupped hands, I lay them against my cheeks, and turned the corner to the newest addition. Grandpop built it shortly before he fell ill. I reached for the knob to open the door, but it was locked.

Tossing all the oddities around in my mind, I knew full well what was in the locked room. But this was Frank here. Could someone be taking advantage of the room while Frank typically wasn't here so much? Except he was this winter.

"This is so weird," I whispered into the empty room. Maybe he was just lonely at home since his wife died recently, and he wanted company, even if it was just the pots and plants. But where was he?

I put my hands on my hips and scanned the shed before I tried the doorknob again. As if it had unlocked itself in the past ten seconds. But since we have a ghost here, it was possible. Except its presence and oddities usually occurred in the boathouse by the lake or inside the inn. Particularly the library and the coffee bar.

The main door opened with a gust of cold air, followed by stomping of boots. "Frank?" I said as I peered around the corner.

"Yumpin yimminy," he exclaimed. "You scared me half ta death." When he realized where I was, he quickly came back to me. "Whatcha doin' here, Miss Andie?"

"Looking for you."

His eyebrows shot up. "Why would ya be doin' that? I'm fine, don'tcha know. Alive and kickin', my plants keepin' me company."

I jerked my thumb toward the door on the addition. "Frank, what's in there?"

He dropped his gaze to the floor. "No idea. Haven't been in there since last summer."

"Do you ordinarily keep it locked?"

"Yes, ma'am. No sense keeping it open if I'm not usin' it."

"Can you open it for me, please? I didn't bring my keys with me. Didn't even bring a coat." My teeth chattered and I wrapped my arms snug around my middle.

"I see that. Come here." He led me toward the front. "Here's a coat for ya. You young people don't know how to dress much for the weather. Heck, scarves draped around your necks like they're meant as a fashion statement or somethin' and no hats so they don't muss yer hair." He shook his head and handed me the coat.

I slipped it on. "Frank, the door to the back room? I have a good idea what's in there. Has someone else been using it?"

"No, ma'am."

"Well, if it's a dead rodent, we need to know and dispose of it. If someone is using the room without your knowledge, I need to know that as well. Open it please."

He exhaled and slowly swiped the keys from the countertop. "There's no way a rodent could get in there and no one else has a key 'cept me an' you." He slid the key into the keyhole and hesitated before opening the door. The room was dimly lit, but enough that I could see it contained exactly what I'd feared—a small marijuana

18

grow. I blew through pursed lips.

"What the devil is this?" he asked, eyes wide.

"We both know exactly what it is, Frank. But by whom?" I stayed silent a moment, wondering what to do. Call the police? That would give the inn a black eye to the community. Then again, it may give us more business. Just not legal business. If I didn't call the police right away, and someone found out before I called, I could risk getting shut down. I sat there on the proverbial fence until a solution descended upon me. "Frank, we need to disassemble this operation right now."

He gasped. "Disassemble it?"

"Yes. Completely. We'll know who the guilty party is by whoever throws the fit."

Frank hesitated with a pained expression. "Miss Andie, there's a lotta money here. Not ta mention a lotta medicinal value at stake, um-hm."

Heavy silence descended on us. Another glance at him and the realization fell on me like a bowling ball. "Something you want to tell me, Frank?"

"I wouldn't say I *want* to tell ya, Miss Andie, but…" His voice grew quieter and trailed off.

I exhaled a sigh of puzzlement and leaned against the door. "Frank, this is no minor offense. And I'm still befuddled that *you*, of all people, are responsible for this. What the—"

"It's legal in a lot of states."

"For medicinal purposes, yeah. But not recreational. And not here yet." A thought hit me, and I gasped and touched his arm gently. "Oh my gosh! Are you sick, Frank? Is that what this is about?"

His shoulders sagged. "Nah. Nothin' like that. But it ain't easy living on one income. Especially with the economy taking such a downturn and all."

I nearly choked. "Well, for God's sake, Frank, ask for a raise."

"I don't wanna be no bother, Miss Andie."

I closed my eyes and took a slow, deep breath. "Disassemble this—*now*. Then come in and see me so we can work something out. I want you here, Frank, not in a jail cell." I scanned the room, and my eyes fixed on some padlocked cabinets along the back wall. "What's in there?" I pointed at them. "And don't lie to me this time. I think that hurts more than anything else."

He cleared his throat, then mumbled, "Product."

"Product?" I said slowly, praying my assumption was wrong. But I knew it wasn't. "Frank…" I gave him the side eye. "Tell me it's not so."

"I'd like to, Miss Andie, but I can't."

I sighed with exasperation, still balancing on the wire of disbelief. Frank, of all my staff, I'd thought was the easiest—stable, no surprises, slow and steady. Did we ever *really* know people? I've worked with clients on that subject, but I'm often guilty of not following my own advice.

"Frank," I said in a low, stern voice, afraid to hear the answer. "Who have you been selling to?"

"No one from here. Promise." He motioned a cross over his chest.

I took a deep breath, pulling it together, before I said, "I don't care how you do it, but I want this gone by the end of the weekend. Whether that's destroying it or taking it somewhere else is up to you. But it'd better be gone from here. That gives you four days."

"So you won't call the police?"

"No guarantees. Frank, you're putting me, and the

entire inn, in jeopardy. Do you realize that? Other than the lie, that hurts more than anything else." I finally stole a glance at him. His slumped shoulders and bowed head trapped me in a web of guilt. I blew a slow breath through pursed lips. "I'm coming back out here on Monday, and it'd better be gone. No trace left whatsoever. Got it? Until then, I'm staying far away and know absolutely nothing about this. I'll deny it to my death."

"Yes, ma'am," Frank said.

I slid my arms out of his massive coat and handed it to him before turning to leave. I stood, my hand on the doorknob, and turned. He hadn't moved a muscle.

"Hey, Frank?"

"Yep?"

Somehow, he appeared more fragile now. "As disappointed as I am about this, I understand why you did it. And you're still my favorite." His lips curved ever so gently, before I turned and ran through the glacial air for the heat of the inn.

When I opened the door, Aspen trotted my way, parking himself at my feet. I reached down and gave him some lovin' while I glanced up at Lily and Simon Timmons in a discussion at the desk. Whatever it was about, Simon appeared a tad heated. *Good Grief.* Some time to get it together before diving into another confrontation would have been nice. I took a deep breath and started that way when my phone rang. I slipped it from the back pocket of my jeans and glanced at the display.

"Hey, Sister Alice. Good timing." I wandered to the parlor and stood in front of the fireplace.

"Can't say that there's such a thing as good timing when I tell you why I'm calling." I groaned inwardly. It was going to be one of these days, was it? When I didn't say anything, she continued. "They found a body in Big Spirit Lake."

"Holy wicked whiskey!" My mind spun furiously. "Who's *they*?"

"Police."

"Hm. Well, on the positive side of things—and I know this won't sound good—but at least it wasn't here at the inn this time. And that someone found it before Aspen and I stumbled upon it when I took him there this afternoon." I'd found a body at the inn last fall, bringing in the Halloween season in an unexpected fashion.

"Keep in mind when you go this afternoon that the police don't need your help. Stay out of their way."

"I'm insulted."

"Stop pouting. You know it's true. We're to keep our own side of the street clean. Not stick your nose in where it doesn't belong."

"I want to fire you as my sponsor."

She snorted with amusement. "Have at it. You're assuming you could find another one."

"Okay, I admit my reaction could be portrayed as insensitive." I closed my eyes and rubbed my temples with my thumb and middle finger.

"It was. God forgives us, thank goodness."

"You, anyway."

Sister Alice had been trying from here to Sunday to get me to go to St. Michael's. I came up with some outlandish but creative excuses. I teased her that if she didn't stop the pressure, I'd go to Spirit Vineyard Protestant. She'd snickered and said, "Whatever works."

"Be sure to hit up the meeting today," she said.

My presence in St. Michael's was mostly limited to

the AA meetings housed there in the basement. Meeting Sister Alice there was the gift that kept on giving. She proved sobriety to be a hoot and one didn't need to booze it up to have fun.

"Yeah, yeah. I know. That's where I get my entertainment." I watched Simon and Lily as I spoke. His irritation was clear, but toward whom or what, I couldn't guess. "What was the cause of death? With the arctic temps this winter, I'm guessing frozen to death."

"Appears so. Some guy found him in the spearing hole inside a fish house. Must have fallen in."

I clenched my teeth, then said, "*Eww*. That must've been quite the shock."

Those spearing holes, big enough for an enormous body to fall into, had always freaked me out. Then I had a thought. "I wonder if they're considering foul play?"

"More likely floated up from under the ice."

I shivered. "That'd be quite a fish story to tell."

"Regardless, they'll send the body to St. Cloud for the autopsy."

I glanced again at Simon, who now stood staring out the window, and Lily, who watched him. "Keep me posted." We hung up, and I strode to the reception desk.

"Hi, Simon. Everything okay?"

He looked at me as if noticing me for the first time. "Toots didn't come back to the room last night."

I hadn't planned on relationship coaching this early. Lily must have read my mind.

"I'll run to the kitchen and grab you a cup of coffee," she told me. "Simon, would you like one?"

He shook his head.

After Lily left, I asked, "Did you and Tootsie have an argument?"

He scowled. "That's absurd. Of course not. We don't fight."

First off, when someone in a marriage says they never fight, it was akin to someone assuring another that there was no judgment. There certainly was. Second, the interaction between them yesterday before teatime wasn't exactly cordial.

"When did you last see her?"

"Just before eleven last evening."

Simon's tone appeared to unsettle Aspen. I scratched his head and kept my hand there. Sometimes I returned the favor and was his ESH—emotional support human. Fair was fair.

"Where was that?"

"The hot tub. I packed it in for the night about ten-thirty, but the ladies and Jerry weren't ready to leave."

"The ladies?"

"Toots, Carmen, and Tina," he grumbled.

I asked the obvious. "Have you checked with Carmen and Tina? Maybe Tootsie crashed on the pull-out sofa in one of their rooms."

He shook his head. "Toots wouldn't do that."

"It doesn't hurt to check with them just to see for sure." Lily just sat from bringing my coffee. "Lily, can you call Carmen and Tina's rooms and ask them to come down to the desk for a second?"

"Tina left early to pick up Jerry. She left their keys and a note on the desk. I'll—"

I shot my hand out to stop her. "Wait. Pick up Jerry from where?"

Lily shook her head. "I don't know. That's what her note said. She wasn't around to ask questions." She picked up the phone. "I'll call Carmen."

She punched in the number for Carmen's room; Simon watched until she hung up; I tried to make sense of Tina picking up Jerry. Did that mean he didn't come back either? I drew a sharp inhale, earning a quick glance from Lily and an irritated one from Simon. Could Jerry have been the body found this morning?

"Carmen will be down in a jiff," Lily said as she hung up the receiver.

While we waited for Carmen, I was unable to get the visual of Jerry in a spearing hole out of my head. Simon leaned against the desk, arms crossed in front of him. I watched him in my peripheral vision. Oddly, he appeared more irritated than worried. When Carmen came into the room, he stood upright and waited for her to reach the desk. Aspen, who had just gotten settled at my feet, now sat up.

"I'm here. What's up?"

Her appearance was like looking in a mirror back in the day after I'd tied one on the night before. Which had been most nights. I shuddered at the memory.

"Is Tootsie in your room?" Simon asked.

She squinted her bloodshot eyes, mere slits. "Why would she be in my room?"

"Because she didn't come back last night," Simon said.

As I listened, a terrible feeling gave birth in the pit of my stomach. The probability that the body discovered was someone from the inn just doubled. What Sister Alice said *wasn't* my business, just became my business.

Chapter 3

"Simon, how did Tootsie seem when you left the hot tub last night?"

"She was perfectly fine. Somewhat plastered, but not so much that it caused me to worry."

After having a close call or two while drunk in a hot tub, I wanted to scream, "How could you not worry?" Instead, I clamped my lips shut, then chose my words carefully. Setting him on the defensive wouldn't help Tootsie. Or any of us.

Marcie came in and stomped the snow from her boots on the mat by the door before coming to stand beside me.

"Something happen?" she asked.

"My wife is missing." Simon's jaw twitched.

"Carmen, did Tootsie come in at the same time you did last night?"

She shook her head, then winced, touching her temple gingerly with her fingertips. "No. She said she was going to make a quick call and have one more cigarette before turning in."

Oh no. I inhaled sharply; my stomach somersaulted. The hot tub cover. I was only seeing disappearing dollar signs, not watching for a body. Had I covered up Tootsie's? "Marcie?" My voice cracked.

Marcie's eyes grew wide. "I'm on it." She turned and darted toward the door.

"Are we missing someone?" a man said from behind me.

I gave a startled cry and turned. I'd become oblivious to anything other than Tootsie potentially at the bottom of the hot tub.

"Yeah, my wife." Simon was eerily calm, his quick mood shift frightening.

"You weren't in the hot tub last night, were you?" I asked the man.

"Noah," Lily said, "this is Andie Rose, owner of the inn. Andie Rose, this is Noah Parker. He checked in yesterday, right before I left."

I extended a hand toward him, remembering his name on the register. Seeing him for the first time, however, his eyes nabbed me instantly, and I got lost there. I realized I was still shaking his hand. I jerked mine back, rubbing the palms of my hands on my jeans.

"Your wife is missing?" Noah asked Simon. "When did you last see her?"

"Last night about ten-thirty." His glance cut to Carmen and back to Noah.

"We'll find her," I told him. I avoided Noah's eyes for fear of getting hypnotized by them. And yet, I snuck the tiniest peek. Self-control wasn't exactly my strength, unfortunately. Aspen nudged my hand with his cool, wet nose, and I released the breath I'd been holding as we anxiously waited for Marcie. I asked Noah, "Is there something I can help you with?"

He appeared amused as he watched me. I ran my tongue over my teeth to be sure I didn't have pieces of breakfast there, then casually brushed the back of my hand under my nose in case of…well, to make sure nothing was there, either.

"It may be the case that you need *my* help," he finally said. "I'm a police detective, here for my final interview at Spirit Lake Police Department. And you," he said, suppressing a grin, "must be the amateur detective Detective Griffin gave me a heads up about."

My cheeks flushed, and I looked down for a moment. "I wouldn't exactly say I'm an amateur anymore."

He raised his eyebrows. "That's not something to be proud of in the short time you've been here."

I shoved my hands in my pockets and drew myself to full height. "I'm no stranger to this town, Mr. Parker. It's not like I'm new to Spirit Lake. My family grew up here. And I've helped Detective Griffin in the past." Confidence had always been my strength, but I was fumbling with it now, like catching a football with frozen hands. Finally, ball caught, I said, "Good luck on your final interview. When—and if—you're hired on, I'll do my best to stay out of your way."

"I'm sure you'll try."

His overabundance of assurance that he would be the next detective, and his dismissal of my help, irked me more than I cared to admit. My typically easy-going nature done got up and walked out the door. I turned my attention to Simon, my back to Mr. Parker, unwilling to entertain his ego. Or get lost again in those hypnotic eyes. What was taking Marcie so darn long? Unless— *dear God, no.*

"Simon—" My attention shot toward Marcie as she opened the door, shaking her head slightly. My relief came out in a gust of breath. Until I thought again about the body found on Big Spirit Lake. "Simon, would Tootsie have gone into town for anything?"

"Not without the car." He shot me a look as if I'd said, "Hey, there's a turquoise camel."

Noah Parker chuckled quietly, but not quiet enough that I didn't hear. I squared my shoulders, intent on ignoring him.

"But the two of you have been here a few times before, maybe—"

"Maybe someone came to pick her up." Noah said, skirting around from behind me and to my side.

"Mr. Parker," I said, a bit smug that I'd figured out something he hadn't. "If Simon's wife never went back to the room, she would have had to go dripping wet in subzero temps."

"My apologies for interfering," he said. "That is so frustrating when people do that, isn't it?"

I caught my breath and bit my tongue to avoid spouting words I'd regret.

"It *is* possible that someone could have met her here from town," Noah said.

I closed my eyes briefly. "That doesn't explain how she would have gone anywhere when she was dripping wet."

"Unless," he said, annoyingly pleasant, "the person brought a change of clothes."

"And, what, she changed in the car?" Okay, I might have said it with a wee bit of attitude.

Simon cleared his throat and his gaze bounced from me to Noah. "Excuse me, but what is going on here? You guys in some kind of competition or something?"

Shame snuck up on me when I realized I'd let myself get drawn into a childish squabble with a guest. Detective or not, he was a guest. I took a moment to find the right words.

"No, we don't," I finally said. "My apologies, Simon." To Noah, "And to you." To Carmen, "How much did Tootsie drink after Simon, Bobby, Jerry, and Tina left?"

"At the risk of ..." *Ahem*. Noah cleared his throat ... "overstepping, who are Bobby, Jerry, and Tina?"

"Bobby is my husband," Carmen said. "Jerry and Tina are other guests here." She said to me, "Tina left shortly after Simon. Bobby decided not to come down with us at all. He wanted to stay up in the room and watch the Timberwolves game. When I got back up to the room, he was already in bed."

The inconsistencies in Simon and Carmen's accounts snagged my attention. "Simon, you didn't mention Bobby wasn't there last night. Nor that Jerry and Tina stayed behind with Tootsie and Carmen."

He pressed his shoulders back. "Pardon me. I'm a little more concerned with my missing wife at the moment, not with what everyone else was doing."

"So how much did Tootsie drink?" I asked Carmen again.

"The rest of the bottle Simon brought down."

Simon blanched. "She finished that whole thing? There must have been at least half of a fifth of vodka left in that last bottle."

"The *last* bottle?" I asked.

"We both finished it off. And, let me tell you, Bobby wasn't pleased with me about it this morning," she said.

I couldn't determine if her glassy eyes were unshed tears of regret or pain. "What'd he say?" I asked.

"Nothing. That's just it. Silent treatment." She rolled her eyes.

I know what that's like. My mother was a master at

doing that with my dad.

"What else can you tell us about last night?" Noah asked. He quickly glanced at me. "If I may ask, that is."

Annoyed, I shook my head and breathed deep. "Of course you may."

"We were just having fun, you know? Girl talk."

"Conversation that Jerry was all too happy to be a part of," Simon said.

Carmen waved a hand in dismissal. "He was only being a good sport about it all. Tina got a little miffed about it, though, and left."

"The guy was hanging on every word my wife said. It was nauseating. Good thing I'm not a jealous kinda guy."

Carmen cleared her throat, then scoffed, "Yeah, good thing."

"Carmen, was Tina jealous of the attention Jerry paid Tootsie?"

She shrugged a shoulder. "I don't know. I don't see why she would have been. It was hard *not* to pay attention to Tootsie. She's hysterically funny and has a mean independent streak. I guess you could say she has a larger-than-life personality. In a classy way, though. She was talking me into pursuing my dream of becoming a flight attendant." Carmen giggled, then instantly stopped and put her hand to her head. "Ouch. Jerry left right after me."

I desperately hoped Tina's continued absence meant she found Jerry. Alive. Until I knew for sure, I didn't want to bring it up and cause a panic. Or speculation of any kind since neither Jerry nor Tootsie returned.

Noah opened his mouth to say something, and I put my hand up, palm facing him.

"Wait. Carmen, Jerry was the last one to be with Tootsie? Did you see Jerry leave?"

"When I got to the door, he was grabbing his towel."

"But you didn't actually see him go into the inn?"

She shook her head. "But it's not like he would have run around outside wrapped in a towel."

"Simon, just curious—if Tootsie didn't come back last night, what made you wait until this morning to inquire about her?"

"Good question, Ms. Kaczmarek," Noah said. "That's what I was going to ask."

I clamped my lips shut and swallowed my annoyance.

We both waited for Simon's answer. He switched his weight from one foot to the other and tucked his hands in the front pockets of his Dockers Chino pants.

He let out a low grumble. "She's taken to sleeping on the pullout. I didn't notice her gone until I got up."

"How long have the two of you slept separately?" Noah asked.

"What does that matter?" Simon squirmed, clearly embarrassed at the transparency of his marital discord.

"It's just that you don't seem particularly concerned. Has she done this before?"

"No, she hasn't. And our nights apart have only been a few."

"So since you got here?" I asked, my brows crinkled.

"Yes." One word and a tone that indicated that line of questioning was over.

Chapter 4

"Listen." Carmen winced as if the mere act of talking hurt her head. "We were having a good time when I left. Perhaps a little too good." She closed her eyes for a moment, then opened them, and blocked the streaming rays of bright light from the windows with her forearm. Oh, how I remembered those days. *Ugh*. When she noticed us watching her, she said, "I'm not used to drinking so much. Neither Bobby nor me hardly ever drink at all."

Simon chuckled. "Can't say that about my Toots. She likes her booze."

Carmen stood taller and narrowed her eyes. "Yeah? I don't see where you can criticize Tootsie. You were toasted, too."

"Except I know when to stop," Simon shot back. "Unlike my wife. And see where it's gotten her."

Aspen, acutely aware of the building tension and Carmen's discomfort, stood and strolled toward her where he briefly camped.

"So you're saying it's *her* fault that she's missing?" Carmen asked, her tone laced with flecks of anger.

"I guess we don't know that yet, do we?" His jaw was tighter than Carmen's defense of Tootsie. "But I do know we wouldn't be standing here right now if she hadn't gotten completely inebriated." He looked at her squarely. "Can you argue against that?"

"How do you know it had anything to do with her drinking at all?" Carmen's headache appeared to either improve or forgotten in the heat of the tension.

I imposed myself between the two of them as they stepped closer to one another and held an arm out toward each. "Okay, this is getting us nowhere and isn't helping find Tootsie." I lifted my phone, still clutched in my hand from Sister Alice's call, and said to Noah, "I'll call Detective Griffin. Proof I work *with* the police, not against them, contrary to what you've apparently been told." *Egad.* If I didn't keep my mouth shut, I would be on his bad side before he even officially started, provided he got the job at all. The shock from Frank's new *hobby* had shaken my solid foundation. Sweet, sweet Frank. I tried to remember if I'd seen any evidence that he'd been using his own product, but all I could think about was the relief that poured over me it was in the winter, a time when guests, like Noah—*especially* Noah—wouldn't be anywhere near the shed.

"I believe you," Noah said, jerking my thoughts back to the here and now. The corners of his lips tugged ever so slightly. "But the fact of the matter is that even if I'm not the detective in Spirit Lake yet, I'm still a trained detective. Use me."

Yet? I opened my mouth to spout a sarcastic comment, then clamped my lips tight at the absurdity of my behavior. The oddities of the morning were causing me to break out of character like zits on a teen.

I finally said, "Would you like to call Detective Griffin?"

"You call him. I'll stay here with the others." He gave a slight nod I perceived to mean he had a specific reason for his decision.

"All right, then. If you'll all excuse me for a moment."

The murky tension from the room followed me into the kitchen, where I was sure no one could overhear my call. Only Tony.

"Detective Griffin?" I said when he answered.

"Ms. Kaczmarek. Not too much longer before you'll be someone else's pain in the backside." I could almost see the old guy smiling on the other end.

"So I've heard. One of your candidates is staying here at the inn."

"Who do you think referred him there?"

I cocked my head. "Thank you, then. But if I've been such a pain in your backside, why would you refer him here? And you're going to miss me, by the way. Admit it."

"Maybe a little," he conceded. "I wanted Noah to get acquainted with his self-appointed assistant before he agreed to take the job. You know—in case it's a deal breaker for him."

"Aren't you hilarious? But the reason I'm calling is serious. Do you know anything about the body that was found in Big Spirit Lake this morning?"

He cleared his throat, and the creak of his chair carried across the phone. "Since I'm the only detective in town—as in the *only* one, Ms. Kaczmarek—of course, I know. Our department can investigate a murder. We're more than capable."

I gasped. "Murder?"

"Oh, good God," he muttered. I could just about see him roll his eyes as his chair creaked again. A creak I'd become familiar with when he leaned back and ran his hand over his face in annoyance. "Keep your mouth shut about that, because we're not a hunnerd percent."

"What makes you suspect murder?"

"I cannot talk about an open investigation. You know that. Especially when it has absolutely nothin' to do with you or your inn this time."

I hesitated, then spit it out. "It might have everything to do with my inn." He grumbled something unintelligible before I continued. "Do you have an ID of the deceased? A guest seems to have disappeared last night—which is how I met your potential replacement." I thought about Jerry again. With no further word from Tina, I was comfortable that she'd found him. When Detective Griffin remained silent, I said, "What's the name of the deceased?"

"That won't be public until notification of the family."

I crossed my fingers. To add a layer of belief that Tina found Jerry, I said, "Can you at least tell me the gender?"

He grumbled, "First of all, I didn't confirm it's murder. We can't jump to conclusions here."

"Well, it wouldn't be suicide. Like the victim would go to some random fish house and jump into a spearing hole?"

He groaned and mumbled something unintelligible, then said, "What's the name of your missing woman?"

"So the victim's a woman."

I blew through pursed lips at the realization that I'd been right about Jerry, yet terrified of what it could mean. I scrambled to think through the brief conversation I'd had with Tootsie yesterday when she scheduled a life coaching session for later this afternoon. She hadn't mentioned any problems with Simon and hadn't appeared depressed. Had she been there with someone? I snapped back to the phone when I'd realized Detective Griffin had said something.

"What?"

Detective Griffin said, "For the third time, what's the name of the missing woman from the inn?"

"Tootsie. Tootsie Timmons."

There was an audible sigh, followed by another groan. "Does that mean you're going to be muddling around in my case?"

My heart sank. "That's who it is then. Tootsie."

"Unofficially. Someone remembered seeing her in the past. Although a name like Tootsie isn't easy to forget."

"Who recognized her?"

"None of your business."

"Detective Griffin, I think I should know if it's someone from the inn."

"It's not. He lives here in town."

"He?"

He exhaled in apparent exasperation. "Ms. Kaczmarek, does nothing get by you?"

"Not much, sir."

"I noticed. I'll be out to your place within ten minutes to speak with the husband."

"Good luck."

"Yeah? Why's that?"

"He's…well, he just seems a little indifferent to his wife's disappearance. And he's got an attitude."

He snorted. "Kinda like you last fall."

"I didn't have an attitude," I argued, vividly remembering my *official* welcome to the town. "I was only trying to help you understand the murderer wasn't anyone on my staff." Another snort. "They—*he* is staying in the Maple Room."

Grandpop and Honey named each of the ten rooms after trees—maple, oak, birch, elm, willow, spruce, ash, cedar, walnut, and pine, and I'd determined to keep the names, nabbing the studio apartment, otherwise known as the Birch Room. If a returning guest called for reservations, they referred to the room name they wanted. Easy peasy.

"On my way." The line went dead.

I slid the scrunchie from my hair to fix it and peered under the hanging cabinets in the kitchen, installed last month at Tony's request.

"Hey, Tony."

"What's this about a body?" he asked, wiping a knife on his apron as he turned toward me and leaned over, elbows on the counter.

"How did you hear me way over there?"

"Your voice carries."

"So what are you saying?" To be fair, it wasn't the first time I'd heard that. My dad used to assure me it wasn't that I talked too loudly, I just had a pitch that reverberates with the vocal tract and the human ear. He even had a name for it—speaker's formant. I think he was just trying to make me feel better.

He shook his head and rolled his eyes. "Nothing. Don't make it something it's not."

I hesitated to say more, remembering my promise to Detective Griffin. Although, technically, I promised I wouldn't tell anyone he thought it was murder, not *who* it was. And besides, this was Tony.

I walked closer to him so no one else heard my *carrying* voice. "It appears they found the body of a guest in Big Spirit Lake. In a spearing hole inside a fish house."

He clenched his teeth together. "Which guest? Do they think he fell in? Helluva way to go." He grimaced.

"Right? It was a she. Tootsie Timmons. Detective Griffin is on his way here right now to talk with Simon, her husband. Don't be surprised if he talks to the rest of us at some point. Just to see what we know."

He sighed and tilted his head back. "Great. We don't know anything anyway. At least the body wasn't here this time."

"That's what I said at first, too. Until I discovered it *is* tied to the inn. But don't say anything to anyone else yet."

Like that stopped me. Sister Alice told me once, *For every person you think you can tell a secret to, that person has someone they can, too, and on and on.*

"We don't have any control over other people's actions, Andie Rose. In your line of work as a life coach, you should know that."

I scrunched my face. "What do you mean?"

"If someone is intent on committing suicide, you can't stop them. At least she didn't do it here."

I clamped my hand over my mouth and hightailed it outta there. I didn't want Tony to think it was suicide, but I'd promised Detective Griffin I wouldn't say anything about the M word. And a promise was a promise. I was nearly bursting to tell someone, though. Sister Alice. She was a safe one to tell. And we could put our heads together to see what we could figure out. Not only was she my sponsor, but she was my crime-solving partner last fall. And her confidentiality duties were doubly strong with being a sister *and* my sponsor, I justified. The irritating naughty angel reappeared on my shoulder and whispered in my ear, "To justify is just a lie, Andie Rose."

I brushed her off and started for my room, then pivoted back toward the front desk, Aspen close on my heels. Lily tapped her pen on the desk in discomfort, and Carmen leaned against the desk, elbows on the countertop, her hands holding her head. Simon stood stiff and stoic, arms crossed in front of him. Noah leaned against the far wall, hands tucked in his pants pockets, as he observed.

I could read so much in this scene without a single word. I broke the deafening silence. "When Detective Griffin gets here, tell him I'll be right back."

"I can keep Aspen with me," Lily offered in desperation.

Aspen looked up at me, the panic in his eyes reflecting dogs understand more than we credit them for.

"Thanks, but he's coming with me."

We ran up to my apartment, taking the stairs two at a time. I closed and locked the door behind me as if a locked door would keep in the secrets that my unlocked lips leaked out.

"Sister Alice." I blurted before she said anything.

"What'dyoudo?" she said so quickly it came out as all one word.

"*I* didn't do anything."

"Then what's got your undies in a bunch? I told you I'd call you when I heard something. I haven't yet."

"My undies are fine, thank you very much. But *I* heard something."

"That didn't take you long, now, did it?" she said wryly.

"The victim is—or rather *was*—a guest at the inn."

"Come again?" Her tone was in utter disbelief.

"Her name is Tootsie Timmons," I said.

"Poor lady," she mused. "I remember Tootsie well. A name like that makes me grateful to have the one I do."

"It's murder," I said.

Sister Alice choked. I waited. "Tea went down the wrong pipe," she finally sputtered. "How do you know who it is?"

"Detective Griffin."

"But *how*? Don't tell me he called you and said, 'Hey Andie Rose, we have a murder on our hands, and we just can't solve it without your help.'"

I chuckled. "He asked if you could help me since we were so successful the last time."

"Lying is a sin, you know."

"I'm not Catholic."

"If you'd go to church, you'd see that sins aren't only a Catholic thing."

I chuckled. "Can't fault you for trying." Despite her cynical retorts, I knew she accepted me as is, flaws and all. We in the Program knew the worst about each other and accepted each other, anyway. At least we tried to. Sometimes. We just made it more fun than *normies*. Those who weren't alcoholics in recovery.

"I need to scoot. Detective Griffin is on his way to talk with Simon. I want to be at the front desk when he arrives."

"I'm sure you do, Sherlock."

"You're just envious because I'm here to get the scoop and you're not."

She harrumphed. "I have to get to work and don't have the idle time you have."

"Fibber. Your time at the hospital is flexible. But I guess if you're going to use that excuse, that's too bad. I was going to ask you to come out here to the inn."

"I'm on my way."

"I thought—" *Click.* "You were too busy," I muttered into the dead line and snickered.

Chapter 5

By the time Detective Griffin arrived, Simon and Carmen had left the room. Noah Parker stayed, claiming he wanted to help Detective Griffin.

Lily put her hand along the side of her mouth, shielding it from Noah, and mouthed, "He's sucking up."

I swallowed a giggle.

Sister Alice arrived a mere heartbeat after Detective Griffin. She breezed through the door, bringing a gust of icy wind with her.

He rolled his eyes when he saw her. "I can only imagine what you're doing here, Sister."

He add something inaudible, but the vein pulsing in his temple told me it wasn't anything pleasant.

She smiled coyly at Detective Griffin and pushed up the bright yellow frames of her glasses with her pointer finger. Those, in combination with her short, half-spiked, half-mussed white hair, she was a sight to behold.

"Good morning, Detective. Last I checked, this was a public place. Anything we can help you with?"

"No," he boomed. I glanced at Noah, who struggled to suppress a grin. Detective Griffin took a breath. "Noah Parker, if you're the next detective for Spirit Lake, this will be your life. Good luck."

"I told you before, Detective, you're going to miss me." As annoyed as he pretended to be, his soft side shone through like light through cracked glass. I knew *I* would miss *him*. "We're having Tony's white chocolate chip almond blondies for afternoon tea today," I told him. "Why don't you come out? You haven't tasted good white chocolate chip almond blondie bars until you've had Tony's. It can be a retirement celebration of sorts. Yeah?"

He breathed a sigh. "Ms. Kaczmarek, you make it impossible to stay angry with you." He turned his attention to Sister Alice. "And the only reason I don't stay mad at you is because you're a woman of the cloth."

Sister Alice smirked. "Woman of the cloth, eh? Can't say as I've heard that one before."

"Don't push it." His grumbling didn't scare anyone though. "I'm going to head up to Simon's room."

"I can call him to come down," Lily said.

"You can use my office again. I'll need to start charging rent, though. It can be my side-hustle."

"Can't afford that on my salary. I'll go to his room. Which way?"

I smiled sweetly at him again. "Allow me. I'll escort you up there."

"Just so you know, you are not welcome to stay while I speak with him."

"Noted."

"Don't act all insulted. I know what you're up to."

"Doesn't hurt a girl to try." Aspen stayed by my side as I led him to Simon's door. "Shall I knock for you?"

"No. I have knuckles of my own."

I held a hand up. "Just trying to be helpful." I turned to walk away, then turned back. "So afternoon tea at three?"

"I'll see what I can do," he said.

"Awesome. It's settled then. It'll be a retirement

celebration, and you'll be the guest of honor."

He opened his mouth to say something, then closed it again. Finally, he shook his head and said, "I'll do my best."

I grinned. "Come on, Aspen." I reached for the side of his neck and ruffled his fur.

When I got back to the foyer, Carmen was by the front desk. She started toward me. Her pain must have subsided, because the lines by her eyes and her lips were more relaxed. That, or she inhaled a good dose of pain meds.

"Andie Rose, can I talk to you for a minute? In private."

"Of course," I said, gesturing for her to follow me. "We can go into my office." I looked at Aspen, who'd laid beside Lily's chair, and decided to let him stay there.

After I closed my office door behind Carmen, I extended my arm toward the chair in front of my desk. I skirted behind my desk and sat.

"It's cozy in here." Her gaze swept the small room and rested on a poster-sized framed photo of Grandad and Honey standing on the back porch of the inn. Grandad was in his bib overalls, his arm looped around Honey's waist. Carmen took in the rest of the room. "Let me tell ya, I can really appreciate gentle lamp light. Those fluorescent bulbs hurt my head on a good day. Which isn't today." She sighed as she leaned back in her chair.

Minnesota winters throttle us with enough cold brutality without adding to it with harsh lighting. And I was a firm believer that lighting determined the atmosphere of a room. I settled in and sat back comfortably in my chair, mirroring her posture.

Mirroring was a technique I'd learned to use that encourages coaching clients to open up by helping them feel more comfortable. It worked nearly every time.

Finally ready to talk, she said, "Tootsie told me last night that she'd made an appointment to see you—you know, as a client—this afternoon."

I gave a slight nod.

"I have something to tell you that Tootsie confided in me last night. In case it helps find her."

Bad news would soon shatter her concern and hope for Tootsie's well-being, and it weighed on me.

"Okay," I said quietly, encouraging her to continue.

"I haven't even told Bobby this yet, and I might not, but …"

She hesitated, and I held my breath, fearing she'd change her mind and not tell me. I had a murder to solve, and I needed all the information I could get.

"This room is kinda like Vegas, Carmen. What you say here stays here." *Unless you admit to murder and I'm obligated to tell the police.*

She took a deep breath. "Tootsie was seeing someone else. Someone here in Spirit Lake."

I blinked hard and sucked my lips in. I hadn't expected that. "Do you know who?"

She shook her head. "This is my first time here, so I wouldn't have known who it was even if I could remember if she said a name. The only reason she did—tell me, I mean—is because she'd been drinking and stuff."

And stuff?

"Makes people talk, you know?" she said. "A good reason I hardly ever drink. Well, except for last night."

Oh, don't I know it. Back in the day, I'd opened my

mouth too many times to count, when keeping it shut would have saved me boatloads of trouble.

"Bobby and I are very private people. We like our personal business to stay personal."

Instead of taking notes, breaking the connection with her, I mentally stored every detail she told me so I could write it verbatim when she left my office.

"Had she seen this person while they've been here this week?" I asked.

"She saw him in town the day before yesterday when they were running around doing stuff. She was going to meet him in town somewhere last night, but by the time me and Jerry left the hot tub, it was too late."

"You're sure she didn't mention a name, though?" I asked in hopes she'd remembered something she hadn't mere seconds before.

She shook her head again. "If she did, I don't remember. Maybe... Will something or other. Or Gary. We were all inebriated, so I wouldn't bet money on either of those."

Gary? I caught my breath. Had the killer been right here beneath our noses? "Carmen, was it Jerry?"

She sighed and massaged her temple with her fingertips. "Of course not. I obviously would have known him. There was nothing between them in the hot tub to indicate anything. Not that I can remember."

I exhaled my relief and waited for her to continue. When she didn't respond, I posed the question, "Considering your state of inebriation, do you think there might have been and you didn't catch it?"

She dropped her hands to her lap and sighed. "I dunno. Anything's possible, I guess."

"Can you recall anything else she might have said?"

47

She stared off to the side as if trying to remember, then twisted her lips. "No. Mostly she encouraged me to get a life outside of wife and homemaker. To go after my dream of being an airline attendant. And to travel." Her face lightened more than it had all morning, her eyes brighter for a mere moment before turning sheepish. "You're positive what's said here, stays here, right?"

"Did you tell the police any of this?"

Her eyes opened wide. "No. And you mustn't either. Promise me, Andie Rose. I don't want to be in the middle of this whole thing. Like I said, Bobby and I like our privacy. But I felt obligated to tell you what I know." When I didn't say anything, she met my eyes, hers desperate and pleading. "Andie Rose, please."

"I promise." Keeping mum was risking a charge of withholding information if Detective Griffin found out. I guess I could count this as a coaching session and claim confidentiality. Not sure how he'd feel about that, but in the name of rationalizing, clients deserved a safe space, right? Sister Alice and I would have to work this angle for all it's worth and claim it was a "hunch" if he asked how we knew. Play the 'women's intuition' card.

"What?" Realizing she'd just said something brought me back to Carmen's presence. I sipped the last of my coffee.

"She'd gotten some marijuana from someone here."

I choked on the coffee, spraying brown droplets on my desktop. I snatched a tissue and began blotting. "From here?" I croaked and placed a hand on my chest. My heart felt like it was trying to climb up my throat.

"Not here at the inn, here in Spirit Lake."

I let out a breath I'd been holding and swallowed. "Thank God." At her raised eyebrows, I said, "I just meant thank you for the clarification. I don't want anyone selling an illegal substance here."

"She smoked it and tried to talk me into it as well."

"Did you?" I asked. When she didn't reply, I held up my hands, palms facing her. "No judgement, Carmen. I've done my fair share in the past."

"You?" Her eyes widened. "I can hardly believe that."

I raised my eyebrows and shrugged a shoulder. "Truth."

She appeared to be weighing whether it *was* true, then giggled. "I did. But don't tell Bobby. I'd hate to disappoint him." Her eyes sparkled with mischief, like she'd gotten away with coming in late for curfew.

"Carmen," I asked after thinking things through, "I know you didn't tell the police about Tootsie confiding in you about her affair. So you didn't tell the police about the marijuana, either, right?"

Her eyes grew huge, and her face paled, as if she'd transformed into the ghost before my very eyes.

"God, no." She began shaking her head vigorously and instantly stopped and winced. "Oh, ouch." After taking a moment to recover, she added, "Especially not that. They'd make it public. I can't have this getting out to Bobby and my children. *Especially* my children. I mean, they're at an age where they've probably tried it themselves, but they don't need to know their mom did. It would mortify them."

I was ashamed at my relief. I had hoped to deal with the marijuana issue by making sure Frank made it disappear without the police finding it first. With Noah on the premises, it might make things a little trickier. Even though Carmen said Tootsie didn't get it from the inn, the police would surely search, anyway.

"I have a question for you. And I'd like you to consider it before giving me an answer," I said, hoping to eliminate a knee-jerk 'no way.'

"Okay," she said warily.

"Are you okay if I mention this to Sister Alice?"

She squinted. "Who's Sister Alice?"

"She's the one you saw in the foyer before we came into my office. The one who was here for tea yesterday afternoon."

"Well, I wasn't exactly paying attention to anyone else."

"Sister Alice knows all the townsfolk and is bound by confidentiality. And she helped me another time in the recent past." She hesitated, so I said, "Take your time in answering. But between the two of us, Sister Alice and me, there's a better chance we'd find out where Tootsie is." A sharp stab of guilt pierced me at the slightly misguided statement. I knew full well where Tootsie was. But I couldn't very well tell Carmen I needed to solve Tootsie's murder. There I went, rationalizing again.

"Do you really think you can find her?" she asked hopefully. "Maybe she left to meet with that guy after all, and she'll come back today."

My heart plummeted. *She may have met with the guy, but she's not coming back. Not alive.* All too soon she'd know the cold, hard truth.

Reminding her of my question, I said, "Sister Alice?"

She sighed. "Sure. If you think it'll help locate Tootsie."

After she left my office, I pondered the news. I

imagined Detective Griffin talking with Simon. Before going back to the front desk in the foyer, I took a detour and poked my head through the doorway to the kitchen to see if Izzy arrived yet. She was fixing her apron, tying it around her waist.

"Hi, Izzy," I called cheerily.

"Hey, Kaz," she called back.

"Tony, can you make extra for afternoon tea today? We're having a little celebration for Detective Griffin." He usually made extra food for meals since we often got dinner reservations from non-guests. But not for afternoon tea. That was a guest perk.

"Why are we doing that?" Izzy, like any typical teen, wasn't fond of the police.

"He's retiring," I said.

She snickered. "What a shame."

I shook my head slowly and smiled. "There will be another to replace him, so no need to be heartbroken."

"Well, I hope the next one won't be so old and crotchety. Griffin's so old he's about to turn to dust."

I smirked and bit my tongue from saying, *If it's Noah Parker, he's annoying, handsome, and annoyingly handsome.* For someone Izzy's age, though, Noah was probably ancient as well.

Instead, I said, "People rarely retire unless they're older."

Izzy shot her arm up in the air. "I'll make the afternoon teatime refreshments and give him a proper sendoff. It'd be the polite thing for me to do."

Tony studied her for a moment. "Why?"

"You know, as an apology for speaking ill of an at-risk adult."

I laughed. "Here I thought it was me who was a pain

in his side."

"Oh, you are," Tony said. "He's said so." He turned to Izzy. "I'm not gonna argue. Finish 'em up. The batter is in the walk-in cooler."

"I'll get on it now," she said, a glint in her eye.

Tony gave her a skeptical look. "You're acting weird."

"Just happy to help him on his journey." On her way to the cooler, she said over her shoulder, "Hopefully, it's a long senile journey and he forgets his way back."

Watching the interaction, I narrowed my eyes. "Izzy, it sounds like you have a history with Detective Griffin."

"He acts like teens partying is the biggest sin there ever was. I mean, come on. What else is there to do in this town?"

"Maybe in Spirit Lake it was. Until the murder last fall." *And another today.*

"Way to kill a mood, Kaz," Izzie called from the cooler.

Chapter 6

"What was that all about?" Sister Alice asked as I returned to the desk. "What'd Carmen want?"

Aspen stood and greeted me, his tail swishing from side to side. I bent to kiss his head and stood again. "If she'd wanted you to know, she would have talked with me out here." I smiled at her, knowing it was driving her crazy.

Unlike Lily, who watched the interaction, eyes crinkling at the corners, Jade ignored us, other than a mumbled, "Hi, Andie Rose."

Sister Alice's blunt honesty about Jade's wardrobe last fall fed a rift between the two, and I held my breath, hoping she wouldn't say anything now to fuel that fire even more. Sister Alice's heart was golden, but gentleness was not her gift.

"Come on," I said. "Let's head into town for the meeting. You can ride with me and come back and get Father Vincent's car afterward." She'd gotten an old beat-up Volvo to use for the winter when she couldn't drive her moped, but the heater had gone out in it just the day before. "When's your car supposed to be fixed?"

"Sometime tomorrow. If we take Father Vincent's car, you can save on gas money to pay for a lawyer. The trouble you get into, you're going to need one sooner or later."

"Nice. Ripping off the priest," Jade said under her

breath. Sister Alice gave her a Duchenne smile, dousing the flame with kindness.

I ignored Jade's comment. "You see, it's not Father Vincent's car that causes me to pause at that suggestion. It's the driver. Aspen's even afraid of you. We can drive separately. See you there."

"Fine. I'll ride with you," she conceded. To Aspen, "I get the front."

"Age before beauty," Jade muttered.

I sucked in a breath and zeroed in on her. "Jade?"

She caught her lower lip between her teeth then said, "All I said was 'sage before duty.' You know, sage as in wisdom, and Aspen's duty to sit in the back."

I held my breath as I waited for what was to come from Sister Alice, but she surprised me.

The corners of her lips curved upward, and she winked. "I underestimated you, dear."

When the expected explosion fizzled out, I released the breath I'd been holding.

As soon as we stepped outside, I stopped and turned toward her.

"What?" she asked.

"What was that in there?" I jerked my thumb behind us.

"I had it coming, I suppose. I know this surprises you, but my straightforwardness isn't always well received."

"Shocker," I mumbled.

I knew the reason she wanted to ride with me was to get information from my chat with Carmen. An AA meeting didn't exactly provide that private moment unless everyone split right after we finished, which rarely happened. And I knew she wouldn't want to wait.

Aspen hopped in the back seat, but not without an attitude that made me feel guilty from here to Sunday. I tried to avoid looking at him in my rearview mirror as I filled Sister Alice in on Carmen's news and about Noah Parker. I'd barely finished by the time we'd arrived at St. Michael's for the meeting.

"You know," she said with a slight cock of her head, "the man wouldn't irritate you so much if you weren't the tiniest bit interested in him."

"Oh, please," I scoffed. "The last thing I have the time or interest in is getting involved with someone. And I can't imagine someone his age isn't married, anyway."

"Yes, because it's so much more likely to be single for someone of, say, *your* age," she said dryly.

"Truth." He appeared to be close to my age, if not a tad older. "But I am not interested," I said with finality. And I wasn't. Just because something on the menu looks good doesn't mean one orders it. Not that I'm opposed to relationships, mind you. After all, relationship coaching is part of what I offer. It's just that I suck at relationships and am much better at helping guide others than following my own guidance. At thirty years old, I didn't see that changing. My mother constantly reminded me I was too stubborn to change my ways. *Thanks, Mother.*

By the time we reached the church basement, two more people were there. Usually, Sister Alice was by far the first to arrive. Since this wasn't one of those times, another had taken the initiative of making the coffee and setting out the sugar-laden treats.

I went directly to the coffeepot and plate of cookies, nabbed a fig bar, and promptly bit half and chewed. Aspen sat at my feet, his attention resting on me expectantly. I lowered the other half to him and snagged another.

Wes Wilson strode up behind me. "Miss breakfast?" He snatched a sugar cookie before putting it back on the plate.

His unusual demeanor took me off guard. He was typically jovial, if not obnoxious. I'd met Wes last spring when I'd made a quick visit with a friend and felt a kinship with him right off the bat. When I saw him at my first meeting here in Spirit Lake, I immediately knew why. We *fun defects*, as we jokingly called ourselves, had internal radar for one another.

"Gross," I said through a mouthful of cookie, looking from him to the cookie he'd put back on the plate.

"Not any grosser than talking with your mouth full," he said. "But somehow you can even make something gross be sexy." He gave a hollow laugh.

I rolled my eyes and covered my mouth until I finished swallowing. "You're sick, Wes." He was acting strange.

I took a sip of coffee. A self-professed coffee snob, the coffee in this room, terrible as it was, appealed to me. It was as awful, and in poor taste, as the stories we told among us. Stories in which only those of us *fun defects* found humor.

"Okay, what's wrong?" Aspen slid into a lying position at my feet.

"Got stood up last night." He shook his head, pointed a finger at himself, and stared at me in mock disbelief. "Me, Wes Wilson, hunk of hunks, got stood up."

Despite the joke, his disappointment was as

transparent as a ghost. Two men and a woman came into the room and joined us at the refreshment table. *This* over a missed date? I hoped he hadn't drunk over it. Maybe that was the underlying cause of his demeanor.

I leaned in and whispered, "Did you relapse?"

He shook his head. "Nah. Nothing that dramatic."

"Getting stood up happens to the best of us, man," one guy said, pouring sludge into a baby-poop-yellow mug. It wasn't hard to be overheard in the eerie quiet of the church basement. Even through the chatter with the typical number of us there, eight to twelve on any given day, sometimes more, the basement still seemed strangely quiet.

When I lived in the city, the meetings were so huge we broke the fire codes. When I moved here, so many of *us* for a small town seemed unusual, and I'd wondered what I'd gotten myself into. I'd convinced myself that it was because Spirit Lake was a tourist town, attracting people from the country over. But when the same people turned up day after day, it blew my theory.

"Tell me someone in the group didn't stand you up," I said, fingers crossed. Awkward was never enjoyable.

"Yeah," said Scooter. "Because we drunks are so dependable."

His contribution to the conversation earned roaring laughter, which echoed off the walls through the darkness of the basement that stretched beyond the lit kitchenette we used. I usually tried to keep my attention from darting toward the blackness. I'd watched too many horror movies and was sure something lurked back there in the dark. On a couple of occasions I'd dared a peek, expecting glowing red eyes.

"Do I know her?" Sister Alice asked, now joining

our circle, which had grown to ten so far.

"Unlikely." He toyed with another cookie.

"Take the damn cookie, Wes." Apparently, my tone startled Aspen, because he bounced into a sitting position and stared at me.

"Young lady," a woman of about seventy said, "you're in a church. Have the decency not to swear."

"Sorry, Phyllis," I said.

"I'm not the one you should apologize to."

I knew exactly what she meant, but the rebellion was strong. "Sorry, Wes."

Phyllis dipped her chin, her eyes leveled on me as though she was ready to chuck her coffee at me, then tittered instead. "You're hopeless."

I picked up the cookie and shoved it toward Wes. "Have you ever stopped to think maybe she stood you up because of your manners?"

"I don't need another mom," he said. "Got one too many in this group as it is."

I inhaled sharply as a thought occurred to me and I stitched together the pieces. Wes's absentee date; Carmen's revelation about Tootsie seeing someone from town; Carmen stating the name might have been Will-something or maybe Gary.

My breath quickened. We don't use last names in the group to promote anonymity, but since it was a small town, most of us knew last names, anyway. Wes's last name was Wilson. My gaze darted to Sister Alice who, seeing my concern, zeroed in on my line of thought.

"Wes—" I paused a moment, leaned in, and nudged his arm. "What's the name of the woman who stood you up? Tootsie?"

At the mention of Tootsie's name, Wes's head

jerked toward me, freeing his arm from my touch. "How did you know that? She's not from around here." And then it appeared to dawn on him. He stuffed his hands in the front pockets of his jeans and bounced his attention between me and Sister Alice. "From the inn. You ladies have time for a cuppa joe after the meeting?"

Luna laughed. "Maybe you can finally answer the question asked in that old commercial with the owl and the Tootsie Pops."

I scowled. "What is this, middle school?"

A hush descended on the room before their attention split, half observing the interaction with Wes, Sister Alice, and myself, and the other half whispering to each other. Sober, we all knew when silence was best. Except despite the group's silence, the basement seemed louder than ever before. And then I realized it was the pounding in my ears. Wes had to be the one who unofficially identified Tootsie's body. The weight between the three of us was enough to sink the Titanic.

"I think coffee later is a good idea," I said.

The general tone for the rest of the meeting was subdued. Even Aspen lay by my feet without suggesting he should have another treat.

Without verbalizing an agreement, the three of us kept mum about Wes's predicament. For now. The rest were bound to find out soon enough. An affair with a married woman, who was supposed to meet him the night before, him on scene the next morning to identify the body—it was all too much for a small town to keep silent. And he would likely become the prime suspect. *Oh, boy*.

Detective Griffin's admission that he thought it was a homicide rang in my head. But did Wes do it? *Could* he? Was he capable of such a thing? I didn't want to think so, but I didn't know. Sister Alice's unusual quietness and furtive glances revealed she and I were on the same page.

After the meeting, rather than linger and chat as usual, everyone left with the plan to hit up the Spirit Lake Café for lunch. Sister Alice, Wes, and I declined, with a promise to catch them the next time. Aspen stood by the stairway as each left, then sprawled on his side on the tile floor.

The three of us were silent as we put away chairs and tidied up the refreshment table. As if restoring order to the room would restore order to life. That or realizing a conversation once opened could never be closed again.

Finally, when we finished, Sister Alice leaned against a square brick pillar. Wes hopped up and sat on the countertop, and I jumped up beside him. He leaned forward, elbows resting on his knees, chin in his cupped hands, as if trying to keep his head from thumping onto the floor.

"Did you do it?" I asked quietly in the large room.

He turned toward me, mouth agape. "Are you serious? What do you think?"

I lifted a shoulder. "She was supposed to meet someone last night. You said a woman stood you up. Now we find out that it was Tootsie, who is now dead, who stood you up."

He squinted, his colorless eyebrows meeting in the middle. "That doesn't mean anything."

"The police will think so. It doesn't look good for you, Wes."

"Are you going to tell them?" he asked incredulously.

"Of course not." At this rate, I'd be holding all the secret cards in this darn case. Too bad I wasn't playing poker.

Sister Alice cleared her throat. "Not to kick you when you're down, but have you lost your ever-loving mind, Wes? A married woman?"

"I know, I know." He scooched back a few inches, planted his palms on the edge of the countertop, and focused down at his feet.

"Apparently you didn't," I said. "It's a good way to get killed by a jealous husband." I shot upright, eyes wide. Aspen lifted his head to see what the trouble was, then lay back down. "Simon. You won't be the only suspect, Wes. Jealous husband and all."

"Is that supposed to make me feel better?" he asked sullenly. "I know getting involved with her was wrong, but it just sorta happened."

"A dog peeing on the carpet is wrong and just *sorta happens*," Sister Alice said, watching him closely. Aspen looked up sleepily at her, then closed his eyes again.

"Aspen's offended at that comment," I said.

"Tell him to get in line with Jade. Wes, what you did goes far beyond that. If Simon is behind this, you realize it could have been you in that spearing hole, right? In fact, it still could. Keep a low profile for a while."

"Tch. Work and home. Got it." His words fell with defeat.

Sister Alice asked what we were both thinking. "How'd it start?"

He ran a hand over his face and groaned. "Oh, cripes ... where to begin." We stayed quiet until he finally took a breath and began. "I met Tootsie two years ago when they were here. We ran into each other at Spirit Brew when I accidentally grabbed her coffee instead of mine. We got to talking, and the rest is history."

"Except it's not," I said. "History."

"Didn't you notice a wedding ring?" Sister Alice said.

"Right?" I said. "That rock on her left hand was hard to miss, Wes."

"I wasn't paying attention to that."

"Obviously" Sister Alice said.

"It's just not something you could have overlooked unless you were focused on her other assets," I said.

He scowled at me. "By the time I realized she was married, I couldn't stop the train. It was traveling too fast."

"Pshaw," Sister Alice scoffed. "You men have willpower; you just don't use it. I bet if her husband walked into the room at the crucial time, you'd have been able to stop that train."

He shot her a visual arrow, which she returned with one of her own. He squirmed.

"So what happened last night?" I asked Wes.

"I don't know." One glance at Sister Alice and me, and he insisted, "I don't. I told you we were supposed to meet, and she never showed up. Not even a text."

"So how was it you were around to identify her body if you didn't know where she was? It's not exactly strolling outside kinda weather."

He didn't answer, just slowly shook his head and ran his hands over his face. "You don't believe I didn't know where she was last night, do you?"

I slid off the countertop and stood in front of him. "I want to believe you, Wes, but you can't ignore how bad this looks. And if it looks bad to people who know you, it will be worse to the police." His gaze dropped to his feet, his weight leaning on his hands which were cupped around the edge of the countertop on which he still perched. "What time and where did you plan to meet?" I finally said, exasperated.

"We have a secret place to avoid nosey people."

"Where?" Sister Alice asked again. "If we're going to brainstorm and help you, 'secret place' doesn't give us a lot to go on."

"A little cabin by the shore that my buddy owns."

"The old Coolidge place?" I asked. He'd mentioned it a time or two in the past and how he used to party there back in the day. It had a reputation way back when I used to visit Grandpop and Honey.

"That'd be the one. But they sold it a few years back."

"So you stayed there last night even though she didn't show?"

He shook his head. "I waited until about eleven, then went home. This morning when I got up and still hadn't heard anything, I wondered if she got there after I left. I didn't want her ticked off that I wasn't there. So I went back to the cabin to see if there was any sign of her. That's when I saw the police activity out on the lake." He paused, then continued. "I had a bad feelin' and went to check it out."

"Did they ask you how you knew her?" He averted his gaze and remained quiet. My jaw gaped open, and I said, "You didn't tell them, did you?" When he still didn't answer, I shook my head slowly, and Sister Alice groaned her dismay. I exhaled a sigh, then said to Wes, "One more thing."

"What?"

"What about my original question?"

He gave me a hard stare, knowing exactly the question referenced. "No, Andie Rose. I didn't do it."

Chapter 7

It had warmed up considerably by the time we left the church, so we drove by Big Spirit Lake and took Aspen for a quick jaunt. The police presence was gone, leaving no sign of which fish house was the *one*. Given the number of people fishing on the lake and the number of ice houses scattered throughout, other than a piece of yellow crime scene tape tumbling across the lake in the stiff breeze, we had nothing to go on.

"I'm gonna call Wes later to find out which fish house was the 'house of murder,'" I told Sister Alice. "I want to snoop and see if we can find anything useful, given the information we got from Carmen and Wes."

"The police have already gone through it. And if the owner of the house is there, they're probably not going to let you in to investigate. Fact is, they'll probably haul the thing to the shore and sell it."

"Well, we won't know until we try." I glanced at her across the car. "Maybe the owner is a tourist and only here on weekends. From what I've heard, some of them aren't even here that much."

"So, what, you'll then plan to commit a B&E— breaking and entering—"

"I know what B&E is."

"No," she said, shaking her head. "There's got to be a way we can do this legally."

"I'll do it. You'll have nothing to worry about."

"Unless you get caught and I have to bail your butt out of jail," she retorted.

"I'll be really careful." I glanced over at her again.

"Watch the road, you felon."

I placed my palm over my heart and snickered. "I'm touched."

When we returned to the inn, Sister Alice went back to town, promising to come back out for Detective Griffin's celebration and that she'd invite Father Vincent.

"And Sister Ida?"

"I've done things more difficult than that, I'll have you know. Like sponsor you."

I blew a raspberry. "Snarkiness doesn't radiate the love I know you have for me."

The smell of hot blondies and gingersnaps met me when I walked through the door of the inn. My mouth watered, and I practically drooled. Aspen graced me with those big chocolate eyes that could make me feel guilty even when I did nothing wrong. He let out a small whine.

"You're a dog, Aspen. Dogs can't have chocolate. You know that. And I'm saying no to white chocolate to err on side of caution." He continued staring at me. He understood full well what I'd said and wasn't one bit happy about it. "Fine." I said. "You can have a gingersnap. But not before it's time." Despite a quiet whimper, he seemed satisfied.

"Hey, Jade. Hey, Lily." I called as I slipped the hat from my head, feeling the static electricity spark from my hair.

Jade snickered. "Nice hairdo."

I slid my hands from my mittens and smoothed it down. "Better?"

She wrinkled her nose and lifted a shoulder. "It'll do. Marcie had to leave early—something about having to pick up her kid from school. Sounds like he got in trouble for something. He's a friend of Izzy's, so no shock there."

Jade had about as much tolerance for Izzy as Lily had for Jade. And yet, as much fun as each had hassling the other, I think they enjoyed the repartee.

I said, "I'll call Marcie and tell her to bring him here for Detective Griffin's celebration. Anyone seen Frank?"

"He left," Lily said. "Seemed a little down at the mouth. Probably the weather. It's got us all in a funk."

Jade said, "Speak for yourself. Nothing usually gets to Frank."

Except losing his illegal second income. Once again, I smacked into the disbelief of it all.

"I'll call him, too," I said. "See if he can join us." I tapped the top of the counter with my palm. "I'm going to check in with Tony and Izzy, then head upstairs for a hot minute. Be back in a jiff."

After getting reassurance from the duo that Izzy finished the blondies, Tony the gingersnaps, and they'd added lemon zest bars for good measure, I headed upstairs to take a beat of solitude before more socialization. I needed quiet so I could process Carmen and Wes's revelations.

I scanned my table and my bed for anything new. Last fall a book we didn't keep in our library sprouted legs—or wings—and found its way through a locked door and into my room. Since no one, except me, had a key to my room, there were no signs of forced entry, and the book wasn't part of our library, it left only one explanation—the ghost. (Aka: Lady Lucy.) That's when

I fell from the skeptical side of the fence to the believing side.

Seeing nothing out of place now, I fell backward onto the bed. Aspen hopped up and laid beside me, his nose on my chest, and stared at me. I rested my hand on his back. "I haven't forgotten your gingersnap, Aspen." He stared at me a beat more, then lay his nose on his crossed front paws.

Unable to focus until I cleared up the biggest question, I took my phone and punched in Wes's number. After learning that not only did the fish house belong to a friend of his—at which I inwardly groaned—but his friend had already pulled it off the lake as soon as the police were done. Sister Alice had been right.

I bemoaned the prospect of the now-missing fish house as well as what this meant for Wes.

"You didn't think of mentioning that bit of critical information to me earlier, Wes? I'm surprised the police haven't hauled you in yet."

"I didn't do it, Andie Rose." His voice was so tight that if we were on the old-timey phones, it would have snapped the cord.

"I'm only saying it will work against you if you withhold the information. Especially from the police, you know?"

He sighed, sounding calmer, if even just a little. "Yeah, I know."

"What's your friend's name? Did the same friend own both the cabin and the fish house? Did he know Tootsie?"

"I think I know where you're going with this. And yes. Joey Peterson and his wife own them. Used to, anyway. They're at the tail end of a messy divorce. She got the cabin, and he got the fish house. He still comes up to use the fish house."

"Has he met Tootsie?"

"Once. Last year."

"Does he stay with you when he's in Spirit Lake?"

"No. At the Raven Motel on the edge of town."

"Yeah, I know where it is. I thought if he stayed at the inn, I might know him."

"Raven Motel is cheaper."

"There's a reason for that."

"His wife got pretty much everything in the divorce, so it's a cheap place to stay. His wife lets me use the cabin but not him." My eyebrows shot up. "She knows I'm sober and trustworthy."

I pinched the bridge of my nose. "Curious…What caused their divorce? Do you think Joey and Tootsie—"

"No, Andie," he said before I could spit out the entire thought. "It's not because he was fooling around."

I pumped a hand in front of me, palm facing down. "Simmer down. I had to at least ask."

"He wasn't even here. He was in St. Paul."

"Then how did he get here so fast to take his fish house off the lake?"

"The police called him. He got here straight away."

"It's at least a two-and-a-half-hour drive from St. Paul, Wes. How was he able to get here so fast and the house off the lake already? He would have had to wait until the police were done with their investigation."

"I told you, he left as soon as they talked to him. In fact, he said he left before they even hung up. They were done by the time he got here. It don't take long to investigate a twelve-by-seven space."

But was he *really* in St. Paul? Could he have been

the one who found her and called it in? I jotted a note to call the Raven Motel to see if they would tell me if Joey was there the night of the murder.

"Have you used it before? The fish house."

"Yeah. All the time. A lot of guys do."

"He doesn't keep it locked?"

"Yeah, he does. I have the spare key. He shoots me a text if someone is gonna drop by and pick it up."

My heart plummeted. It was bad enough that his prints would be all over the fish house. Now he added more incriminating information. I pinched the bridge of my nose and closed my eyes. Wes was living outside jail bars on borrowed time.

"I know what you're thinking, Andie Rose."

"Do you, really?" I heaved a heavy sigh.

"Yes. Whoever did this woulda had to bust the lock to get in, because no one picked up the key."

"You're a genius."

"It wasn't an impressive lock. A first grader could have opened it without a key." A moment of silence hung in the air before he said, "Whoever did this somehow tethered her to the spearing hole. I wouldn't have done that. I mighta been a boy toy to her, but I really cared about her. Whoever did this is sick." His voice quivered.

I let out a long breath and said quietly, "Completely."

After we hung up, I needed air and a distraction for my brain. Aspen needed his promised gingersnap, so we hiked downstairs to find Izzy setting up the final touches on the refreshment table. I sidled up beside her and she quickly glanced toward me as I snatched a ginger snap and discreetly slipped it to Aspen.

"You sure are taking a special interest in this

celebration," I said. "Happy to be sending him on his way?"

"You have no idea." She gave a dramatic teenage eye roll. "I know there will be another one, but he can't be as crotchety as Griffin."

"*Detective* Griffin," I corrected.

"He doesn't respect kids, so I don't have to respect him."

I could see her point. When I was her age—and the first part of my twenties—I didn't so much respect cops either. As far as I was concerned, they were out to destroy my life; a life that eventually nearly destroyed me.

"Um, Izzy," I said, hesitating as I put the pieces together.

"Yeah?" She finished the last of her setup and turned toward me. Her dark hair, pulled back in a scrunchie, made the hazel starburst in the center of her green eyes pop out even more. But it was the color of her lips that grabbed my attention, and I couldn't take my eyes away from them. I used to prepare the dead for viewing at a funeral home by doing their hair and makeup, and while I had some odd requests for lip and nail colors, I'd never seen this one. "What color is that lip gloss?"

"Pucker-Up Pink." She formed her lips in a pouting *O*. "Like it?"

"On you." The confidence it took to wear that impressed me. I'd never had that at her age. I'd always found ways to fly under the radar, unnoticed, so I could do my—well, whatever it was I wanted to do at the time—undetected. Mostly. Honey knew, though. I could tell by some of her comments. Yet, she'd never judged me. "Grandparents love their grandchildren unconditionally," she'd said. "Doesn't matter what they do. And remember that grandparents are the best listeners," she'd always said, probably hoping I'd fess up. Mother, if she had an inkling of what I'd been up to, would have turned the other way so she wouldn't have had to deal with it. Dad? He confronted me on more than a few occasions but was a *learn from your mistakes* kind of dad.

Remembering what I'd wanted to ask her, I said, "Izzy—"

"What?" she asked, as though I was holding her up from something important.

"When you said the police don't respect kids, have you experienced that first-hand?" She tossed a glance over her shoulder toward the kitchen. Probably looking for a quick escape. "I'm here if you ever want to talk, okay?" *Honey would be so proud.*

"I don't need a life coach, Kaz. I'm fine."

"Not as a life coach. As a friend. If you ever want to talk, no judgment, I'm here."

"Okaaayy." She drew out the word as though I'd lost the last marble in my noggin. "Is that it?"

"That's it," I said, worried that Izzy was on her way to adopting my addiction issues.

"Ms. Kaczmarek," a familiar voice said behind me. Izzy's attention toward me flew out the proverbial window and onto the person speaking—none other than Noah Parker. "Smells delectable in here. Could smell it the minute I opened my car door to come in."

"Thank you. We like to keep our guests happy." I glanced toward Izzy to introduce the two, but nearly choked on the laughter that bubbled up. Her eyes and mouth were the same shape, and she stood immobile.

She was clearly smitten with the new potential detective. "Noah," I said, struggling to swallow my cachinnation. "Meet Izzy, our sous-chef and the one who did most of today's baking." I grinned at Izzy. "Izzy, this might be the next Spirit Lake detective."

Chapter 8

Izzy's cheeks quickly matched her lips. Finally, she broke free of the trance and reached to shake his extended hand. Unable to suppress it any longer, I giggled, earning me a glare, but it held little weight through her star-struck eyes.

"Good job, young lady," he said. "But aren't you awfully young to be a sous-chef?"

Despite her clearly smitten demeanor, a defiant glint sparked in her eyes. "I'm the best chef you'll ever meet."

"I can't disagree with her," I said, enjoying the show.

She finally let go of his hand. "I need to get back to work. Tony can't run the kitchen without me."

Amusement danced in Noah's eyes. "You'd better go then."

Turning to leave, she grabbed my arm, yanked me a few feet away, then whispered in my ear, "He's so hot."

I snickered. If he landed the detective job, I hoped her infatuation wouldn't lead her toward behavior that led to seeing him more often.

Izzy disappeared behind the kitchen door, and I walked back toward Noah, who stuffed half of a blondie in his mouth. My eyebrows shot up.

After he swallowed, he said, "These are amazing."

"Apparently." I snagged another gingersnap and discreetly slipped it to Aspen behind my back.

"I saw that," he said and winked before he jammed the rest of it in his mouth.

"I'm sure you did, being a detective and all," I said wryly. "When is your second interview?"

"Tomorrow first thing before I head back home."

"Where's home?" Aspen, who must have swallowed the cookie in one bite, peered up at me expectantly.

"I think your companion wants another."

"No more," I said, scratching the top of Aspen's head.

He openly admired Aspen. "Beautiful dog. I noticed him earlier. Is he a golden?"

"Red retriever. My service dog."

His eyes darted toward me. "Service dog?"

"Yep." I could have kicked myself for offering up the last tidbit. My mental issues were none of his business. Detective Griffin came through the door. Saved. I waved at him over Noah's shoulder. "I'd better go greet the guest of honor."

The number of people who'd shown up to celebrate with Detective Griffin made clear that word about the celebration flew around town. With the volume that Tony and Izzy baked, the goodies were dwindling quickly. On more than one occasion, I glanced toward the kitchen where Izzy stood in the doorway watching. She had it bad for Noah Parker.

Detective Griffin appeared genuinely pleased as he munched on gingersnap after gingersnap, chatting with people between bites. Wish I'd known earlier how much he liked them—I wouldn't be above bribing him with them for the information I wanted. Both Sister Alice and I preferred the lemon bars and ate our fair share. The blondie's, though, remained mostly untouched except for what Noah and one other guest consumed. Note to self—maybe we won't serve them regularly.

Izzy had refilled the refreshment trays, and by the time they were all but empty, most of the inn's guests retired to their rooms and the visitors from town had left. Half an hour later, Detective Griffin, Noah, and Sister Alice and I were the only ones left. Jade watched in silence from the desk. Lily, who received a call from her daughter, was fixing to leave to pick up her grandchildren from school.

"Another cookie Detective?" I asked.

He patted his belly and waved his hand as if swatting at a fly. "No, no. If I eat one more, I'll bust. And now that I'll soon become a poor retired man, I won't have money to buy bigger clothes. And food. Good God. It's a shame what they charge for the stuff that keeps us out of the hospital."

I chuckled. "You're welcome to come and eat here anytime. On the house. Another bar, Noah? Or a lemon zest bar? You don't have the same excuse as Detective Griffin."

He held his hand up, palm facing me. "No. I've already had too much, and I'm ready for a nap." He yawned, more relaxed than I'd seen him since he'd been here.

After Noah stood, Detective Griffin did the same. "I'd better get back to the station." He gave me a side hug that warmed my heart. "Thank you, Andie Rose. I really appreciate the trouble you went to for me. But I won't miss the trouble you've caused me."

Smiling, I leaned into him. "I'm sure you won't." I pulled back. "Do I still have to call you Detective after you're retired?"

He nodded toward Noah. "You'll likely be calling *him* Detective. Spirit Lake isn't big enough for two." He snorted. "Well, it wasn't before you came along."

I elbowed his ribs gently. "I keep telling you you're going to miss me."

"You'd better go rest, Parker," he said. "You're falling asleep on your feet. I'll see you tomorrow first thing."

He shook his head and grimaced. "Think I'll do just that. Hope I'm not coming down with something. But I'll be there regardless, wearing a mask if I need to." He saluted Detective Griffin and left toward the stairs, retreating toward his room.

"You know," I said to Detective Griffin and Sister Alice, "there might be something going around. A few people were acting a little weird." I poked Griffin's arm with my forefinger. "I'm good at this detecting stuff." I realized Frank's absence from the celebration, and I inhaled sharply. *Crap*. I'd seen this kind of weird before.

Detective Griffin regarded me carefully. "Why do I get a feeling something popped into your head I should know about?"

I shook my head vigorously, my cheeks hot. "Nothing. Nothing at all."

He narrowed his eyes. "I don't believe you. You're going to give me my last gray hairs."

I clamped my lips together. "Just remembered something is all. No big deal."

He guffawed. "Right. I'll find out, eventually. I didn't see Simon down here. Not that I'm surprised."

"Are you looking at him for his wife's murder?" I was hopeful that discussing the murder would rid the unease in the pit of my stomach that I couldn't shake.

He sniggered. "You don't stop, do you?" His attention turned toward Sister Alice, then back to me. "And I thought I told you to keep your mouth shut about the potential foul play."

I bit my lower lip. "You did. But Sister Alice and I tell each other everything. Well, *I* tell *her* everything. She can't really tell me everything because of confidentiality and all that."

Detective Griffin snorted. "Somehow, I don't believe that."

"So are you?" I pressed. "Looking at Simon."

"I can neither confirm nor deny."

"That's no answer."

"Exactly." A corner of his mouth twitched upward.

"What about the owner of the fish house where they found Tootsie?" Sister Alice asked, pushing up the orange frames with her finger. "Or the guy who broke in and found her."

"Yeah," I said. "From what I've heard, a lot of people use that fish house. Kind of a community fishing hole."

Detective Griffin scowled. "How did you hear that already?"

"I have my ways. What about Carmen? Although," I continued without giving him a beat to answer, "it would have been pretty impossible for her to carry a body out there. Unless said body was on a sleigh of some sort. But then, where would she ever find one of those since this was her first time here? I think we can rule her out."

"*We?*" Detective Griffin tipped his head back, groaned, and rubbed the back of his neck. "*We* aren't doing anything, Andie Rose. The police are handling it. Please, for the love of God, stay out of it." He turned toward Sister Alice. "You, too."

"I only go with her to keep her out of trouble." Sister Alice jerked her thumb toward me.

He exhaled an odd combination of amused irritation. "Thank you for this send-off. It was nice. And you're right."

"About Simon?"

"No." He slipped into his coat and zipped it up, the zipper straining over his belly. He pulled his hat on, ear flaps dangling over his ears, stuffed his fingers into his gloves, and started for the door.

"About what?" I called after him.

He opened the door and called over his shoulder, "I might miss you a little when I'm gone."

I pumped a fist in the air. "I knew it."

His reply, a short cackle, rode in on the stiff wind that blew through the door as he closed it behind him.

As soon as he left, Sister Alice nabbed her coat and slid her arms into the sleeves.

"Leaving so soon? I thought you'd come with me to bring Aspen for a walk."

"The sun's going down fast, and it didn't get as warm as predicted. Besides, Father Vincent needs his car."

"All right then." I fetched her hat and gloves from the desk. "Talk soon."

"Try to stay out of trouble, will you?"

"You crush me with your lack of faith."

She eyebrows bounced up. "There's nothing wrong with *my* faith."

As soon as the door closed behind her, Jade stood

and stretched. "I didn't think either Detective Griffin or Sister Alice were ever gonna get out of here."

"Two of your favorite people. And Izzy and Tony…see the common denominator here?" I chuckled, and she rolled her eyes. "Sister Alice has a heart of gold, Jade. She's just a little rough around the edges."

"A little? Can you say understatement?"

I sighed, choosing my next words carefully. "I don't say this in a mean way, Jade, but you're not exactly Princess Diana." She snorted her response. "All I'm saying is we all have our faults. Every one of us. When people get upset with others, it's on them, not the person they're upset with."

"Is that some of your life coach mumbo-jumbo?" she asked.

"It's called wisdom." I laid a hand gently on her shoulder. "I'm not asking you to be friends with Sister Alice, only that you try to see what's in her heart."

She mumbled something unintelligible, and I gave her shoulder a gentle squeeze. "I'm going to go check in with Izzy and then be in my office for a while."

She nodded. When I'd walked a few feet, she said, "Hey, Andie Rose?"

I turned. "Yeah?"

"Thanks for the free session." She didn't look at me when she said it, but I detected a ray of sunshine in those words.

****

The following morning birthed warmer temperatures, providing me hope that the cold snap was finally ending.

I hopped out of bed, dressed in long underwear, jogging pants, hoodie, parka, earmuffs, and my warmest running shoes. After Aspen and I ate breakfast, I snapped his harness on, sans the leash, and headed outside by way of the back stairwell.

Opening the door brought with it a deep breath of fresh, frosty air. Northern Minnesota, despite its sometimes-brutal temps, had the cleanest air of anywhere I'd ever been. The sky was crystal clear and dotted with millions of stars. The sun would begin its ascent before we reached the trail around Big Spirit Lake. We trotted around the building toward my car. In warmer temps, we jogged to the trail. Not today.

I shivered as I thought of the icy wind coming off the lake. But Aspen had been such a trooper through the cold snap. He deserved to go where he enjoyed it most.

I opened the passenger side door and scratched his head before he jumped in. He settled on his haunches, so tall and proud, while I fastened the seat belt around him. Sister Alice teased me mercilessly about buckling him in. "He's a dog, Andie Rose," she'd scoffed. "Back in the day, we didn't even have seat belts for children. If someone had a pickup truck, the kids piled in the back."

"Yeah, but we're not in the stone age anymore," I'd teased her.

By the time we reached the lake and traipsed through the snow to the trail, the sun's dazzling rays began their ascent. I stood in awe and stared, hardly able to take in the full beauty. The pristine snow on the ground, the deafening silence, condensation from each breath gently rolling from my mouth and nostrils, and the freshness of unpolluted air. It was all like poetry. Aspen focused on the rabbits and squirrels. As soon as he began chasing one, he stopped to study another; chased that one, then stopped when he saw another, confusing himself silly.

"Aspen, give yourself a rest." My voice echoed in the stillness.

After an exhilarating walk, we headed back toward the car, my senses alive and alert to begin the workday. As soon as I'd belted in Aspen, then my own seat belt, my phone rang.

"This is Andie Rose."

"Was this some sort of sick joke?" The angry tone shattered the peacefulness.

I frowned and shook my head. "Noah?"

"Yes, this is Noah. What in the hell did you do?"

Performing mental gymnastics, I struggled to understand what he was talking about. I hadn't done anything or talked to anyone, and even if that was the case, wouldn't Detective Griffin be calling me?

Finally spent, I said, "Noah, I have no idea what you're referring to."

"No?" he barked, not sounding like himself at all. "I lost the job because I failed the pee test this morning. Cannabis. There was a reason I felt the way I did yesterday. And it wasn't the flu."

My stomach tanked, and I wanted to vomit as I listened. I had been right. *Frank, I am absolutely going to kill you.* Yet, I couldn't believe Frank would have done this. *Couldn't or wouldn't, Andie Rose?* After a deep breath, I pressed my lips together to keep my breakfast in.

"On my way back to the inn right now. Fifteen minutes tops."

"It's a little late for that." The line went dead. His tone made me want to stay in town and hide my car somewhere until he checked out of the inn, was on the road, and beyond the horizon.

"I think I'm in deep trouble, Aspen." I slid my fingers through his silky fur for comfort and to ease my narrowing vision, preventing a panic attack. Aspen slipped out of his belt and laid his head on my thigh. He watched me with innocent eyes. "If Noah had been a dog, he wouldn't have had the chocolate. So it's *his* fault." Funny how a dog's eyes can communicate not-so-subtle messages. And right now, his eyes said, *humans are so weird.*

On the drive back to the inn, thoughts of the prior afternoon tumbled through my head like rocks in a polishing machine: Izzy, all too happy to finish baking the blondies; Izzy, all too happy to be rid of Detective Griffin; Izzy, all too happy to make sure the celebration was a bang; Izzy, all too happy in general. Izzy, Izzy, Izzy. *Argh.* I thought of Frank's grow and his stash, his absence, and his promise that he'd never sold a single ounce of his supply to any guest. But he didn't say anything about the employees. Surely, he wasn't stupid enough to sell to a minor. *Was he?*

And then I obviously lost my mind as I howled with laughter, startling poor Aspen, who'd been perfectly happy watching out the window. I laughed until I cried and my side ached, then had to force myself to stop before I cried for real about all the potential repercussions.

I pulled off to the side of the road for a moment. So many *what-ifs* circled me at a dizzying pace. What if I lost my business license? What if I'm slapped with criminal charges? What if the place that had been in my family for so long, the place Grandpop and Honey took such pride in building, crashed down around me? What if my neglect ruined Noah's life? What if … Anxiety swept me up in its clutches. Suddenly a fist formed in the pit of my stomach. "Holy wicked whiskey!" I shifted my car back into drive, stepped on the pedal, but barely remembered the rest of the drive back to the inn.

When I pulled into the parking lot, I snapped my phone from the center console and dialed.

The phone finally picked up and a sleepy voice said, "Yello?"

"Izzy. Get your butt to the inn. Now."

Chapter 9

By the time Izzy arrived, my anger had transformed into guilt, thanks to Noah's scolding. While Noah ranted, finally running out of steam, I kept mum. There's no reasoning with someone who's in a tirade. When he'd finally stopped, I was so grateful for the break, I didn't dare risk getting his dander up again by saying anything.

Head down when she came through the door, she unzipped her coat. When she saw Noah, she stopped dead in her tracks. Her hair was a hot mess, and she was still in her pajamas—flannel bottoms that read *Go sit on a* with a picture of a cactus plant, and pink suede snow boots. Her cheeks flushed, and in one fluent move, she ran a hand over her hair and clutched her coat together with the other.

When she finished her dramatic entrance, she stood still as could be, avoiding Noah's direction.

"What's wrong?" she asked.

Never would I have described Izzy as timid, but there was a first for everything. Assuming she knew why I called her in, my guess was she feared for her job. I scowled. *She should have thought about that earlier.*

"In my office," I said. "I don't think anyone coming down for breakfast needs to hear this."

"Okay," she all but whispered.

I turned toward Noah and beckoned him to follow.

Lily watched without uttering a word. My staff had

never seen me angry. To that point, since sobriety, few people have seen me angry. But the possible consequences of her actions on the inn, the business Grandpop and Honey built with decades of love, warranted anger.

Once inside my office, I closed the door behind Noah and Izzy.

I pointed to the chair opposite mine. "Please sit, Izzy." Aspen sat, too. I cleared a chair in the corner of the room of books, papers, and a coat and pulled it over for Noah. Finally, I skirted my desk and sat on the edge of my seat.

Silence hung in the air, as pregnant as a rain cloud begging to burst. I took a few deep, calming breaths before trusting myself to speak.

"Do you want to tell us anything about yesterday afternoon, Izzy?"

Noah looked from me to Izzy and back to me. "What's going on?"

Izzy stared down at her hands as she twisted a ring on her middle finger back and forth. Probably sending me a subliminal message.

"Izzy?" I said, trying to maintain my cool.

"Tell you about what?" she finally said so quietly I could hardly hear.

I forced myself to remain as calm as possible. Which wasn't easy. "You know about what."

Noah's eyebrows raised. "I don't. Anyone want to fill me in?"

I squinted my eyes, flabbergasted. He'd rather believe *I* spiked the blondies rather than a seventeen-year-old kid? He was a detective, for crying out loud. And if these were his detecting skills, Spirit Lake was in a steaming heap of trouble. His confusion, however, caused me to second-guess my presumptuous accusation. Even though I hadn't outright verbalized it, the allegation was undeniable. *What if I was way off base?* Guilt invaded me like weeds choking a garden. A *weed* garden.

Izzy hung her head low, still twisting the ring. "I'm sorry. It was a prank meant for Detective Griffin."

"What?" he said incredulously. "Why would you try to get a detective high?"

Her lips turned inward, all but disappearing, as if forcing herself to be quiet. But I knew the answer. The full realization dropped one piece at a time until the puzzle was whole.

"Revenge," I finally said. "Detective Griffin busted you for smoking weed, didn't he?"

Her nod was barely perceptible.

"Good God, Izzy." Noah's voice was tighter than the ring Izzy was now trying to remove. He stood and paced, ran one hand through his premature gray hair, the other in a fist on his hip. "I'd remind myself to never get on your bad side, but now that's a moot point because I lost the job opportunity. All because of your so-called *prank*."

"Where did you get it from?" I held my breath. *Don't say Frank. Don't say Frank.*

"Frank," she whispered.

And there it was. Out loud, no less, in front of Noah. Was there no end to the poor discretion of a teenager? I exhaled my grief, tipped my head back against my chair, closed my eyes and pinched the bridge of my nose. "When?"

"A few days ago."

That would have been before I talked with Frank, but apparently all the shelves weren't stocked in his brain if he's selling to a minor. Or even *giving* it to her. I was likely to lose two good employees in one fell swoop. Not to mention the reputation of the inn.

Taking a minute to mull over the situation, I said, "Izzy, that was before you knew about the retirement celebration."

"Yeah." Her voice was a mere whisper.

"Who is Frank?" Noah asked.

I swallowed the lump in my throat and kept my mouth shut.

"The gardener," Izzy admitted.

I blew through pursed lips, and she raised her shoulders and palms in a nonverbal *What*?

"Go figure," Noah said dryly. "The gardener growing marijuana."

"He's a seventy-eight-year-old gardener," I said and shook my head in disbelief. "And no, he's not senile. He's kind, thoughtful, helpful, and sweet."

"I bet he is," Noah said.

The tension in the room nearly suffocated me. "Noah, I don't know what to say." I sank into my chair.

He heaved a sigh and sat down, leaned forward, and rested his forearms on his thighs. "Well, if there's a silver lining here, it would be that I am still in for the job." He stabbed a finger in the air toward Izzy. "Because you, young lady, are going to call Detective Griffin and tell him what you did. Now."

I groaned with the force of what that meant. The incident had to be reported to Detective Griffin, who would then investigate the situation with Frank. Izzy too. Frank could go to jail for possession, possession with intent to sell, contributing to the delinquency of a minor, cultivating, and God only knew what else. And Izzy—she's facing juvenile detention.

"Do we have to tell Detective Griffin?" But Noah's expression told me what I already knew. "I understand. It's not fair for you to lose this job because of something you didn't do."

Fear of the close call of lost sobriety buzzed into my head, and the situation became very personal. "Izzy, what if I had eaten those blondies? Or anyone else with addiction issues." Like Sister Alice. Even if it was only half. "Do you understand what that could have done? I only have six, almost seven, years under my belt. Others may have longer, but that doesn't mean it wouldn't cause a relapse."

"I'm sorry, Kaz," she whispered, her eyes filled with silvery tears, the starburst in the center of her eyes shining. "Am I fired?"

I exhaled, buying time to get my renewed anger in check. "Given the consequences of what your *prank* cost all of us, *that's* what you're worried about? Mr. Parker here might have lost his job opportunity—and it wouldn't be as easy for him to find another job. Not with something like this on his record. Unlike you, he's not seventeen."

"Thanks for adding insult to injury," Noah muttered. "Although there's not enough money in the world to make me want to be seventeen again."

I glanced at him, then back to Izzy. "Frank…" My stomach turned at the thought and his potential jail time. "Did he approach you with it?"

She shook her head. "No—"

"Oh, thank God." I fell against the back of my chair,

hand to my chest.

"I saw him one day bringing things in and watched him for a while. I wanted to know what the old man was doing, so I snagged the master key and went to peek."

"When was this?" I asked, making a mental note to lock the master keys in a drawer to which only *I* had the key.

"A couple of weeks ago."

She slid down farther into her chair, her bottom on the edge. Her pajama bottoms gave me the idea to slip a cactus underneath her before she slipped completely off the chair and onto the floor. Now *that* would be a suitable punishment.

"Where's the rest of what you took?"

"Wasn't much left, so I threw it away." Her flushed cheeks and refusal to make eye contact screamed *liar, liar, pants on fire*.

I clenched my jaw. "Neither Noah nor I are stupid. Where is it?"

"My bedroom," she murmured, barely audible. "I'll bring it to you if you promise not to tell my mom."

I cocked my head to the side and crossed my arms in front of me. "Eh. I think you'll get it to me no matter if I tell your mom or not."

She groaned. "I'm in so much trouble." After a loaded pause, each of us lost in the possibilities of our own dilemmas, Izzy asked, "So am I fired?"

After a long sigh, I said, "I don't know, Izzy. I need to process all of this. And then talk with Detective Griffin." I glanced at Noah. "Preferably before you do."

"So long as you talk to him before noon today, because I'm not leaving town without getting this straightened out."

I exhaled slowly and rubbed the back of my neck. "I'll call him now." I looked at Izzy. "Go home, Iz. When I've decided what to do, I'll call you. Do not come back here until you've heard from me. You're under house arrest."

She kept her face lowered, swiped her cheeks with her palms, and stood. "Yes, ma'am."

Noah closed my office door after Izzy, then turned toward me. "Well done. I hardly had to say anything."

"This wasn't a simple prank, Noah," I said, swallowing my fear. "Pranks don't potentially destroy lives and cost people their jobs. And then there's probable jail time for a dear old man."

"Well, to be honest, the prank didn't cause that. Your *dear old man* did. But I'm sorry about the close call for you. Detective Griffin may have mentioned your AA affiliation. Also, the inconvenience that if someone tells you something in a meeting, you cannot tell him who said it."

I rested my attention heavily on Noah. "AA stands for Alcoholics *Anonymous*. That Detective Griffin told you anything at all strips the anonymity part. That's why we don't allow outsiders like you in meetings. You don't know how to keep things quiet."

He nodded. "Message received." He turned to leave, then pivoted back toward me. "Why do I get the idea that you knew about Frank's grow operation?"

"How would I know where your ideas come from?"

His lips curved in amusement. "Smooth answer." He stood still, his attention toward the floor, hands tucked in his front pockets. "Did you?"

I blew a breath from pursed lips. "Noah—" I paused before deciding honesty would be less damaging at this point. "Yes. I knew about it." He didn't say anything, so I continued. "I came across it yesterday, scolded him until he felt the way I did when you lit into me earlier—which disappoints me. No one deserves to feel that way." I cocked my head. "Eh, except Izzy. Anyway, I gave him until Monday to get rid of it, whether that meant bring it to his house or destroy it, or I would call the police."

"So, in other words, you gave him a choice of how to destroy it." I kept silent. "You can't just move a grow like that, Andie Rose. The plants need to be kept at a certain temperature and humidity level, and in these temps—"

"I'm well aware of how growing weed works, Noah."

"Do you, now?"

I wanted to swipe the smirk from his face, but worry about Frank, the inn, and Sister Alice having unknowingly imbibed after thirty-plus years of sobriety zapped what little energy I had left. Not to mention my close call and Noah possibly losing the job … And Izzy. So young, beautiful, and brilliant, yet so stupid. I'd hit up a meeting today for sure. Resentment was enemy number one for an addict, no matter how many years sober. And my resentment level right now was off the charts.

"I hear Brewski's has Pub Quiz night on Tuesdays. If I'm lucky and still get the job, maybe we could try it some evening. I bet you'd be a mean contender."

Sighing, I stood and stretched my arms behind me. "I don't normally hang out at pubs, Noah."

"Of course. My bad."

I shook my head slowly, catching my lower lip between my teeth. No sense upping my resentment by one. "No problem. It's not something normal people remember. But if you'll excuse me," I gestured toward the door, "I have a couple of phone calls to make." *The first one to Frank*.

Chapter 10

Frank gripped the armrests of the chair opposite me and winced as he lowered himself into the seat. "This cold weather is heck on the arthritis." His aura told me he hadn't a clue why I called him in. His eyes, more sunken than usual in his smoky-quartz-colored skin, appeared strained as he settled in. "What's up, Miss Andie?"

I tapped my pen on my desk blotter as I carefully constructed how to start. "We had a problem yesterday afternoon concerning your decisions." I sounded like a schoolteacher chastising a student for skipping an exam. I blinked in dismay. Frank's white arthritic knuckles clutched the chair, and he heaved a sigh.

"Miss Andie?"

I blinked and shook my head. "That came out wrong. Let me start over."

"I think I know what this is about, mm-hm."

My eyes grew wide. "You do?"

"Yes, ma'am. Got a call from Izzy this morning."

I pressed my lips together while giving him a sidelong look.

"She said it was best if she ratted on herself before someone blamed me for what she did. Said she'd found, um—" He cleared his throat, rocked forward slightly, then back. His grip loosened a little, and color returned to his knuckles. "I thanked her for letting me know, and she offered to help me get rid of it. Leave no trace of evidence. As a matter a fact, she wanted to do it straightaway this mornin'. She's meetin' me here in half an hour, um-hm."

Engrossed in processing the unexpected information, nothing came to my lips except, "Huh."

"Said it would keep us outta trouble. And it had to be done anyway, so I accepted the help. Probly her way of making an amends."

I gave a sardonic smile. "I know what amends are, Frank."

"Yes, Miss Andie, I suspect you do. I'm proud of you for all your hard work."

His grandfatherly accolades warmed me. And that ticked me off. How can I draw a firm line when his approval was all it took to make me crumble? I breathed in through my nostrils, out through my mouth, briefly closing my eyes before speaking again.

"Amends are about others, not oneself. When you're genuinely sorry for what you've done rather than what you get out of it. Speaking from hard experience." Ironically, I'd learned that if it's done with others in mind instead of self, expecting nothing in return—not even forgiveness from the other person—I get something out of it anyway. Something priceless—freedom from self-destruction. Life is full of ironic, peculiar lessons. That said, I wasn't convinced Izzy's apology was about *her* instead of Frank. But who was I to judge?

"I sure hope young Izzy doesn't get in trouble because of me," he said. "Since I'm the one who did the wrong thing and all."

I choked. "Apparently you haven't heard the complete story." I filled him in on the extent of Izzy's *innocence*, and he heaved a sigh.

"I see," he mumbled. "So what I did was more serious than I'd anticipated."

I squinted and shook my head slowly. *Enable much, Frank?* "Frank, Izzy's behavior had nothing to do with you. It had to do with *Izzy's* choice. Do you understand that?"

"But it wouldn't a happened if—"

"No, no. Stop right there." I shot out my hand, palm facing him. "Izzy concocted some cockamamie scheme. She would have carried that out with or without your— stash. Do you get that?" It baffled me that the same conversation I'd had with a seventeen-year-old, in somewhat different verbiage, I was now having with a seventy-eight-year-old. He stayed quiet, probably thinking I'd lost my *ever-loving mind*, as Sister Alice says. "Take Izzy up on the offer to help and get it done fast. I have to call Detective Griffin." I looked at Frank pointedly. "But first I have to take care of something that needs my *immediate* attention, so that call to the detective will have to wait a little longer." Stupid on my part, I know, but at this point, I was willing to stoop to any level to save the inn.

It took a hot minute for the unspoken message to strike him. Suddenly, he pushed himself up from the chair. "I'll get started right away."

"And Frank?" I said as he reached the door. He turned his head my way, hand still on the doorknob. "When this all blows over, let's talk finances and see how we can work something out."

He gave a barely perceptible nod and left. If I knew Frank, he wouldn't allow a raise—or any kind of help— after this debacle. Of course, that said, I apparently didn't know Frank at all, or this debacle wouldn't have left me so thunderstruck. But as the saying goes, desperate people take desperate measures. I wondered how desperate Wes or Simon were. Desperate enough to kill?

Since Izzy offered to help Frank, my admonishment to not come back until I call must have, to her, applied only to the inn and not the entire grounds. A misunderstanding I wasn't about to clarify with her now. I wanted this taken care of immediately, for all our sakes. Realizing my own enabling tendencies, I sank down into my chair and groaned loudly. As I've already said, I never had been good at taking my own advice.

For the next hour and a half, through the windows in the foyer that faced the woods toward the shed, I watched the buzz of increased activity. Besides Frank and Izzy, there was also a boy about Izzy's age in the mix. Her poor judgement had no bounds. I closed my eyes, tilted my head back, and rubbed the back of my neck with one hand. *Oy Vey*. Could this get any worse? I bit my lower lip and watched his taillights until they disappeared.

Izzy's heart was in the right place—partially—and she was a child genius, but her ability to think logically was that of a seventeen-year-old. A child. Is that someone I wanted as an employee here at the inn? I was leaning more toward the negative. Sister Alice had told me more than once, "Don't judge other people because they sin differently than you do." At the time, I didn't fully understand what that statement meant. But I sure did now.

A short time later, Izzy drove past the inn to the long driveway leading toward the road. She sunk low in her seat and pulled the brim of her ball cap low. *Seriously*? I rolled my eyes. Next, Frank got in his truck, gave me a thumbs up signal as he drove out—which I returned—before turning toward the office to call Detective Griffin.

Before punching in the last number, I paused and took a deep breath. *Here goes nothin'.* Hoping it would roll to voicemail, I sucked in a breath when he picked up.

"Griffin."

I swallowed the lump in my throat. "This is—"

"I know who it is. And it's never a good thing when you call me here."

"Never say never," I said, trying to lighten his dark expectation.

"What's it this time?"

So much for that. "Um—well—I'm not sure how to say this."

"Usually the best idea is to spit it out before figuring out how to spin it. But I assume the spinning began before you picked up the phone."

The idea struck me that if I started with the part that Noah's failed pee test wasn't his fault, that might help. So I gave him the song and dance first, careful I didn't inadvertently say something to dig the hole deeper. The line was silent except for his breathing. "Detective Griffin?"

"Yep. I need to put you on hold for a minute."

"But—" Elevator music piped through the line. We played it at the hotel I used to manage, hoping it would relax the waiting party, but usually it had the opposite effect.

I closed my eyes, inhaled deeply, and did the four-square breathing technique I taught clients. *Four in, hold for four. Four out, hold for four. Four in, hold for four. Four out, hold for four.* When I'd begun relaxing, the music stopped.

"Noah is in my office now."

"So you already knew everything before I called, and you just let me go on?" I was sick that I'd gotten so worked up about telling him, and he already knew.

"Nope. He made an appointment to come in and see if he could make a plea for another chance. I had you on speakerphone. You were on hold while he filled in the gaps of your story. You know, the parts you left out."

Great. I had assumed I was on speaker because of the tinny echo, but I sure as heck didn't think Noah was there listening in. My mind began spinning. If Detective Griffin let Noah listen in, that meant he'd hired him. And then it occurred to me—Detective Griffin had lied to me. Noah must have told him, and Detective Griffin *did* know. "You've already hired him. That means he *told* you why he failed the pee test."

I heard his chair squeak, the squeak I knew by now that happened when he leaned back so far only his toes touched the ground.

"Nope, he didn't tell me. He evidently trusted you to do that. He's nicer than me."

"So why'd you hire him if you didn't know it wasn't his fault?"

"I haven't told you I did."

"You didn't have to." I remembered his preference for the gingersnaps. "Why didn't *you* have any blondies?"

"No, I didn't know about the laced *refreshments*," he said. "That's what you were getting at, wasn't it?"

"No. But that begs an answer."

"Nut allergy. Plain and simple. And I don't answer to you."

"Noah?" I said, assuming he was still in the room.

"Here," he said as if in roll call.

"Are you the next detective in Spirit Lake?"

Detective Griffin jumped in. "Ms. Kaczmarek, has anyone besides me told you you're nosey?"

"In school, they teach kids curiosity is a good thing."

"This isn't school." His response was more of a bark, and after a beat, he said in a gentler tone, "Yes. Noah Parker is Spirit Lake's new detective."

"And you're heavy on my radar, Andie Rose," Noah said.

Detective Griffin said, "We'll be paying young Ms. Carter a visit in an hour, and then we'll be out at your place to search the gardening shed and to speak with Mr. Flowers."

The formality of using Izzy and Frank's last names said he'd once again crossed from casual to detective mode.

"Yes, sir."

Collecting my thoughts, I stared out the window at the surface of the thick blanket of snow, madly sparkling in the sunshine. I picked up the phone and left Frank a voicemail about what I'd learned from Detective Griffin, and that I'd see him soon. Frank picked it up just as I was hanging up.

"Miss Andie."

I put the phone back up to my ear. "Hey, Frank. I just left you a voicemail."

"I was on the phone with Detective Griffin. He wants me at the inn for an interview. He's gonna search the shed, um-hm. Sure glad we got—"

I quickly cut him off. "Say nothing more."

Clearly stunned into confusion by my outburst, he

remained silent. The police would subpoena our phone records, and I wanted to play it safe. Calling my employees wouldn't cause any red flags. Except calling Frank might, given the timing was so quick after my conversation with Detective Griffin.

"We'll talk when you get here."

"I'm on my way home from the dump. I'll be there right after I change."

After we hung up, I laughed until I thought I was gonna pee my pants. And I couldn't stop as I imagined all the high animals foraging through the dump for food.

Finally collecting myself, I realized I hadn't told Tony that Izzy wouldn't be in for a while, and that we might need to start the search over again. *Oy Vey.* I pinched the bridge of my nose and closed my eyes. But then something occurred to me and they flew back open—Tony was Izzy's supervisor. Had he known about Izzy's prank?

Chapter 11

Tony wasn't in the kitchen. Since lunch had already been served, he was probably cleaning up the dining room. Aspen wandered off toward the front desk, so rather than lending Tony a hand as I usually would, I took advantage of his absence in the kitchen and nosed around for any sign of something amiss. Like marijuana, for instance. I sighed. When this whole stinking nightmare was over, the inn might get closed down.

By the time Tony finally arrived, I'd searched what I could and plunked myself down on a stool at the long center island.

"Hey." He breezed right on by me and toward the oven. "I was in the dining room."

"I gathered that."

"Thanks for the hand," he teased over his shoulder. "Izzy isn't here yet, not that I'm surprised, so I'll get a start on the refreshments for afternoon tea." When I didn't say anything, he turned toward me, leaned against the counter, and wiped his hands on the towel hanging by the belt of his apron. One glance at my face and a scowl spread across his. He knew a lot more than I thought he might.

"About yesterday—"

"Yeah, about that," he said.

"So you heard."

"Some of it."

Each answering with brevity, waiting for the other to expound on the situation, I finally caved. After finishing the highlights, if one could call it that, he simply stared at me as he processed the complete disaster. Finally, he looked upward and shook his head slowly.

"Izzy called to, quote, fill me in, unquote." He emphasized with air quotes. "But she neglected to tell me the part that she's not allowed to come back until you've told her she can. Would have been nice to know she's not coming this afternoon. Or possibly ever again." He huffed and shoved his fists on his hips. "I'll do what I can, and supplement as needed, with some things I stored in the freezer. I think I have scones, raspberry blondies, and cheesecake bars. There might even be some cranberry cream cheese bars. I made them all so we won't have to worry about Izzy's additives."

I sighed and shook my head slowly as my stomach grumbled. "It would horrify Grandpop and Honey at what has all happened since I've taken over."

"Probably."

"Thanks. Do the world a favor and don't become a counselor, okay?" I said sullenly. "I'll call Sister Eunice to see if she can fill in until I sort out this mess."

He muttered something unintelligible. "That'll work."

I frowned. "I thought you liked Sister Eunice?"

Before I hired Izzy, Sister Alice recommended Sister Eunice help us until we came up with a permanent solution. As Tony had been with Izzy initially, he didn't trust Sister Eunice to step up to bat. "Not just anyone can do this job, Andie Rose," he'd grumbled. "We have a reputation to uphold." Thankfully, Tony had come around and enjoyed her help. So when I found Izzy, he pushed back against it, wanting to keep Sister Eunice. Times changed, I guess.

"I do. But I don't particularly appreciate the constant upset in my kitchen."

"I get it. But what am I supposed to do?" When he didn't answer, I said, "Sulking won't solve the problem. Do you have an opinion on Izzy?"

He inhaled slowly, letting it out equally slowly while looking directly at me. Or rather, *through* me. I waited.

Finally, he said, "She's a pain in my butt, but she's good. And she's reliable." I thought my eyeballs might pop out of their sockets. He tilted his head to the side. "Usually. But come on, Andie Rose. She's a seventeen-year-old kid. We both knew what we were signing on for when we hired her."

I sucked my cheeks in as I waited to see where he was going with this.

"People gave both you and I second—and third and fourth—chances when we screwed up, right? Where would either of us be if that hadn't happened? How about returning the favor to someone else?"

In the stainless-steel countertop of the kitchen island, I saw the blurred vision of my face. I touched my palms against both red cheeks. "Touche." I stood and walked toward the door, then turned. Tony hadn't moved. "Hey, Tony?" He jutted his chin out in a nonverbal, *Yeah*? "Have you ever thought about becoming a life coach?"

He chuckled and turned back toward the oven, saying over his shoulder, "Two minutes ago, you suggested I don't. Besides, they're too needy."

Despite the heaviness hovering over the inn, his humor was a welcome relief. Heck, truth be told, if I was Izzy's age, I might have even been a conspirator, a thought that made me chuckle at the irony.

After calling Sister Eunice, who had agreed to be here within the hour and volunteered to help indefinitely, I started back toward the front of the inn and fell deep in thought. Turning a corner, I nearly ran headlong into Carmen. We both yelped and thrust our hands out in front of us, Bobby skidding to a halt before slamming into Carmen.

"Babe, you okay?" he said, one hand on her back, the other on her bicep.

"Yes, just scared me nearly to death." Carmen faced me. "We were talking about Tootsie and how it still seems so surreal. It's all made me a little jumpy." She took a deep breath. "Have there been any more developments?"

"The detective can't tell me anything while the investigation is open."

"So you don't know what might have happened then?"

I shook my head. "I only know what you guys do." Aspen sat patiently at my feet, and I briefly scratched his head. "He probably knows more than me."

"Humph." Bobby grumbled.

Carmen poked her finger up in the air. "The ghost. Why didn't we think of that before? Can't you, like, summon it or something? Call it however one calls a ghost? It's got to know something."

I clamped my lips closed, struggling not to laugh. Finally safe to open my mouth, I said, "I'm pretty sure that's not how the whole ghost thing works."

"Why not? Can't we do a…a séance or something?"

Once again clamping my lips, I glanced at Bobby, who stared at me in expectation.

"Umm…" I inhaled slowly and ran my tongue over my lips. "I'm not into witchcraft and have no clue how a séance works."

"Well, can't you look it up?"

So briefly I couldn't know if it happened at all, the lights blinked three times.

Carmen's head jerked upward, eyes wide, as she stared up at the lights. "There! Isn't that something a ghost would do?"

Or the weather, I thought. But it had gotten my attention and piqued my curiosity, too.

After waiting a few moments, and nothing else happened, she said, "I need to get back to the kids, Andie Rose. And my daughter's horse. But the detective told us and Simon to hang tight until he gives us the green light. The ghost could speed that process up."

I exhaled and blinked slowly.

Bobby cleared his throat. "Clearly you're not going to help us with this by trying to do some," he waggled his fingers, "woo-woo to conjure up the ghost, so I guess it's a good thing our reservation extends for another two days. Not that we want to be here at all anymore."

Carmen held a hand up, palm facing me. "Nothing against you."

"I get it. But I can't imagine Simon would *want* to leave."

"I disagree," Bobby said. "Why would he want to *stay?*"

"For starters, because it's his wife. If that were me, I'd want answers."

Carmen said, "When I talked with him earlier today—"

Bobby's jaw muscle tensed. "When was that?"

She knit her eyebrows together. "Well, I don't know the exact time, Bobby. Sometime earlier, obviously. I knocked on his door to be sure he was okay and to see if he needed anything. He said he wanted to be left alone."

"I'm sure he did. But honey—" His jaw relaxed as he sighed and wrapped an arm around his wife's waist. "We can't worry about Simon right now. For all we know, he's the one who did it. You need to stay away from that man." Worry lines creased his forehead as he asked me, "They *are* looking into him, aren't they?"

"As I said earlier, I don't know who they're focusing on. It's an open investigation, so—"

"I heard them arguing in the hot tub last night," he admitted. "Even though it was freezing outside, I cracked open the window to get some fresh, unpolluted air in the room. We don't have that in the city." He said to Carmen, "To be honest, I was embarrassed for them with the little I heard. I'm surprised you didn't excuse yourself and come back to the room."

"It was just a lover's spat. Nothing serious," she said.

He raised his eyebrows. "The part I heard before I dozed off didn't sound like nothing serious. And I'm sure Jerry and Tina didn't think so either. Maybe that's why they split."

"Do either of you know where Tina was picking up Jerry early that morning?"

They both shook their heads, and Carmen said, "Jerry probably went into town to see what he could hook. He's a player."

Bobby's head swiveled toward Carmen. "You know Tootsie was having an affair, right?"

Carmen inhaled sharply. "How did you know that?"

"Simon told me."

I gasped. "Simon knew?"

"Yeah. He said he didn't think Tootsie knew he was aware of it."

"How did he find out?" I asked.

"Didn't ask him. It was already awkward as it was, to be honest."

"Did Jerry and Tina know about it?"

He glanced at Carmen and back to me, lifting his hands, palms skyward. "I don't know. You'd have to find them and ask. They stuck more to themselves. The only reason I know is because of my wife and Tootsie hitting it off. But it was someone here in Birch Haven, I know that. That's why he pushed to come back here. He wanted to catch him and put an end to it. Now I wonder if it was Jerry, and Simon *did* put an end to it."

Oy Vey. My heart rate spiked to dangerous levels. This just got a lot more interesting.

"Put an end to it? How?" I finally asked.

His eyebrows knit together as he considered the apparently dumb question. "Well, after what's happened, it's pretty obvious, isn't it?"

"Did Simon tell the police any of this?"

He shook his head. "I don't believe so. But I'm not surprised. That would be like turning himself in. I told the detective, though."

"Yeah. It would be," I murmured. Maybe there is a possibility of clearing Wes after all. "Bobby, did Simon tell you who it was?"

He shook his head. Carmen's pallor revealed her

unease.

Carmen leaned into Bobby. "I think I need to go lie down."

Bobby kissed the top of her head. "I'm sorry, love. That's why I didn't say anything to you before this. I know you really liked her."

I forced a smile. "I'm sorry your vacation has been so unfortunate. Let me bring afternoon tea and refreshments up to you so you can rest."

"Okay." She trudged away, Bobby behind her, a protective hand on the small of her back. I was fairly certain Carmen wasn't the killer. She was too timid. Naïve even. Not to mention shocked at the newly disclosed news that Simon knew of the affair.

Going into the dining room, I gazed through the wall of windows facing Whisper Lake. Other than the inn, the only buildings that were on the shoreline were two cabins and a small house on the opposite side. Snow blew across the top of the snow packed frozen surface, developing into small drifts, reminding me of the meringue on a giant lemon pie.

There were only three fish houses—one belonged to the inn, one had appeared this year for the first time, so I wasn't sure who it belonged to, and one to the house from across the lake. The house belonged to an 87-year-old man with dementia. A few months ago, his fifty-something-year-old son and his wife moved in to care for him. They'd stopped in a few times since then for dinner and the coffee shop. Parked beside their fish house was a yellow Ski-Doo snowmobile. I made a mental note to invest in one for personal use. Grandpop and Honey had one here when I was a kid. That was the best part of coming here in the wintertime. But I wouldn't allow

Sister Alice to drive it. No way. I chuckled at the thought of her behind the handlebars of a snowmobile.

Whisper Lake was a hidden gem, limiting traffic. Big Spirit and Little Spirit Lake were bigger and well-known for their fishing and swimming beaches, giving the inn's guests more privacy to swim, waterski, and fish here in quieter waters.

A gust of wind picked up some loose snow, and a funnel hovered over the ice, dancing as it blew across. I crossed my arms in front of me, rubbed my biceps, and shivered as I thought of Tootsie's fate. I hoped she had been dead *before* she ended up in the lake. What a horrific way to go. For the umpteenth time, I mentally scanned the brief conversation we'd had about scheduling her life coach session for any hints to help determine what happened. But, yet again, I came up blank and frustrated.

My gaze drifted toward the boat shed and through the small window. I hoped to glimpse Lady Lucy, but the search yielded nothing. I twisted my mouth in disappointment, turned from the window, and toward the desk in the foyer; the lights blinked again. "I saw that," I whispered. "The least you could do is make yourself useful, Lady Lucy." The bulb directly above me flickered and went out. "Of course." I chuckled.

When I reached Lily and Jade, I asked, "Anyone seen Frank yet?"

"His truck is out there, but I haven't seen him," Lily said. As if on cue, the front door opened, and Frank blew in with a swirl of snow.

"When Detective Griffin gets here, you guys can use my office," I told him.

"Good enough." He brushed snow from his sleeves

and stomped his boots on the *Welcome Inn* door mat in front of the door.

He sported a calm demeanor, yet he avoided my eyes. There wasn't an ounce of fear there, but something that almost appeared … conflicted. I wondered if he understood the severity of the situation. Or he didn't care. That concerned me much more.

"Frank, can we talk a minute?" I asked.

"Sure thing," he said.

He followed me and Aspen to the parlor. The fireplace had been on for a while, keeping it toasty warm. Aspen slid down onto his front legs, rump in the air, then followed with his hind legs.

After making sure no one else was within hearing range, I said, "Frank, do you understand what's going to happen today?"

"Yes, Miss Andie." He stared into the fire, then back at me. "I accept responsibility for what I did and'll take whatever punishment comes my way. But…"

I waited for him to continue, and he gave a heavy sigh. "Well, I can accept my punishment, but young Izzy gettin' in trouble because of what I did, and that it could harm the inn—well, that's harder. I been here a long time; was a young man when I started for your grandpop and Honey."

I affectionately touched his arm. "We'll get through this, Frank."

"I'as thinkin' that maybe it's time I retire. Go live with my daughter and her husband. Just hate to be a burden, ya know."

His eyes glistened, and tears crept into mine. "Frank, if that's what you want to do, you know I'll support you. But I'm begging you not to do it on account of this." I flung my arm outward. "*This* will pass, and we'll all be fine." *But would we?*

"Detective Griffin's here," Jade said from the doorway. "So is that hottie, Noah. Yummy."

She fanned herself with her hand. I raised an eyebrow, and she grinned.

"Tell them we'll be right there."

The sound of Detective Griffin's ringing phone reached us, followed by his brief one- and two-word grumbled responses to the speaker on the other end. "Uh-huh." "Yep." "No." "Not good." "Okay." "Uh-uh." "Thanks." "Yep, bye."

Footsteps stopped at the doorway. When I turned, his eyes pierced mine. I squirmed.

"Just got a call from the medical examiner. Seems we have a bigger problem on our hands."

Chapter 12

Holy wicked whiskey! Now what?

Detective Griffin studied Frank and appeared to be at a loss for words. My heart sank to my toes, and I felt like a liar telling Frank everything would work out. Whatever the new information Detective Griffin received about Frank, I knew he had done nothing to Tootsie. I had to help him.

"Whatever you think Frank did, he didn't do it."

Detective Griffin cut a glance at me. "I'll be the one to determine that. And I need to speak with Ms. Carter and Mr. Valentino, too." He looked at Frank. "Starting with you. In private."

"I got nothin' to hide, Detective," Frank said. "And I can't afford no lawyer."

I shot my hand out toward him. "Not so quick, Frank. Detective Griffin, what's this new information you've received?"

He cleared his throat. "Unless you're his attorney, which you're not, I need to speak with Mr. Flowers in private. May I use your office?" When I stared at him, he said, "Or I can take Mr. Flowers down to the police station."

"Can I have a word with you first?"

Noah shoved his hands in his pockets. "This isn't a compromise or a negotiation, Andie Rose."

My eyebrows shot up. "Are you on the case now?"

He remained silent; I heaved a sigh at what that could mean. I'd shared information with him I wouldn't have been so forthcoming with had I known he would be involved. Not to mention that Izzy told him she got the weed from Frank. *Tchah.* "You haven't *officially* started yet, have you?"

"Just helping out."

"So you *are* on the case." When he didn't reply, I said, "Either you are, or you aren't."

"I'm not on the payroll yet," he said. "That's the only answer I have for you."

I blew through pursed lips and shook my head. Could this situation possibly get any worse?

Detective Griffin to the rescue. "Tell you what—I'll talk with you so long as you don't try collect information about the investigation that will interfere with my job."

Good enough for me. I turned toward my office and crooked my finger for them to follow me. "Come on."

"Mr. Flowers, you can wait for us here," Noah said.

Aspen followed me into the office, Noah and Griffin behind him. I stepped aside and waited for both to have a seat. I closed the door after them and took the chair behind my desk.

"So what'd you want to talk about?" Detective Griffin asked.

"What have you found that implicates Frank?" I leaned back, toying with a pencil between my fingers, preparing myself for what was to come.

We had a mini staring session, each willing the other to break. Finally, he sighed and said, "Fine, it won't hurt to tell you that the preliminary toxicology screen came back." He fell silent.

"And?"

"And what?"

I grumbled in frustration, then resorted to begging. "Stop toying with me. Please. This is Frank we're talking about. He's not capable of harming *any*thing."

"The victim had a massive amount of THC in her blood."

I gasped and my heart plummeted. "Is that what killed her?"

Noah witnessed our exchange in silence. Probably taking notes on the best way to placate me and keep me out of his hair.

"From what I know," Detective Griffin said, "THC won't kill a person, but high enough amounts can cause emotional distress, high blood pressure, unintentional injury, extreme confusion—"

I tilted my head, baffled where he was going with all this. "So it could have been her own doing and not murder? But how would she have gotten there? They found her on the opposite side of the lake that's nearest the inn, and her car is here."

"I know."

"So, what, she got super high and, in her *extreme confusion,* walked to the lake and caused *unintentional injury* by falling into a spearing hole in a random fish house?"

"Her BAC—blood alcohol content—"

"I know too well what BAC stands for."

Detective Griffin crossed his arms in front of him and tipped his chair onto the back legs. "I'm sure you do."

Ouch. "No need to make this personal. Can I ask what the cause of death was?"

Detective Griffin appeared to weigh his next words

carefully, apparently deciding I was trustworthy. That, or he didn't care because I wouldn't be his problem anymore.

"Her BAC suggests probable alcohol poisoning."

I sat forward, crossed my forearms, and rested them on the desk. "That still doesn't tell us how she got onto the lake. Or how she was anchored to the fish house. She obviously didn't do that to herself."

His face turned red, and he locked eyes with Noah. He turned back toward me. "How did you hear about that? I haven't released that information."

I swallowed the lump in my throat. I'd possibly sunk Wes. "Someone overheard."

"Who might that someone be?" Detective Griffin said. "No one was around when we revealed that."

I caught my lower lip between my teeth. "Must have been the guy who found her."

His eyes narrowed. "I would have sworn him to secrecy."

"Pshaw." I dipped my chin, my lips in a tight line. "Like that happens in a small town. Unless you threatened him—"

"Which I all but would have." He grumbled and sat back in his chair. "Is that who told you? The key witness?"

"I don't remember where I heard it," I lied, hoping Wes would forgive my big mouth.

"You don't remember, or you can't tell me?" He glanced at Noah. "Some things in Ms. Kaczmarek's world are anonymous." He returned his stare to me.

"Something just occurred to me."

"I'm sure it did," Detective Griffin said.

"You said you *would* have sworn him to secrecy,

and you *would* have all but threatened him. Does that mean the guy who found the victim is flying in the wind somewhere?" His eyes leveled on mine.

"You tell me since you seem to know who it was."

"Have you issued an alert so people can be aware?"

"Who was it?"

I shook my head and admitted, "I don't know. I assumed you would."

"That's still part of our investigation. But how about you let me do my job, kid." We held a tight gaze for a moment. "The guy called from a burner phone. So if you know who that was, telling me would be best for you, unless you want to get charged with withholding evidence in a murder investigation."

I thought about Jerry. Had it been him? This conversation caused a degree of disbelief in Wes's story. How *did* he know Tootsie was anchored in the hole? I hadn't thought to ask him when he told me. Unless the guy who found her told Wes. Worse, was Wes the one who found her, and it wasn't a break-in at all as he claims? Did Wes and Jerry know each other? Oh, boy. So many scenarios played out in my head, none of them good, and I couldn't shut them down. I closed my eyes tight, then opened them again. Who'd have thought drugs and alcohol would become my biggest problem well into sobriety? "This isn't good," I murmured.

"Sounds like you understand now," he said. "While the manner of death is homicide, as you already know, until we hear more from the medical examiner, we're guessing the COD—cause of death—was drowning. With outrageous amounts of alcohol and THC present, it's likely they were a contributor to her death. If there's any chance the particular marijuana she, er, *enjoyed*, came from the gardening shed, the inn will be liable. Not to mention Mr. Flowers and Ms. Carter."

Holy wicked whiskey. I absently glanced out the window and said quietly, "I might need to get a lawyer for the inn."

I inhaled and exhaled through pursed lips, eyes closed. When I opened them again, I said, "Detective, we had another guest who might not have returned to the inn that night."

The muscles in his jaw tightened and the end of his nose and tips of his ears grew red. "Why are you first telling me this now?"

"Because his wife checked out first thing in the morning to go pick him up. Since she had the car, he couldn't have taken it anywhere. But she hasn't come back, so I'd assumed she found him. But now I question the extent of their involvement."

He stabbed a finger in the air toward me, his mouth a thin line. "This. This right here is what is called withholding information, Andie Rose."

I averted my gaze and swallowed. "I'd a thought everyone would have been questioned by you before now."

His face grew so tight I thought his reddened bulbous nose might pop right off. "How about you let me handle the investigation the way I see fit. And that means I'll talk with people in the order of most importance."

"Sorry," I mumbled, glancing back up at him. "But it might be nothing. Like I said, his wife checked out to go pick him up, so she obviously knew where he was. Right?"

"How about you let me decide that." He took a moment to calm his butt down. "His information please."

His tone let me know the sought-after calm hadn't reached his brain. I retrieved Jerry and Tina's contact information from my files. "I've tried calling them to be sure he was okay, but it just goes to voicemail. And now the voicemail box is full."

"Because of you." He rubbed his eyes with his forefinger and thumb before he stood and held up a legal document.

"A search warrant?"

"Yep. For the entire premises. We'll start with the shed."

I heaved a sigh and swallowed the lump in my throat. "Can you do it discreetly? So guests don't see what you're doing."

"We'll do what we can," Noah answered. "And I'll put out a BOLO on the missing couple. Be on the lookout."

I raised my eyebrows. "I know. I'm not stupid."

Detective Griffin tipped his chin toward his chest and stared at me.

My cheeks flamed, and I stood. "One more question if I can ask?" I quickly spewed my question before he could say no. "I understand why you have to talk with Izzy, but why Tony? He wasn't in on this whole marijuana debacle."

"I wouldn't call murder a debacle."

I rolled my eyes in exasperation. "You know what I mean."

"Mr. Valentino could have known about it. In fact, I'd be hard pressed to believe he *didn't* know. He's Ms. Carter's supervisor."

I silently prayed to God that Frank and Izzy cleaned out that gardening shed good, leaving no trace behind.

When they stepped toward the door, I said, "What would be the charge? For Izzy and Tony."

Noah avoided the question, but Detective Griffin held my gaze a moment before saying, "Murder in the Third Degree."

"What?" I sank into my chair, my legs weak. "How?"

"Even if someone had no intent to cause someone's death, they're held liable. Quoting the statute, 'proximately causes the death of a human being by, directly or indirectly, unlawfully selling, giving away, bartering, delivering, exchanging, distributing, or administering a controlled substance classified in Schedule I or II, is guilty of murder in the third degree and may be sentenced to imprisonment for not more than 25 years or to payment of a fine of not more than $40,000, or both.'"

Clutching the arms of my chair, I exhaled and felt the color drain from my face. "I'm sure you'll understand if I don't see you out. I need a moment."

Both men nodded and walked out the door. After one last glance at me, Noah pulled it closed behind him.

I leaned over my desk and rested my head on my folded arms. As soon as I'd regained my composure, I forced myself back into a positive frame of mind. I picked up my phone and called Sister Alice; she answered on the first ring.

"What's going on over yonder at your place?" she asked. "I hear there's trouble at the homestead."

"You have no idea. How did you hear about it, anyway?"

"I didn't hear about anything more than that. Hence, why I asked you."

First, I filled her in on my conversation with Carmen and Bobby, after which she didn't utter a sound. "Let me help you process this little tidbit," I said. "If Simon knew about Tootsie's affair and wanted to find out who it was so he could end it, that seems like the perfect motive. And he definitely had the opportunity."

"He looks equally guilty as Wes. Except we know Wes."

"But do we?" I asked with skepticism. "Wes had information that no one outside of the investigation could know."

"Which is what?"

"That the murderer anchored Tootsie's body in the fishing hole."

"I see," she said. "Did you tell the police what Bobby said?"

"No. After the bombshell Detective Griffin dropped on me, that part fell into my rearview mirror. Besides, Bobby said he told them about it."

"Dish about said bombshell," she said.

I passed along the news about the preliminary tox screen. "He said it could take up to six to eight weeks, maybe longer, to get the full report for any other substance that might be present in her blood."

"Spirit Lake has never been so interesting until you moved here," she said dryly.

"I'm not sure Detective Griffin would call it *interesting*. Sheesh. After this, he'll decide he won't miss me at all."

"Can you blame the man?"

"In my defense, it's not like I wish for this stuff to happen. It didn't in the city I came from."

"I must disagree, Grasshopper," she said, clucking

her tongue. "The city always has more crime. You just weren't aware of it, because with everything else that happens in a city, this stuff wasn't shoved in your face there. And it didn't happen right next to you. I'd take small town life to a city any day."

I leaned over my desk, my head resting on the arm that wasn't holding the phone. "Hmm. I'm finding out that small-town life is dangerous to one's health."

"You could have accepted the loveless marriage proposal last fall and moved back to the city."

My ex-boyfriend proposed to me last fall, but it was more of a business proposal. I let him down gently, but it still hadn't ended well.

"Humph." I shook my head. "I'm fine right here, thank you."

At a knock on my door, I bolted upright.

"Oh, shoot. I gotta run. I forgot Detective Griffin wanted to use my office. He said for interviews, but what he really meant was interrogations. Hold on."

"I can tell you're thrilled about it."

"To death." I hung up over the start of her protest.

"Andie Rose?"

"Come in." I called, after he'd already begun opening the door. He and Noah each lowered themselves into the same chairs they'd all too recently vacated. I waited expectantly, bracing myself for the delivery of more bad news.

"Interesting thing," Detective Griffin said. Noah's amusement disappeared.

"The marijuana in the shed—" Noah began.

"What marijuana in the shed?" I asked, feigning innocence.

"Poof." Detective Griffin said, tossing his hands into

the air. "Gone. Kaput. No sign. Except that doggone smell." He narrowed an eye at me. "I'm sure I don't need to tell you what I'm talking about."

I widened my eyes and shrugged, maintaining my ludicrous innocence. "How would I know what you expected to find out there in the first place?"

"Yes, I'm sure you don't," Noah said.

Detective Griffin groaned and said to Noah, "This. This, right here, is what I was talking about and what your job will be like here in Spirit Lake."

The struggle to be stern was evident. It reminded me of the time I wouldn't fess up to my dad about who backed the car out *through* the garage door. As mad as he was, he found it somehow amusing that I had the gall to deny something that was blatantly obvious. I'm still confounded about that to this day. Maybe it had to do with the fact that I was nine years old and daddy's little girl. Thinking about my dad made me happy. And sad, too. I missed him and hoped that my mother would get over herself and he'd come with her for a visit. Of course, he probably wanted the break as much as she did.

Detective Griffin said, "I'm so glad you think this is so amusing, Andie Rose."

"It's not you, sir." I ran my hand through my hair, fingers catching in a tangle. I winced. "Ouch."

He leaned forward, elbows resting on his knees. "You know, the funny thing is, I called young Ms. Carter, and she suddenly developed amnesia and said she doesn't remember where she got the, uh—"

"Weed?" I said, helping him.

"Don't you think that's strange?"

I opened my eyes in wide innocence. *Yeah, right.* "Why? It's not unusual for one's memory to fail when under duress." I thought of Grandpop and Honey and all the hard work they'd put into making this inn such an immense success, how I didn't want to disappoint them, and how much *I* loved it here. I had to do whatever it took to save it.

"We'll be bringing out a narcotics dog from an agency we contract with."

I swallowed a gasp. I hadn't counted on that. "Oh."

"Since Mr. Flowers' side hustle potentially links to the murder, it'll be soon." A Cheshire grin appeared, then disappeared equally quick. "That appeared to have gotten your attention on the matter."

I cleared my throat. "Um, you said 'not long' … that's kind of subjective. How long is 'not long'?"

A corner of his lip turned upward ever so slightly. Amusement? Irony? Victory? I couldn't tell. I wished he'd eaten some blondies. A *lot* of them.

"Don't worry, Andie Rose. Noah here is staying on the premises for one more night, anyway. He can be sure no one gets to the shed before the dogs do. I'll go get Mr. Flowers now."

I stayed anchored at my desk. Noah left first. When Detective Griffin got to the door, he paused, turned, and said quietly, "Andie Rose, this is nothing personal. I'm just doing my job. You're a good kid."

I snickered and said wryly, "You obviously haven't talked with my mother."

I swallowed the lump in my throat, peered down at Aspen who was sweeping the floor with his tail, then glanced at the blotter on my desktop. Honey's birthday would have been in three days.

Chapter 13

Desperate to get this twisted chaos disentangled, I decided to pay Simon a visit. You know, just to be sure his stay is a pleasant one and all. After all, I'd promised Carmen I'd bring afternoon tea and refreshments up to her room. I could do the same for Simon. *Voila.* Aspen was lapping up love from Jade, so I let him stay there.

In the kitchen, Tony was preparing to leave for the day, finishing up his prep work for early the next morning, and Sister Eunice was putting the final touches on the afternoon teatime refreshments. I snagged a couple of plates and cups with saucers.

Tony asked. "Hungry? Or a testament to my skills?"

"It's called being a guest-centered host," I said. "I'm going to bring some up to Carmen. She'd rather not come down and socialize today."

"The second one for Bobby or you?"

"You sure are a curious fella. But in answer to your question, no. The second is for Simon." I'd been so focused on Carmen and talking with Simon, that I'd forgotten all about poor Bobby. I nabbed a food tray and a third plate, cup, and saucer. "But since you mentioned Bobby, I'll bring his as well."

"Tell Bobby he's welcome." He chuckled and watched me balance the tray. "Need help?"

"Nope. I got it. I used to be a cocktail waitress during college."

"Shocker."

Heading up the stairs with the tray balanced on one hand, it was eerily quiet as I passed the library and down the east hallway toward Simon and Carmen's rooms.

One room didn't have anyone in it, nor anyone scheduled for a few days; Noah was with Detective Griffin; the guests from two rooms had checked out, Tina had checked out early to go get Jerry—wherever that was—and the others were out and about somewhere. The cleaning staff wouldn't be here until this afternoon.

I was grateful the incoming guests hadn't heard about the latest events and canceled their reservations. That Tootsie's body was found in the lake and not at the inn helped matters, I supposed. But I needed to get answers before all the work my grandpop and Honey did to build the stellar reputation of the inn was for naught.

As I neared Simon's room, an ominous chill crept down my back. I knocked on Carmen's door first. Bobby whipped it open.

"Come on in," he said in a hushed tone.

I passed by him and set the tray down on a desk tucked in the corner and set his and Carmen's tea and cookies on the small space beside the tray. Bobby saw the remaining plate and cup I'd left on the tray. "Are you joining us? I can wake Carmen." He turned toward the small bedroom.

"No, no." I whispered quickly. "I don't want to wake her. This one is for Simon. I assumed he wouldn't be up for socializing, either."

"He left." I turned toward Carmen, now leaning against the doorjamb, arms crossed in front of her.

"Oh?" I said, sounding more like a question. "It'll probably do him good to get out of the room for a while. Did he go into town?"

"No," she said, "I mean he *left* left. As in back home."

She crossed her arms tighter against the apparent

chill in the air; a chill I felt as well, but not from the elements of nature.

I squinted as I tried to understand. I must have heard incorrectly. "He went back *home*?"

She gave a barely visible nod. "He left about an hour ago. Said he had to plan Tootsie's cremation."

"Did he now." I said, more to myself than to Carmen. "And Detective Griffin was okay with that?" I turned toward Bobby for some kind of confirmation that Carmen's information was indeed true.

Bobby cleared his throat and turned toward the tea, handing one of them to Carmen, who wrapped her pale hands around the mug. She'd bitten her nails to the quick.

Bobby said, "I—well, I—"

"He didn't talk to Simon. I did," Carmen said.

My eyes widened. "You went back over there?" It surprised me that Bobby was comfortable with that. "Alone?"

"Bobby went to get my book from the car."

"And?" I pressed.

"I felt an obligation to check on him and be sure he was okay," she finally said.

I studied her carefully. "Why would you feel an obligation toward Simon? Moral obligations usually occur when someone feels guilty about something."

Bobby protectively stepped in front of Carmen. "Your insinuation is ridiculous, Ms. Kaczmarek. Thank you for the tea, but she needs some more rest. This has been a traumatic experience for her."

My mind swirled with scenarios. "Let me know if there's anything you need." I got to the door and turned toward Carmen, who was now standing beside Bobby. "Carmen, have you told the detective that Simon left?"

She shook her head. "Not yet. But I will."

"Why the wait?" I asked as gently as I could so Bobby wouldn't shut the door in my face to protect his wife. *Protect her from what, though?*

"Wanted to give him some time, I guess."

I studied her momentarily as I tucked the inside of my cheek between my teeth. "I'll let the cleaning staff know. Enjoy your tea." I closed the door behind me and heard the lock click and the safety chain slide into place.

I stood stock still with my ear to the door. Aspen trotted up the hall and sat quietly beside me.

"Why did you tell her you felt obligated?" Bobby asked in a harsh whisper. "You may as well have raised your hand and jumped up and down, screaming, 'It was me. It was me.'"

"I can't in good conscience let Simon take the fall, Bobby. Not completely."

"Why not?" he shot back. "He doesn't have any small children at home. We do. They need you."

"Bobby—" Her voice broke. "I'm not about to let him take the fall alone when I—well, it's bad enough that, you know—"

Aspen, who'd laid down a moment ago, decided now, of all times, to whimper, a signal to let me know he needed to go outside. I should have realized that was the reason for finding me, but I'd been too focused on being nosey.

The metal click of the lock, the screech of the security chain, and the door whipping open happened so quickly I hadn't even had time to come up with an excuse for lingering there.

Bobby stared down at me, a pained expression on his face. Carmen's hand covered her mouth, her eyes wide.

"Have you been standing here the whole time?" he asked.

I shook my head, desperately searching for words. "No. I forgot Simon's refreshments on your tray. Since he's not here, I'll just take them with me back to the kitchen."

"You came back for the tray." His skepticism made it more a statement than a question.

I nodded and tugged at a sleeve. "Yes. But don't worry about it." I waved a hand in dismissal. "Just set your dishes on the floor outside your door when you're finished, and the cleaning crew can pick them up when they clean Simon's room."

Bobby scrutinized me as he appeared to decide whether or not he should believe me; Carmen swiped at her eyes with sleeves pulled over her hands.

I gently tugged Aspen's collar. "Come on, Aspen."

After taking him outside, we headed straight for the coffee bar. I needed some serious caffeine. It wasn't unusual for town residents to peruse our unique coffee shop. But with tourism down during the brutal winter months, the coffee shop often stood lonely apart from the inn's guests. And, of course, it was then that guests heard the espresso machine when no one was behind the bar.

I grabbed the largest cup available and made myself a peppermint mocha latte, with an extra shot of espresso. Aspen's long tongue ran over both sides of his schnoz as he looked at me expectantly while I made a pup cup of whipped cream for him. He devoured it before I'd even fully set it down. He was a picky and dainty eater for most things, but whipped cream wasn't one of those.

After a quick trip through the foyer and a quick

check-in with the kitchen to be sure all was well, given the circumstances, Aspen and I marched back to my office, closing and locking the door behind me. I had three phone calls to make, two of which I couldn't risk anyone hearing. I plopped down in my chair and swiveled it to gaze out the window as I called the first—Detective Griffin. As I waited for him to answer, I focused on the snow; the peaks from the drifts once again reminding me of meringue. Which, in turn, brought to mind the lemon bars served at Detective Griffin's retirement celebration, which caused me to recall the entire debacle said celebration had caused. So much for nature's relaxing qualities.

"Detective Griffin."

I startled at his sudden bark.

"Hi, Detective. This is Andie Rose." I held my breath a beat while he sighed.

"What now?"

"Have you heard from Carmen yet?"

"About?"

"Simon."

"I'm busy trying to solve a murder, as you know. Cut to the chase and tell me what it is she was to tell me."

So she hadn't contacted him yet. Interesting. Then, when I remembered what I'd overheard and her lack of communication over Simon's disappearance, I gasped. "Oh, my God. They're in on it together."

"In on *what* together?" Detective Griffin asked, making me realize I'd said it out loud.

"Simon left to go back home to plan Tootsie's—"

"He *what*?" Then he said to someone—my guess it was Noah—on his end, "Simon Timmons split. See if you can catch him."

"Yeah. He left for home about an hour and a half ago."

"Why on God's green earth didn't you tell me this before now?"

I jerked my chin downward. "Because *I* didn't know about it. And before you get all butthurt, do you want my help or not? Because I'm getting whiplash here."

"Only when I ask for it."

"So since you didn't ask for me to tell you—"

"Andie Rose," he intoned, his patience wearing thin. "I think we both know what is welcomed and what is not."

"I'm sorry," I said earnestly. "Interfering isn't my intent, only trying to save my grandpop and Honey's love child—heck, *my* child—this inn. I can't be a big disappointment to them."

The line fell silent. Then he said, "Do what you must, but getting in my way won't help you. Are we clear?"

His admonition sounded like the many my father had given me during my teenage years—firm but gentle. Without outright saying so, Detective Griffin had just given me permission to help, albeit with parameters. At least that's how I chose to interpret it.

"Yes, we're clear as vodka," I said. "Thank you."

"We'll be there shortly to search his room again." He grunted something unintelligible.

"Wait," I blurted. "One more thing. Have you found Jerry and Tina yet?"

"Workin' on it." The line went dead.

Me too. I took a breath before the next call and punched in Izzy's number.

"Hi Andie Rose." Her voice was almost a whisper.

"Did you call to fire me?"

I took a deep breath and sat back in my chair. "No, Izzy. I'm calling to ask when you'd be able to come back?"

"Really?" she squealed in delight, a bipolar change from when she'd answered.

"But one more stunt like this, and you'll be gone. Understand?"

"Yes."

"Be here for your normal shift tomorrow. And Izzy?" I said before she hung up.

"Yeah?"

"You can thank Tony. And don't get too excited—the way things are going, you might be in juvie before long, and there might not even be an inn to come back to when you're out." The thought of either made me sick to my stomach.

"Way to kill a mood."

"The truth is often hard to hear."

"Doesn't mean you have to say it out loud," she grumbled, another bipolar shift. "But thanks, Kaz. I won't let you down."

Yeah, right. Teens were a pain. Not to mention unreasonable and moody. And Izzy wasn't even nearly as bad as I had been. The thought made me roll my eyes. I was more grateful than ever that I didn't have kids—especially a girl like I had been.

After I drained the last of my lukewarm mocha, I called Sister Alice again. I glanced at my watch. She should be well out of the AA meeting by now—I'm sure I'd get an earful from her for missing it—and either doing something for Sister Ida, Father Vincent, or at the hospital. I was just about to hang up before it rolled into voicemail when she answered.

"Hey." She sounded out of breath.

"Hi. Are you busy? If you are, you can call me back when you're free."

"Not busy anymore. At the moment, Sister Ida is at the newspaper and Father Vincent is out on house calls."

Sister Ida worked at Lakes News and Reviews in town. Sister Eunice had worked there temporarily as well, but they let her go last fall, which worked well for the inn because she was available to help in the kitchen as needed. At least until she went to work somewhere else.

"Hospital?" I asked.

"Nope."

Her vagueness made me even more curious. "Were you with another sponsee?" She gave a hearty laugh, and I pulled the phone from my ear a few inches and winced. "My ears."

"Then don't say something so ludicrous. I don't have time for another sponsee. Sponsoring you requires all my extra time."

I guffawed. "Whatever."

"So what's the scoop? Anything going on in your neck of the woods?"

I filled her in on my visit from Detective Griffin.

After a pause and a loud sigh during an exhale on her end, she said, "We'll need to work fast to keep *all* of you from getting charged with third degree murder."

"I'm not a suspect in Tootsie's murder."

"Yes, at least there's that," she said dryly.

Next, I told her about my visit to Carmen and Bobby's room. When I got to the part about Simon bolting from Spirit Lake, she stopped me.

"Hold on, there. Only a guilty person would get out of dodge. And why the quick cremation? It's not like Tootsie's going anywhere."

"But wait until you hear this." I told her what I'd overheard through Carmen and Bobby's door, including getting busted.

Sister Alice sighed. "That dog is a godsend for so many reasons. Except when he's not."

Aspen tucked his nose between his front paws and whimpered. "You hurt his feelings," I said.

"How?"

"You called him a dog, for starters."

"Mary, Mother of God," she muttered.

In my mind, I could see her eye roll and a slow headshake. "What are you doing right now?" I asked.

"Going to pray for you."

"Sarcasm is your superpower, isn't it?" I chuckled. "I'm going to nose through Simon's room now. If you want to join me, I'll wait a few minutes. But it's gotta be quick."

"I thought Detective Griffin told you he's sending someone to search it again."

"He did. That's why it's gotta be quick."

"So that means you shouldn't go in there."

"Like you wouldn't?"

"That's different."

I snickered. "I'm sure it is. Besides, Detective Griffin didn't explicitly tell me to stay out. And he did sorta give me permission to investigate on my own, so long as I don't get in his way."

"Hate to tell you this, Grasshopper, but you're riding the fence on this one and falling on the wrong side. It's a terrible idea. But I'll be right there."

I grinned. "I knew it. One more thing."

"I'm afraid to ask."

"Wear the brightest frames you have. We need a little brightness around here."

"I'll wear my neon orange ones just for you."

"You're too kind." Despite teasing her, that's exactly what she was—kind. But sometimes her tough exterior impeded others from seeing it. Like Jade, for example. And Sister Ida.

Chapter 14

Sister Alice hung up from Andie Rose and rested her hands on her hips. Her life had never been as lively as it had been since Andie Rose moved to town. Offering to be her sponsor came with a lot more than twelve-step work. Yet, she couldn't imagine her life *pre*-Andie anymore, either. The girl brought ... well, she brought *spirit* to Spirit Lake. So full of questions, curiosity, and fire. Although the population of the town dwindled since her arrival.

Wes hadn't shown up for the AA meeting nor answered her call afterward. She thought of what Andie Rose said about Simon and gasped, her hand flying to her mouth. *Oh, no.* What if the real reason Simon split so fast is because he killed Wes? She had to get over to Wes's house lickity split for a welfare check.

Zipping up to the front of his house—a shack not much bigger than an oversized fish house with peeling paint the color of apple cider vinegar—she got out and hustled up the front steps. She could see why he hadn't brought Tootsie here. It would have been a one-nighter, if even that.

She rapped her knuckles on the door and waited. When he didn't answer, she clenched her hand into a fist and pounded louder. Still no answer. She scurried from window to window, her nose to the glass, hands cupped around her face, hoping to glimpse something—

anything—that told her he was okay. The inside was much like the outside, so she couldn't tell if there'd been a struggle. She went back to the door, wrapped her hand around the doorknob, hesitated, then turned. It was unlocked. She pushed the door open and stepped inside, eager to get out before someone called the cops on some crazy window-peeping lady. Wouldn't that make headlines: *Sister Alice in Spirit Lake, Minnesota, arrested for being a peeping roamin' Catholic.* She heaved a breath and quickly scanned the room before turning a corner to find the bathroom and bedroom to be one, separated by a curtain. "Oh, boy," she muttered.

She pushed aside the curtain to the bathroom and gasped at a blood-soaked washcloth in the sink, still wet. She sighed. "Oh, Wesley. What have you gotten yourself into?"

"What are you doing here?"

Sister Alice swiveled around and sprung into a fighting stance, nearly tumbling over as she did. She hadn't even heard the door open. Peering through glasses knocked askew, she was face to face with Detective Griffin.

"What are you doing here?" he asked again, a deep guttural sound coming from his throat.

She unclenched her fists and straightened her knees, then her glasses. "Welfare check."

"Yeah? I think you were interfering with my investigation." He narrowed his eyes.

"Well, I'm sure it's not the first time you've been wrong."

"When's the last time you've seen Mr. Wilson?"

"Yesterday."

"Where was that?"

"Can't say."

"Ah, yes. The whole convenient, anonymous excuse you and Andie Rose use to withhold information."

"It's not an excuse, Detective. Now, shall we stand here and exchange barbs or do you want me to show you what I've found? Personally, Wes's safety is more important to me than your territory war." She stepped aside, revealing the bloodied washcloth. "I pray Simon Timmons didn't get here before we did."

He cursed under his breath, quickly glanced at Sister Alice, and grumbled, "Sorry. But you can go now. I'll take it from here."

"I'm kindly asking you to find Wes Wilson, Detective. Alive."

"Sister?" he said before she closed the door behind her. When she turned toward him, he struggled to maintain a straight face. "Wondering what you were posturing to do when I came in."

"Sneak up on me again, Detective, and you might find out. Sister or not, a woman has to protect herself." She quirked an eyebrow at him, turned, and left.

****

What felt like hours after talking with Sister Alice, she poked her head around the corner of my office door. I bolted out of the chair and around my desk and glanced at my watch. "It took you forever."

"I had to use the ladies' room before I left. It might surprise you, but even sisters do that. And I had a bit of a run in with Detective Griffin at Wes's house."

I tucked my chin down. "You what?"

She filled me in on the troubling news.

"Oh, man. What if Simon bolted because he hurt Wes? Or worse?" I covered my mouth with my hand.

"Come on. We have to get up to his room."

"What's the rush? Detective Griffin is bound to be tied up for a while."

"Yeah, but what if Noah comes? They might have split up." I grabbed her arm and pulled her toward the stairs, saying over my shoulder, "And here I thought you were finishing an episode of Forensic Files. And by the way." I glanced at her again. "Does Sister Ida know you watch that?"

"Nope. It's not wrong, and I refuse to bend who God made me to fit into another person's mold. Given that, I don't see that she needs to know anything. We clear?"

"Clear as gin." I glanced at her when we reached the library. I placed a finger to my lips and said quietly, "The last thing we need is for Carmen and Bobby to see us going into Simon's room."

"Quiet isn't my specialty. I guess I'm like Aspen in that respect. Where is he, by the way?" she said in a harsh whisper.

I put a finger to my lips, then pointed toward Simon's door at the end of the hallway. "The point is not to snag anyone's attention when we sneak into the room," I said, my voice barely audible. "And Aspen's with Jade. He didn't want to get busted for a B&E."

When we reached the door, I turned the key. It clicked, and I sucked in my breath. I pushed open the door, ushered her in, and closed it behind us without a sound. This time I left it unlocked to avoid the click. When Bobby and Carmen's door whined opened, I caught my breath and listened closely. My eye against the peephole, Carmen stood in the doorway and observed the hallway, then turned her attention directly at Simon's door. She crossed the hallway and reached for the doorknob. I clenched my hand around the handle on my side, preventing it from turning, then I ducked so she wouldn't see my eyeball watching her through the peephole like some horror movie. My keys scraped against the door, and I squinched my face and waited, keeping my grip firmly on the door handle.

A light tap on the door made me jump, and I clasped my hand over my mouth.

"Simon?" Carmen said in a harsh whisper. "Is that you?"

Sister Alice and I locked eyes and stayed completely still.

"We need to talk, Simon. Now."

She tried turning the knob again, and I could almost hear her breathing on the other side of the door.

When it had been silent for a few seconds, I peeked through the peephole again as she glanced over her shoulder before quickly retreating to her room. She closed her door without a sound.

Allowing myself to breathe, I gulped air.

"I'm not sure what all the secrecy is," Sister Alice said, this time in a quieter tone. "You own the place. You can be anywhere you doggone choose to be."

I pressed my lips together. I didn't have an answer because I knew she was right. But something in my gut told me to keep it a secret.

"I was thinking on my way over here," Sister Alice said. "From what you've told me, I wonder if Carmen and Simon were in on the murder together. Perhaps," she raised an eyebrow, "Simon was having an affair of his own."

I nodded. "I thought the same thing. But I hate to think Carmen would do that. I kind of like her."

Sister Alice tucked her chin and studied me over the top of her glasses. "Speaking as your friend, but also your sponsor, don't judge—"

"Others' sins by your own," I said, finishing the statement she'd told me more than a few times over the past several months. "I know, I know."

"Acceptance—"

"Is key," I finished for her again. "Again, I know." I peeked through the hole in the door once more, satisfied that the hallway remained empty.

"You have the knowing part down pat. Now let's see you put it into action." She kept her gaze trained on mine.

"I want a different sponsor," I muttered. But I knew she was totally right.

I handed her a pair of latex gloves. She looked at me quizzically. "What about you?"

"They would expect my fingerprints; not yours."

She shrugged a shoulder and pushed her hands into them. We searched the small space, careful not to disturb anything. If we picked something up, we put it back the same way we found it. We opened drawers, the door to the small closet, peeked under the bed, and under the plaid cushion of the reading chair. All his and Tootsie's things were gone, so there wasn't much to search through. He'd even taken a few things that weren't his, staple items we kept in every room. Like the remote to the tiny TV and the alarm clock. *Weird*.

"What were you hoping to find?" Sister Alice asked.

"Anything incriminating—blood, signs of a struggle …"

"Well, we're not finding anything resembling those things. This room is emptier than an alcoholic's bank account."

"Shh." I said, surveying the room once more.

The door opened, and we both jumped. We turned to see a red-faced Detective Griffin.

"Holy wicked whiskey. You scared me to death."

His gaze leveled on mine. "That's because you're guilty of doing what you're not supposed to be doing. Interfering with *my* investigation."

"I wasn't interfering. Not exactly. You didn't come right out and tell me to stay out of here," I yammered. "I wanted to assure everything was ready for the cleaning crew when you're finished."

Sister Alice gave me a *that's-such-a-lame-excuse* look over the top of her glasses; I returned it with one that said *then-come-up-with-something-better*. And she did.

"She had to check if there was anything that needed a special crime scene cleaning company. Like blood." Detective Griffin simply stared at her. "Tourism is down in the winter months so Andie Rose can't afford to be down a room."

She was good. And not even a lie. Not completely. Had we found blood, or any bodily fluids, really, that's outside the scope of our normal cleaner's responsibilities.

Detective Griffin tipped his head toward Sister Alice's gloved hands. "If this was an *innocent* room visit, care to explain those?"

"Self-protection. If we found something, I wasn't going to get it inadvertently on my hands." She held her hands up, then dropped them again.

"It wouldn't be to keep from contaminating the scene with your fingerprints."

"Trust me, Detective. I'm a sister."

He scowled.

"I have eczema, too. Terrible, terrible thing in the winter months." She stuffed her hands in her pockets. "Instead of getting in a snit about us legally in a place Andie Rose owns, what did you find on Wes?"

Noah came through the door and in a low tone, said to Detective Griffin, "Nothing."

Worry lines creased Sister Alice's forehead, and she said quietly, "That's not what I wanted to hear."

"We'll keep looking. The lab will test the blood on the washcloth." Detective Griffin's tone was empathetic for a split second, then all business again. "Did either of you remove, move, or touch anything. Like I'd get the truth," he grumbled to himself.

"I may be blunt in speech, Detective, but I don't lie," Sister Alice said.

I shot her an *it's-going-to-rain-fire-on-you* look. She and I had mad nonverbal skills.

Detective Griffin motioned toward the door. "Go."

The door slammed behind us as we left. I flinched and said, "This is where the saying 'don't let the door hit you in the backside on your way out' applies. Except it darn near did."

Carmen and Bobby's door whipped open, and Carmen stood in the doorway, her knuckles white on the doorknob.

"What were you doing in Simon's room?" she asked.

"It's not Simon's room anymore. But regardless, I let Detective Griffin in."

"What does he want in Simon's room?"

"Solving a murder."

"He's innocent," she said.

"And you would know this how?"

Carmen jumped at Bobby's voice behind her.

I shrugged and put my palms up. "I don't know what to tell you. But Detective Griffin and Mr. Parker are in there if you have questions for them when they finish." There were more questions I wanted to ask them, but not with Griffin and Parker right here. "Gotta run. Let me know if you need anything."

Carmen held my gaze a moment and closed the door.

When Sister Alice and I turned the corner, I snickered. "Eczema? Isn't telling him you don't lie, right after you told a lie, a double lie? Is there, like, a special kind of punishment for sisters who do that?"

She glanced at me, eyebrows raised. "I *do* have eczema."

"For real?"

"Andie Rose," she said, shaking her head slowly, "would I lie?"

Was she messing with me? I studied her as we walked, trying to read her, and caught myself right before I tumbled headfirst down the stairs.

"Your mama should have named you Grace." When we reached the last step, Sister Alice's phone rang. She glimpsed the screen. "It's Wes."

"Let me talk to him." I reached for her phone, and she jerked it back.

"Wesley Wilson. Where are you?" She listened for a moment. "What was that bloody washcloth from in your bathroom?" A pause. "I went there to find you. You weren't at the meeting, and you weren't answering my call. We thought Tootsie's husband got to you before he left town. After seeing your place, spending money on oneself isn't a bad thing. And if you hope to have a relationship with someone someday, preferably someone who's NOT married, you need to clean it up." Another pause and brows knit together. "Well, are you all right? That was a lot of blood."

I was getting impatient, and my heart was about to leap out of my chest. "Where is he? Is he okay?"

She listened and then said to me, "Wes said to keep your pants on."

"Tell him if he'd kept *his* pants on, literally, I might add, we wouldn't be in this predicament. Is he okay? Put him on speaker."

Sister Alice listened to Wes again, then said, "Well, under the circumstances, running away right now is your biggest mistake." Pause. "So long as it's legal." Pause. "We won't get caught up in aiding and abetting." Pause. "Okay, then. We'll see you tomorrow." Another pause and she hung up.

"What the hell?" I asked. "Why didn't you put him on speaker?"

She tilted her chin and stared at me over the top of her orange eyewear. "Excuse me?"

"The Bible says the word hell," I muttered.

"It's about context, dear. Besides, I'm trying to teach you patience."

"It's not working. So what did he have to say? What about the blood?"

"He smashed a glass in his hand and was in the ER getting stitches. He's in quite a quandary. The police discovered he was the one the victim had an affair with."

"What? But how? What else did he say? Wait. Don't tell me yet," I blurted. "Let's go sit in the coffee shop. I need some caffeine."

"Heh. You need a valium is what you need. Give that dog of yours a break from vicarious anxious trauma."

She had a point. I had been pretty needy with the little fella lately. "Better to be addicted to Aspen than a narcotic."

I wasn't one to get worked up about most things, but this wasn't just any old thing. She followed me down the hall past the parlor and toward the green neon sign announcing the coffee bar. I employed part-time baristas to cover this area of the inn. The one presently on duty was busy wiping down the equipment.

She turned toward me, and I held a hand up. "I got it, Wendy."

She smiled. "Hey, Andie. Let me get it for you and earn my wages. It's been like a ghost town in here today."

I smiled. "Okay then." During the second half of January and the month of February, I staffed the coffee shop fewer hours per day, sometimes not even every day.

"In reality," Sister Alice said, "Wendy doesn't want you to mess her cleaned machines."

Wendy grinned and asked me, "The usual for you?"

"Yep. And for her," I jerked my thumb toward Sister Alice, "anything that might make her a little less salty."

Even Sister Alice chuckled. "At my age, I'm afraid that's a lost cause." She looked pointedly at me. "It's a good thing God forgives, eh?"

"Yeah, yeah. Message received," I said with a wave of dismissal. Through my recovery, I held a belief in a higher power, but that higher power didn't look the same as Sister Alice's.

We settled into one of the four tables, the one tucked

146

cozily in the corner, adjacent to a table that held an all-season holiday tree. Each holiday had its own decorations. January had only translucent snowflakes of several sizes emitting rainbows of colors in the sunlight. I think it was my favorite of all.

As soon as Wendy left from bringing our coffees, I leaned in. "So give me the deets from your conversation with Wes."

"From the phone call just now or the one from last evening?"

My jaw dropped. "You didn't tell me about the call last night."

"You didn't ask." She chuckled at my squinched face. "Besides, I didn't exactly have the time since I got here, and it was too late to call last night. The police called him into the station and questioned him. They found out about the affair. They asked for an alibi at the time Tootsie was murdered. He said he'd call us if anything transpired and if he needed our help. I told him so long as it was legal, and we weren't aiding and abetting."

"Heard that part. Do you trust he didn't do it?"

She seemed to ponder that a moment. "I want to. But I also know what humanity is capable of. And that we really don't know people no matter how much we think we do."

I hesitated a moment, then had to ask, "Do you think Wes was the one who found the body and called it in?"

"Hmm…" She appeared to think on that before adding, "We've never asked that, did we?"

"No. I can't imagine the police didn't ask him and somehow rule him out." I narrowed my eyes and focused my attention past her, deep in thought. "I'm going to ask.

What did he tell them about his whereabouts?"

"The truth."

"Yeah, but how *much* of the truth?"

"That they had seen each other occasionally."

"And?" I asked, giving her the side-eye.

"And what?"

"Anything else?"

"They didn't ask for anything else."

"What about that whole lie by commission and lie by omission thing? Aren't both lies?"

She snorted. "When have you been concerned about that?"

I reared back at the insult. "Since I got sober." Then I dropped my gaze, took a sip of my latte, and added quietly, "I just conveniently forget once in a while." I glanced back up at her and smiled sheepishly. "That's why I have you as a sponsor. To unload on."

"You know something, Andie Rose? When I first met you, I thought you were such a sweet, innocent, gentle human being. Then I realized that was how one could describe Aspen. You're just ornery."

I giggled. "If it's progress and not perfection, shouldn't half-measures avail us at least fifty percent?"

She snorted. "For once, I got nothin' to come back with."

"Once, indeed." I grinned and reached out and placed my hand over hers. "I hope you know I really appreciate you."

"Oh, I know," she said. "Besides God, who else would invest so much time in you?"

Aspen wandered in and stood beside me. I smiled at him. "Aspen does." I stifled a snicker while mustering my most innocent expression before I grew serious again. "Truly, I appreciate you. When the music fades and the silence settles, I know I can count on you to still be there."

Sister Alice, not one to accept compliments well, turned away. "Helping you is my gift to your grandpop and Honey. They saved my life."

"So it's not because you love me?" I gave her a mischievous grin and held my thumb and forefinger mere millimeters apart. "Even this much?"

"Almost that much." A corner of her lip pulled into a wry smile.

My phone rang, and I snatched it from my pocket. I looked at the screen, then at Sister Alice. "It's Wes. Watch this. I'll show you how to switch it to speaker. Hey, Wes." Background noise on his end made it hard to hear him. "Everything okay?"

"If you consider I got to make one call, and it was to you and not a lawyer, I hope everything's okay."

I swallowed hard at the abrupt change in mood. Things had just gotten serious again.

Chapter 15

"You in the clink?" Sister Alice asked.

"Good, you're there too," he said. "I figured as much. Two calls in one. I need help, guys."

"Sounds like it," I said. "Tell us what happened."

"I need you to find me a lawyer. And fast."

Discomfort pricked my conscience. As much as I believed Carmen and Simon were in on it together, what if I was wrong and it was Wes? Just as much evidence, if not more, pointed to him. I realized Sister Alice had said something, and it snapped me back to Wes's dilemma that had also become ours.

"Repeat that," I said to Sister Alice. "My mind took a one-minute day trip."

Wes said, "Do you even think I'm innocent, Andie Rose?"

"Do you ever use a burner phone?" I blurted.

"What are you talking about. Hasn't everybody at one point or another?"

"Are you the one who found Tootsie and called it in?"

He gave a derisive snort. "What kind of lunatic question is that?"

"A simple one, Wes."

"One I can't believe you're asking me. You don't think I'm innocent, do you?" He heaved a sigh. "I shoulda called someone else."

"I didn't say that, Wes. Besides, what me and Sister Alice believe doesn't matter, only—"

"*You* don't believe me either, Sister Alice? Where's the faith here?"

"My faith is in God," Sister Alice said.

"I could use a drink," he muttered into the phone.

"All I meant," I continued, "is that whatever information and evidence the police have leading them to what *they* believe happened is the only thing that's important. So maybe start with what they found and the reason you're sitting behind bars right now."

"Sister, did you tell them where I was? They showed up at the hospital."

"I did not," she said. "But I can't imagine they wouldn't have checked the hospital when they saw the blood. Seems the fine new detective lied to us," she said to me.

Wes cleared his throat. "Doesn't matter much now, does it? All that matters is I get out of this place. I'm innocent."

The amazing aroma of roasted chicken and freshly baked bread permeated the air. My stomach growled and my mouth watered. Awful for wanting food at a time like this. I pushed my coffee cup aside and peeked at my watch—five-thirty. My mind had insisted on traveling, and I thought I'd missed something again.

"What?"

"I didn't say anything," he said sullenly.

"What evidence do they have, Wes?" I asked again.

"Can you just get me an attorney? Every alcoholic has an attorney on speed dial. Mine just happened to have retired."

"I have more time under my belt than you do and

haven't needed one since long before I moved here. And I'm not sure attorneys were even a thing when Sister Alice needed one." The joke got a somber chuckle from Wes and a look from Sister Alice that scared me.

With this whole marijuana debacle at the inn, which ironically directly correlates to the reason Wes needs an attorney, I wondered if using the same one would be a conflict of interest. "We'll find one for you after you've told us what they got on you. And, no, we didn't tell them anything, just so we're clear. What happens and what's said in the rooms stays there."

"I know you didn't. But they were closing in like hyenas, asking me questions I couldn't get out of. You know the kind—no matter the answer, they'll think I'm guilty. I tried to skirt around it until the two of you could find out what happened to Tootsie, but we all see where that got me."

"Time," a male voice called out on his end.

"I gotta run."

"But we still don't know—"

"Just please find me a lawyer," he pleaded. "I gotta go." The line went dead.

Sister Alice and I stared at each other.

I put my hands up, palms facing the sky. "We have no clue what went down, so what kind of lawyer do we get?"

"A criminal one," Sister Alice said, exhaling slowly.

I rolled my eyes. "Obviously. But one who specializes in what? Murder?" It felt like I swallowed a rock at a realization—that's the kind of attorney Frank and Izzy—and possibly even Tony would need.

Sister Alice slapped her palm on the table and abruptly stood. Aspen flinched. "Chin up, buttercup. No time to get down at the mouth. We have work to do. And by the time we're through, we'll all be fine."

But would we? What if the marijuana had something to do with Tootsie's death? What if she got it from the inn, and the inn got shut down? And even if we weren't legally at fault, what if Simon filed a civil suit against us and I lost the place?

Fearing I'd vomit, I quickly swallowed. "I should have chosen the Colorado inn. Marijuana's legal there."

"What?"

I shook my head. "Nothing. Did you notice Wes didn't answer my question about finding Tootsie?"

She drew her eyebrows together. "Yep. Caught that."

"Do you still think he's innocent?"

She sighed and slowly shook her head. "That's for the police and lawyers to work through. Even if he *is* guilty, it's not for us to judge."

I tried to absorb her sense of calm. If one could be guilty by association, could one also be good by association? I touched her shoulder, just in case.

****

That evening I had an appointment with a client—the Lakeview Pharmacy owner's wife, Mary, who was desperately searching for self-worth after her only child was in prison for illegal activity while he was running the pharmacy for his father. "Motherhood was always my greatest joy," she said. "I feel like such a failure."

I had all I could do to stay on track and be present in this moment as she unburdened her heart, hoping for guidance in climbing out of the giant black hole of perceived failure. My mind kept wandering to find answers that would save my inn and keep both businesses afloat. If I couldn't, I'd wind up coaching the homeless—my could-be peers.

"Andie Rose."

I pulled my attention, a ten-pound weight, back to the room. "I'm so sorry, Mary. You were saying?"

"It seems to me you could be the one who needs a little help right now. What can *I* do for *you*?"

Ugh. Speaking of failures. Maybe someday I'd learn to follow the wisdom I dished out. Or not.

"Honey," she said in an earnest, motherly tone. "I might be a failure as one, but I'm still a mother. I have a sixth sense about these things."

I sighed. "I am so sorry, Mary. Obviously, this session is on the house." I cleared my throat and adjusted my position, so I leaned in toward her. "Your son was an adult when he broke the law for fast money. They were his choices and his alone. No one has the power to make a person behave a certain way and we're certainly not responsible for another's choices. But we have the power to make our own right choices." As I spoke, my brain screamed, *Listen up, Andie.* "I have the perfect homework for you this week before we meet again next Friday." Her eyes brightened with hope as I explained the power of simple affirmations, explaining that I wanted her to even take it a step further into incantations.

Her brows knitted together. "What's that?"

"Reciting your affirmations, out loud and with feeling, in front of a mirror. Ten times a day."

She giggled. "My husband will think I'm off my rocker."

I chuckled. "I'd do it when he's not around. And if you're in public, wait until you're not."

Another giggle. "We're selling the pharmacy, you

know."

"Yeah?"

"Mm-hm. It's too much for us, and with my son in prison …" Her tone turned wistful. "Well, we decided it's time. If it doesn't sell, we'll just close'er on up." She abruptly stood and lay a hand against her chest. "Oh, Andie Rose, I cannot wait to get started on this homework. Thank you so much for your help." She leaned in and quietly added, "You're a little brighter now too, don'tcha know. Perhaps you should take your own advice and do those magic incantation thingys this week, too." She observed Aspen who lay gnawing at a peanut butter bone clenched between his front paws. "I need to get me a dog."

I chuckled. "Incantations are far from magic. They take work, consistency, and dedication. And yes, I highly recommend animal therapy."

As I walked her to the door, I thought about the pharmacy and the big uprising that had occurred with Mary's son at the helm last spring. Which led me to think about the pharmacist brother of an acquaintance I'd made in Birch Haven. Her super *cute* pharmacist brother, Max Winters. I'd met them both last spring while temporarily crashing at my cousin Babs' apartment until I officially took ownership of the inn.

I stopped and turned toward her. "Mary, I might have a lead on a buyer for you. I'll see what I can do."

She clapped her hands together. "Oh, you're just full of goodness today, Andie Rose."

"Well, I don't know for sure. But I'll make some inquiries and get back to you." I blushed as I thought about Max.

"Let me know what you find out, then. And thank

you."

After Mary left, I scrolled through the contacts until I reached Melanie, my Birch Haven friend's name. When she picked up, I said, "Hey, Melanie, this is Andie Rose. Remember me?"

"Andie Rose." she exclaimed. "How could I not remember? Being suspects in not one, but two murders together, is a unique bond one doesn't easily forget." She groaned. "Those days are in my rearview mirror. For now."

"Say what? What do you mean by *for now*?"

"Babs told me you've already got the Spirit Lake police department on their toes."

I chuckled at her sudden change of direction. "Just making sure they're earning their wages. How are you? Babs told me you're pregnant."

"As big as an elephant and ready to pop. But I'm grateful a human's gestation isn't as long as that of an elephant. I couldn't imagine going through this for eighteen to twenty-two months."

I cringed at the thought of even one month, then told her about the pharmacy, hoping to get the unbearable long pregnancy thought out of my head. "So I thought you could let Max know, in case he wants to branch out."

Melanie snickered. "You just want my brother in Spirit Lake. You were pretty adamant last spring that you had a boyfriend and not looking. Has that changed?"

"Fifty-fifty. No longer have a boyfriend and still not looking. But even though Spirit Lake is beautiful, adding more beauty isn't a bad thing." I grinned.

"Do you want his number so you can call him directly?"

"No. If I'd wanted to do that, I would have called

Winter's Pharmacy instead of you."

"Oh, I get it. You're calling me to get to my brother. And here I thought you needed my help in solving a murder."

I let out a howl. *If she only knew*. "Last I heard, Levi banned you from finding dead bodies." Melanie's husband, Levi, a homicide detective with Birch Haven PD, finally found a brilliant way to keep her from getting in the middle of his investigations. A baby.

She scoffed. "I'm not sure which makes him happier, that I'm out of his way or for the baby. I'll pass along the word about the pharmacy to Max."

After extending my gratitude and hanging up, I allowed myself a few glorious moments of daydreaming about Max's almost electric green eyes. Then I sighed and pulled myself up from the chair. I still hadn't gotten replies from messages I'd left two attorneys as possibilities for Wes. I glanced at the clock. Seven-thirty. They wouldn't call anymore tonight. In fact, by the time I'd left the voicemails, they'd probably already left the office for the day.

I thought about Wes sitting in jail. Had he been the one to find Tootsie and call it in anonymously? Was Carmen strong enough to survive if she landed in jail? That's if the police are even considering anyone else for the actual murder. And where did Tina pick up Jerry? Maybe the police weren't even out to find them anymore, content with Wes as the suspect. And what about Simon? If I was wrong and he wasn't involved in his wife's murder, would he file a civil suit against me and/or the inn?

Then a thought nearly bowled me over. I jumped up, slipped into my coat, and slid a red knit hat on my head.

The drug-sniffing dogs hadn't been here yet. If I opened all the windows in the shed, maybe it would get rid of any detectable scent. Highly unlikely, but better to try something than do nothing at all.

As I passed the front desk, Jade was straightening things up for the night. She frowned. "You're going out now? It's dark."

"Not far. Just need to check something outside."

She nodded toward Aspen. "For as much trouble as you've been getting into, you need a guard dog, not a service dog."

"Ha. Truth. If you're gone by the time I get back in, have a good night."

"Where are you going?" she asked.

"The less you know, the better."

"Well, that's not concerning at all," she snapped.

I waved at her and started for the door, Aspen by my side. "See ya." I called over my shoulder as I headed for the dark shadows of the property.

Chapter 16

The parking lot, the landscaping, and the recreational area on the lakeside each had unique and adequate lighting. But since no one typically used the gardening shed in the winter months, when the dark hours were most of them, that area of land was unlit. I planned to fix that this upcoming summer.

The light from my heavy-duty flashlight bounced over the snow in front of me as I swished it from side to side. At least I had Aspen with me. Except he was only interested in rabbits and squirrels, neither of which was any danger. Even if he caught one, he'd never injure it. He'd rather play chase. I agreed with Jade, a guard dog he was *not*.

When we reached the gardening shed, the flashlight's beam grew dimmer and flickered. "Of course," I muttered. I hoped the beam would last until I finished inside the shed. Outside, at least I had the moonlight. Though only a sliver tonight, it shone on the snow, causing it to glow.

I bumped the flashlight against my palm, and after another flicker, the light grew brighter again. Tucking the flashlight under my arm, the beam shining on the door, I unlocked the door and slipped inside the darkness. The pungent smell of Pine-Sol scented marijuana assaulted my nostrils, and I wrinkled my nose. It was akin to those odor-reducing bathroom sprays.

Nothing like a giant whiff of Hawaiian Paradise smelling poo. *Gross.*

I reached for the light switch but stopped short. I didn't want the windows illuminated from the outside announcing my criminal behavior. So instead I found an old, heavy pot and propped it against the door to keep it open in case my flashlight called it quits.

I did a quick once-through of the entire shed, not so much as a leaf left behind. I swept the floor and shelves with the dimming beam, determining that I'd come back out here at first light when I could safely use the light in the shed as an extra precaution. For tonight, the windows.

I started toward the one small window in the back room where the grow was before tackling the windows in the main shed. After a visual sweep of the room, I stepped back into the main shed to grab the big box fan from the corner to help hasten forcing the smell out and bring in fresh.

While I searched for an outlet in the back, I couldn't help but wonder whether I was helping my case or hurting it? I was sure the law would consider this hindering an investigation, but it *was* kind of stale and humid in here, I justified before the little voice in my head named conscience said yet again, *To justify is just a lie, Andie Rose.* I shoved it aside for now.

I strategically placed the flashlight, directing the beam at the window, adjusted the fan just so, then crossed to the window to lift the lower pane. It wouldn't budge. I stood on my tippy toes to check the lock, only to find there wasn't one. The window was simply stuck; sealed shut as if no one had opened it for decades. Except this room hadn't been here when they built the original shed. Grandpop added it on later. I tried again with no luck. At five-foot-eight-inches, I was taller than the average woman, but not tall enough to get a good grasp on the high window.

Hands on my hips, I grasped the flashlight and scanned the room for something to stand on and found a five-gallon bucket just outside the door of the room. I set it underneath the window, bottom up, and perched the flashlight back where it had been, when the light flickered again. Once, twice, and then a third time as I held my breath. Finally, it stayed lit, albeit dimly, a trite occurrence in a horror movie. And those never ended well.

I stepped on top of the overturned bucket and reached again. The light flickered, and a noise came from the main room. I swallowed a yelp, sucked in my breath, and held completely still. The last thing I anticipated was a rat scurrying back here. I'd take a bear any day over a rat. I shuddered and waited, but there was nothing more except the wind howling outside. "Get a grip," I mumbled in the dimly lit room. The future of the inn, the legacy that Grandpop and Honey left behind, was at stake here. There wasn't time to be a coward.

Another attempt at prying the window open, tugging and yanking, when a crash and clang came from the larger and primary room. I screamed. This time the adrenaline rush created greater strength, and the window slammed open so fast I nearly tumbled from the pail. Just as I caught my balance, the door to the room banged shut. Too late, I realized my mistake of not propping this door open as I did the front door. A gust of wind sweeping through the shed was all it took to blow the door closed. I gasped and Aspen barked. But *was* it the wind? The deadbolt slid into place, putting to rest my question; the wind doesn't lock a deadbolt. My heart thumped. The ghost? No. She had helped me in the past. She wasn't harmful. *Was she*?

"Hey," I shouted. I reached for my phone to use the flashlight app when I remembered I set it on the shelf to the left of the main door when I went in search for something to prop the door open with. *Grrr.* "Andie Rose Kaczmarek," I muttered in frustration. "Why didn't you set the flashlight down and use your phone to begin with, dummy?" I exhaled loudly, realizing I could either sulk or *do* something about it. Choosing the latter, I ran for the door. The flashlight's dim beam shined the other way, and I tripped. My hands shot out in front of me, and I caught my balance just before falling headlong into God only knew what. At this point, I welcomed the light. I pressed my hands along the wall until I felt the switch and flipped it up. Nothing. I shuffled toward the flashlight, aimed it upward. The socket was empty. *Of course it is.* Frank probably didn't even know about it. He had his own light system in here and most likely didn't use the primary source. I exhaled my frustration through pursed lips and held my palm against my forehead, then back to the door.

"Hey." I shouted again and pounded with a fist. I placed my ear against the solid wood door, but all was silent except for the foraging from a rodent. Aspen scratched on the floor in front of the door and whined.

I glanced at the faintest of light from the window across the room. Hope rose to the surface. I could climb out, then go around, unlock the door, and let Aspen out. *Yes.* No. I heaved a sigh of defeat and dropped my chin. That plan was impossible. Even if I *could* pull myself up to the window to crawl out, no way could I get my body through that tiny window. I had my father's height and athletic build of his youth.

Okay, think Andie Rose. No worthwhile options came to mind, so I worked on the door some more, tugging, pulling, placing a foot against the wall for leverage, and pulled some more. This door was not budging. I crouched while I reconfigured a plan. Aspen's wet nose touched my cheek, and I wrapped an arm around his neck, taking comfort by burying my face in his fur.

I looked back at the window, grateful my eyes had adjusted to the fragment of remaining light. The window was our only hope of getting out of here. But how? Aspen wouldn't even fit through that thing. If the inability to escape forced us to stay out here all night, we would freeze to death. Aspen had since ceased his frantic desire to get to the critter on the other side. We were utterly and completely alone in these sub-freezing temps. I shivered, blew hot air into my cupped hands, and vigorously rubbed them together. My fingertips burned. I tugged my mittens from my pockets, blew warm air into them and slipped them on. The window was our only hope.

Once again, I stepped onto the overturned bucket, laid the flashlight on the sill, then turned it off, hoping to save the remaining fraction of battery life. I began hefting myself up, but I couldn't get leverage with my mittens on. I took them off and tossed them on the floor. Blowing into cupped hands once more, I grasped the window ledge and pulled. No luck. After taking a minute to catch my breath, I grumbled, "I seriously need to get moving on a workout plan to build up some muscle again. I'm getting soft."

Just when I thought I'd made it, the window gave way and crashed down on my fingers. I yowled at the starburst of pain that sliced through my fingers, a sound that would make a feline jealous. I fell to the floor, and the flashlight flipped off the sill. Unfortunately, on the other side and in the snow.

"Grr," I yelled into the darkness. I held my hands between my thighs to help ease the pain, if even a little. Aspen planted his rear on my lap. Fingers throbbing, no flashlight or cell phone, I leaned forward and buried my face in his fur again as he leaned into me, doubling as a blanket for warmth and security.

When my fingers froze enough to dull the ache to a throb, I gingerly slipped them back into my mittens. When I regained my strength, I took a deep breath, got back on my feet, and kicked on the door, yelling at the top of my lungs. Why hadn't I yelled bloody murder out the open window? Not one of my brightest moments. "Ay-Caramba!" I shouted in a fit as I plopped onto the floor. It was as if my brain matter was frozen. Aspen's nose nuzzled my cheek. Leaning into him, I said, "I'm sorry, buddy. You got yourself a nutcase for a human." I took a deep, centering breath to clear my head. Maybe kicking the walls instead of the door would yield better results. Standing back up, I saw Aspen, still on his haunches, staring up at me. "I will get us out of here, bud. I promise."

I pummeled the heel of my foot against an exterior wall and kicked with all my might. This *had* to be related to Tootsie's disappearance. Or maybe there was a weed-buying customer getting back at me for shutting down his or her source. No way could it be someone wandering around thinking trapping someone in a shed would be a fun time. Unless it was a guest, people wouldn't even know about the shed. Carmen or Simon? Jerry or Tina?

I pushed the button to light the face of my watch—almost nine o'clock. All the staff had left by now; no one would be outside to hear me yell and kick. Giving it one more try, I yelled as loud as my lungs allowed, my throat raw, and waited, legs crossed at my ankles, since I couldn't cross my fingers.

"Andie Rose?"

Halleluiah. There was hope. Forgetting about my fingers, I clapped. A fresh wave of pain brought stars.

"Frank?" I cried out. "In here. I'm in the back room of the shed. Someone locked us in." Aspen barked in agreement. I wrapped my arms around his neck and giggled. Relief or frozen to the point of hysteria, I couldn't be sure.

The door opened, and I threw myself at Frank and wrapped my arms around him. Tears sprung a leak at both the pain level from my fingers and knowing Aspen and I would live.

I pulled back from him. "What are you doing here? How did you find me?"

"I thought I'd open the windows to get the smell of the plants out before the detective brings those sniffin' dogs out."

"That's what I was doing."

"I found this." He handed me my flashlight, now completely dead. "How'd you get stuck in here?" he said as he shined the flashlight around the room.

A flashlight? Frank *knew* the bulb was out? I shook my head to clear the rubble. *No. No way.*

As I spilled the traumatic experience, the words

falling all over themselves, he removed his ratty wool fingerless gloves and gently lifted my hands to inspect my fingers. I flinched at the pain from his touch, and he let my hand go.

"You're gonna have some bruisin' on those fingers. You should probly get 'em checked out. Lots of bones in the hands, ya know."

"Yeah. I can feel every one of them right now." My enthusiasm from the rescue simmered, overshadowed by who did this. Another prank from Izzy? Doubtful. This would have been taking it too far, even for her. Pranks weren't sinister. Someone would have had to follow me to know I was even out here. I hadn't even told Jade. That gave Wes a double alibi—unless he'd been released from jail on bond, eliminating the need for me to find him an attorney. Maybe he thought I knew too much and had someone watching the inn. I had to warn Sister Alice.

"Miss Andie," Frank said, concern etched on his weathered face. "Why didn't you just open the door and leave?"

"I told you. It was locked."

Frank scratched his temple then tugged an earlobe. "Miss Andie, the door wasn't locked."

I sucked in a breath, unable to release it until the room began to spin. "It was locked, Frank. I know it was. The deadbolt even clicked."

He cupped my shoulder with his large hand, his facial features softening as if he thought I'd lost my last brain cell. That or—no, not Frank.

Chapter 17

I snatched my cell phone from the shelf by the door, removed a mitten and, with my thumb knuckle, gingerly touched the speed dial number assigned to Sister Alice. Frank removed the door block and shut the door. I inhaled sharply.

"What are you doing?" I threw the weight of my body against the door to push it back open and tumbled out. Aspen trotted out after me.

"Just keepin' the heat in while you make yer call."

No longer knowing who to trust, I hustled toward the inn, stealing a glance over my shoulder at Frank. Sister Alice didn't answer, so I left a message at the tone.

"Call me ASAP. As in 911. That doesn't mean call 911, it means call me—oh forget it. You know what it means. Just call me."

"Miss Andie," Frank called from behind me. "What's wrong? You still want the windows open?"

"Yes, please," I said over my shoulder. I wanted to protect the inn, but I couldn't if I was dead. And right now, I wasn't ruling anyone out. That included Frank.

That deadbolt wasn't on the door before. Did Frank install it? And why? Was it because I discovered his undercover criminal operation? Maybe he figured I'd verify the room was clean before the dogs came. Or maybe, like me, he was only trying to stop the dogs from picking up the scent. But I knew the door was locked. I heard the deadbolt slide into place. Could it have been Lady Lucy giving me an escape? If so, she could have at least let me know. Possibilities swirled around in my head like a snow devil.

When I leaped up the stairs to the front door, I turned to see if Frank was behind me. He wasn't. Maybe he was hiding somewhere.

"Andie Rose, you're ridiculous," I scolded myself as I tried to maneuver the knob with the heel of my hands. "He's probably just in the shed opening the windows." The pain in my fingers turned from slicing pain to a throbbing ache. Whether that was good or bad, I didn't know, and there wasn't time to think about it right now. Frank was one of my favorite humans in the world. There was no way he would hurt me or anyone else. *Would he?*

My phone rang, and I swallowed a yelp.

"Sister Alice?"

"What's the 911?" she answered groggily.

"Were you sleeping? You were sleeping." I answered my own question. Now that I was in the safety of the inn, I felt foolish for calling. I'd allowed myself to become unhinged because of an anxious imagination. "Sorry. Calling was a mistake."

After some rustling around on her end, she said, "Well, seeing as you did, tell me what's up? Besides me."

"Go back to sleep. I'll fill you in tomorrow." If it *was* Wes, he couldn't get inside her house. *Could he?*

"I'm already awake, Andie Rose. Fill me in."

"Someone locked me and Aspen in the gardening shed. Frank found us, and here we are. And the window slammed down on my fingers, smashing them. You locked your doors and windows, right?"

"What is going on, Andie Rose?"

"I think it might be Wes."

She made a grumbling sound in the back of her throat. "You're confusing the ever-loving sense out of me. Is Wes there?"

"Not now, but he might have been. And if he is bent on getting rid of me for knowing too much, he'll be coming after you, too."

She exhaled a sigh. "Andie Rose, start at the beginning and tell me every detail before I come out there and lock you in the shed myself."

And so I did. Every. Last. Detail. And the line fell silent. "Sister Alice?"

"You seem to have gotten someone pretty hot under the collar," she said. "And Frank finding the door unlocked is concerning. I don't suppose you called Detective Griffin."

"No."

"What about Noah? He's right there at the inn. Call his room or knock on his door."

"Interfering with evidence is not exactly something I want to announce to the police," I shot back. "Besides, at this time of night? He'll think it's a booty call. No, thank you." I started for the stairs to my room.

Sister Alice snickered. "And why would he think that, Grasshopper? Have you been giving him signals?"

"No." I said with more force than I'd intended. "They're supposedly coming out in the morning with a dog, so I'll fill him in then. I want him to inspect the lock and to dust for prints, too. Until then," I said as I closed my door behind me, sliding the deadbolt into place, "I'm secure in my room and not going back out until Tony is here."

"Where's Frank now?"

"I don't know. Maybe I should go out and be sure he didn't get locked in as well."

"Maybe you shouldn't," she said dryly. "Right now, you don't know Frank isn't who locked you in to begin with. Keep your nose clean and your fingers intact. Your only job is to stay in your own lane. You seem to have trouble with that."

"You're not any better," I said. "It's not like I've had to beg you to help me."

"Yeah, but I'm not my sponsor. I'm yours."

Despite the gravity of the situation, I couldn't help but snicker before once again growing sober.

"If Frank gets locked in and freezes to death overnight, I could never forgive myself."

"At this point, missy, we don't know who locked *you* in. So stay put, huh? I'll be there before I head to work at the hospital tomorrow so we can poke around some. Being familiar with the place, you might see something the police won't even notice."

I rubbed my eyes with my thumb and forefinger. "Just watch your back."

"And you yours," she said. "Now get some sleep. I'll be by first thing in the morning."

I examined my crimson-colored fingers and moved them slowly, grimacing. Getting a single blink of sleep tonight would prove nearly impossible. Hoping to tackle two issues at the same time, I popped some nighttime extra strength pain reliever and began getting undressed, a painful and tedious process, being maimed and all. As I did, I continued pondering possible suspects, and when I thought about Frank, I put my clothes back on. I knew what it felt like to be locked out there, not knowing if I was going to see morning. If Frank wasn't the suspect, the culprit could have locked Frank in, too. I couldn't do that to him and live with myself afterward if he didn't. Live, that is.

When the next thought popped into my head, I gasped. Frank had the key to open the deadbolt. The same deadbolt he'd said wasn't locked when he arrived. I'd assumed he was the one who had installed it, but given I now had proof, it caused extreme uneasiness. I paused again, waffling whether I should leave my room and go out there, ultimately deciding I had to. If Frank was the one who locked me in, why would he come back and rescue me? My suspicions leaned toward Wes again.

Letting Aspen stay curled up on my bed, I crept down the hallway and past the library when I glimpsed someone tiptoeing down an adjacent hallway. Coat on, black hat covering his head, and his back toward me, I couldn't make out who it was but knew he was going toward Bobby and Carmen's room. Bobby? But the build was wrong. Too short. Had Simon returned?

As I pulled back and peeked around the corner, I placed my hand on the wall to steady myself. Pain sliced through my fingers. "Ouch," I said under my breath. I jerked back behind the corner and plastered myself flat against the wall and waited. Footsteps padded closer, paused, then retreated, and it was quiet again. I poked my head around the corner as the person removed the hat and disappeared behind the door. Carmen.

I hurried down the hallway and once again put my ear against her door. Someone moved about quietly on the other side. "Carmen," I whispered. The sound on the other side of the door went deathly silent. "Carmen? I know it was you. Can we talk?"

Still nothing. Another try yielded the same silence, so I continued my way to check on Frank, this time with a heavy-duty flashlight to double as a weapon. I tucked my phone inside my mitten against the palm of my hand. When I reached the front door, I spotted Frank. He walked down the drive and hopped in his truck, which was parked in a tree-lined nook off to the side. I exhaled my relief and went back to my room, hoping—no, praying—that the pain reliever kicked in soon. (Sister Alice would be so proud, even if desperation led to the prayer.)

Aspen, lying on his side across my bed, watched as, with still-throbbing fingers, I struggled into my green and black long underwear and matching top I'd gotten from my parents for Christmas two years ago. To keep my hair in the morning from looking like something Aspen threw up, I attempted to braid it, but recoiled from the pain. Instead, I wrapped my fingers with ace bandages and snuggled under the covers, pulling them up to my chin as best I could. Typically a side or back sleeper, tonight I tossed from side to side, on my back, then side to side again, finally landing on my stomach, head off my pillow and flat. Lying there for what seemed like hours, I lifted my head to see the green numbers on my alarm clock. A paltry one hour had passed. I flipped onto my back again and lay staring at the ceiling. The light of the moon spilled across the foot of my bed and on the floor, brighter now than in the shed when I'd needed it.

"Where are you, Lady Lucy?" I whispered into the semi-darkness. "Some help to work through this hot mess would be nice. And if you're gonna unlock a door to help me, let me know next time, would ya?" The numbers on my alarm clock flickered, and I froze. Was that her? Instead of fear, it was oddly comforting. It's not like she had ever harmed anyone. The only frightened people were those afraid of ghosts to begin with. And with the inn's reputation for being haunted stretching far and wide, guests couldn't help but know about it.

I grasped the covers between the palms of my hands, tugged them tighter under my chin, and closed my eyes. The PM part of the pain reliever was failing miserably tonight. Maybe it wasn't designed to silence adrenaline. As I lay staring at the ceiling, the lights on my clock flickered one more time. Thoughts of Wes in jail trespassed my mind. Was he still locked up, or had they released him on bail? Was releasing a murder suspect on bail even a thing? I thought of Carmen sneaking down the hall toward her room, dressed as if she'd been outside. And then there was Simon. He'd been in such a hurry to split and to get Tootsie's body cremated. Why? He'd said he wanted to put her to rest and move on with his life as best he could. Did that mean with Carmen? If Bobby knew that Carmen and Simon had killed Tootsie together, did he know they were together as a couple? I wouldn't think so, because if that was the case, he wouldn't be protecting Carmen.

The snow devil in my head spiraled into a snow tornado, so I ceased all thoughts as best I could by entering my nearly always-successful four-square breathing. *Four in; hold for four; four out; hold for four. Four in; hold for four; four out; hold for four.* I continued until my eyelids grew heavy, and I stood on the ice outside the fish house, minus Aspen. An unseen presence propelled me toward harsh fluorescent lighting that streamed through the tiny window on the door. I walked slowly toward it, my heart rate gathering speed far north of safe as I did. I stopped in front of the door, raised on my tiptoes, and peered inside the small window and gasped. Wes was inside plunging someone down into the hole as the person flailed and fought back. I pounded my palm on the window and grasped the handle for the door. Oddly, there was no pain in my hand. But the door was locked. Again I pounded on the door as well as kicked with all my might.

"No," I screamed. "Wes, no." The woman thrashed about, and I pounded and kicked until my foot went through the plywood. The woman in the spearing hole turned, and I cried out as I saw myself in that hole, ice hanging from my hair and eyebrows.

I swallowed a scream and bolted to a sitting position in absolute panic, my breaths coming in gasps. Despite my hair plastered to my head with sweat, the temperature in the room felt glacial, and I couldn't stop shivering. I untangled myself from the bedding, twisted in knots, and wrapped them tightly around me, not caring a hoot right now about my injured hands. In fact, I barely noticed them. What I *did* notice, and appreciated more than ever, was as I curled into a tight ball, my knees to my chest, Aspen curled up beside me, his snout tucked in the crook of my neck.

Before long, the room felt too warm. I shed the blankets, turned onto my back, and stared at the ceiling again. "Sorry, buddy," I whispered to Aspen. He wasn't happy with the disruption of his comfort. I glanced at the clock—only twelve-thirty. *Ugh.* Torn between wanting to fall asleep so the night flew by faster and fear of sleep,

I decided that if I was to function properly the next day, I needed some zzz's.

Chapter 18

I woke to Aspen nudging my cheek with his nose, his tender brown eyes level with mine. I laid my forehead against his, then hugged his neck. When I pulled back, his gaze stayed on mine, communicating loud and clear he needed to go outside. Now. I turned off the alarm to avoid the obnoxious beep. I groaned and closed my eyes, burning from lack of sleep. One more glance at Aspen, however, and I couldn't resist those baby browns.

His tongue lapped my face before I'd even sat up. "Eww." I wiped the back of my arm across my mouth. "I don't know what you've been licking while you waited for me to wake up." He tilted his head and stared at me with innocent eyes, a move that melted my core every time. I sighed and scratched his neck. "Come on." He leaned forward, his front legs resting on the bed, wiggling rump in the air, then lifted his head and gave a quiet howl. I chuckled. "Patience. I need to get dressed first." As if he understood, he lay down and settled in, his gaze following my every move. The pain in my right hand was tolerable, the pain in my left, not so much. Thankfully, I was right-handed.

Finally dressed, a two-minute task that took ten this morning, I led him down the stairs and into the darkness. Morning darkness was never as ominous as nighttime. Besides, I'd regained my composure after last night, except for my fear of losing the inn. That would be the ultimate disappointment and insult to Grandpop and Honey.

I shined a flashlight and scanned both sides of the doorway and then over the massive back yard. Aspen whizzed in record time, then investigated the snow-covered ground around the bonfire pit like a hound. Dim light filtered through the curtain on a window to my room above me. I glanced at the hot tub, then down by the boat shed where the beam of my light couldn't quite reach.

Aspen zoned in on something by the bonfire pit, his nose rooting in the snow. "Aspen," I called in a loud whisper. "Stop foraging for food like you're starving."

I glanced toward the second floor where all the rooms were located, catching a flicker of light in Carmen and Bobby's window, slightly ajar. Right before I turned away, the curtain fluttered, and a hand snaked through where the curtains met in the center and pulled one side open enough to reveal half of Carmen's face. When she saw me watching her, she pinched the curtains closed again in one swift move. If Carmen heard my hushed call to Aspen, wouldn't they have heard a struggle in the hot tub? That led me to believe it hadn't happened in the hot tub at all. If they hadn't heard anything, someone might have captured Tootsie when she was in town meeting Wes. This wasn't good for him at all. And what about Jerry? I still didn't know what to think about Tina needing to go pick him up. From where? She still hadn't returned my calls. If Jerry was the last in the hot tub with Tootsie, what happened after that? None of the pieces were fitting together to get even a glimpse of the picture.

I kept my eyes trained on the window a minute longer when leaned against my legs, apparently ready for breakfast. After one more glance toward Carmen's window, seeing nothing more, Aspen and I trotted up the stairs to our suite.

By the time I fed Aspen and dressed in presentable clothes—which today meant no buttons or laces to tie, only a red pullover sweater, jeggings, and red slip-on boots—my hands ached. A ponytail or braid was completely out of the question, so my curls hung loose down my back beneath a knit hat. I hadn't even been able to make the bed. A trip to the doctor had to be in the plans this morning. By the time I'd applied black eye liner and blackest black mascara, two staples I never left without, *no matter what*, the fingers on my right hand hurt more and the ones on my left were nearly intolerable. I re-wrapped them as best I could and popped four ibuprofen tablets before Aspen and I headed down to the kitchen for coffee.

Tony was hustling to finish breakfast preparations and cutting vegetables for soup as part of the noon meal. Aspen stayed in the doorway, and I crossed the kitchen to the enormous coffee pot. Height usually wasn't an issue for me, but having to reach with both hands, I knew how it felt to be vertically challenged. I grasped a mug between the heels of both hands.

Tony stopped what he was doing and frowned. "What happened to you?"

"Long story," I muttered. "Can you please pour me some coffee? I'm not above begging at this point."

"Sure. Need me to pour it down your throat, too? And don't eyeball me like that. I'm joking."

"At least one of us got some sleep last night."

"It clearly wasn't you." He poured a mug of coffee, and I grasped it between my hands, the bandages a barrier from the heat. After the first sip, I closed my eyes and groaned, "Mmm. This is exactly what I needed."

He leaned against the counter and crossed his arms in front of him. "So, are you going to tell me what happened or just leave me guessing?"

"Someone locked me in the gardening shed last night."

He narrowed his eyes and looked at me sideways. "Why were you out there last night to begin with?"

I took a deep breath, plunked down on a stool at the island, then launched into the complete story. When I finished, he stared at me in silence.

"Do you think it could have been Frank?" he finally asked. "I didn't think the old guy had it in him to hurt anyone. Although," he added without waiting for me to respond, "technically he didn't hurt you, the window did. And he, quote," he made air quotes with his fingers, "rescued you," he put his fingers back down, recrossing his arms in front of him, "from freezing to death. But what's with the door? Did he unlock it?"

I tossed my hands up. "Dunno." I wanted to talk with Tony about Wes, but I couldn't do that without violating Wes's anonymity. "Coulda been Carmen who locked me in." I told him about her weird behavior in the hallway last night and again this morning in the window.

"Anything on Jerry and Tina?"

"Nope. I've tried calling a few times, but now their voicemail box is full."

Tony shook his head, blinking slowly. "You need to hire a bodyguard. Have you ever considered that?"

"Huh," I said, focusing on the vegetables rather than him. "Nah," I said after a minute, turning my attention back to him. "I don't want anyone following me around."

He pushed himself away from the counter and snatched a towel, tossing it on his shoulder. "Well, if you're not careful, Izzy will have her chance to own the inn because you won't be around."

****

By the time Sister Alice arrived, I was on my second cup of coffee.

"Anything new since we last talked?" She stomped the snow from her boots and tucked her gloves in her coat pockets, then hung her coat on the rack beside the door. "On second thought, don't answer. That's a scary question to ask you."

"But since you did," I answered with a wink, "I started a beautiful fire in the parlor fireplace so we can have a fireside chat. Coffee?"

"I'll wait until you catch me up so I don't get indigestion."

Once we settled in the two wingback chairs that flanked the fireplace, I filled her in on the latest. By the time I finished, my coffee had grown lukewarm and Sister Alice's face was pinched.

"Well?" I finally said.

"The things you get into in a matter of a few hours frighten me deeply."

"I didn't get into anything."

"No need to get defensive," she said.

"What if the same person who locked me in, locked Frank in, too? I couldn't, in good conscience, leave an elderly man out there to freeze to death. Or anyone, for that matter."

"I'm so relieved you clarified that," she said dryly, then sighed. "But in your defense, I guess we can agree that you acted on behalf of someone else and not selfishly."

I stabbed four bandaged fingers at her. "Exactly. But here's a question that popped into my head. If Simon and Carmen were seeing each other, maybe Simon swiped the remote control from the bedroom TV and the alarm clock because it was faster, easier, and less risky than trying to clear Carmen's prints from them."

Sister Alice cocked her head. "Except if that's the case, and her prints were only on those two things, that makes little sense."

"Maybe," I said, lifting my fingers in the air and wincing at the stab of pain, "the nightmare is a clue that Wes is the guilty one."

"Nightmare?" she asked.

"Forgot to tell you that part." After I did, I said, "Maybe the dream means he bonded out and is coming for me because I know too much."

She shook her head. "That doesn't make sense either. You only know what you do because *he* told us."

"How is that different from a killer confessing everything to his victim before he kills her?"

"Because the murderer kills his victim right after the confession. He doesn't let her get away and blab first."

I set my cup on the table between our chairs, wrapped my arms and bandaged hands around myself, and shivered. "What a comforting thought."

I swatted away what felt like a mid-winter viral cloud hanging above us. This was no time to feel defeated but to stay grounded.

"I'm going to get another cuppa joe," I said. "I'll be right back. Want anything?"

She raised her eyebrows. "Instead of spending all my prayer time asking for your protection, why don't you give me the answer to who killed Tootsie? Soon I'll have to seek volunteers to help with that."

I briefly touched her shoulder with my bandaged paw. "We will. I know it. Find who killed Tootsie, I mean, not the prayer volunteer part." When I spun around toward the kitchen, I said over my shoulder, "See if Wes will join you on your prayer chain."

"Go." she ordered. She tipped her head toward Aspen, lazing in front of the fireplace. "Leave your security blanket with me."

Turning the corner from the parlor, I ran smack into Noah, startling both of us. I got the better end of the deal since he now wore the remaining coffee from my mug on his sweater and jeans. I only hoped he wouldn't take revenge on me while he helped investigate this case.

My cheeks hot and my brain's cylinders misfiring, I furiously wiped the coffee from his sweater with my ace bandages. "I'm so sorry."

"Just get me a towel," he said, then pressed his lips together. He went to swipe at my hands with his and stopped short, reaching for them instead, eyes round.

"What happened to you?"

Instinctively, I jerked my hands away. "Nothing."

His brows furrowed. "That's not *nothing*."

"My fingers tried to stop a window as it slammed shut. The window won."

He winced and he clenched his teeth as if feeling the pain. "How?"

"I was trying to get some fresh air."

"You'd better have those windows inspected before it happens to a guest, or you'll be facing a lawsuit one of these days."

If I'm not already. Desperate to change the subject

before he asked more questions—like how it happened and where—I said, "What are you doing here? Um—I mean not here at the inn, obviously, but down here. Breakfast isn't for another half hour."

"I'm an early riser and came down to grab me a cup of coffee when I heard the two of you talking in here and came to see what you're conspiring about so early."

I shook my head vigorously. "Nothing. Sister Alice just stopped by for a cup of coffee on her way to work."

He stuck out his chin in hesitant acknowledgement. "You sure that's all it is?"

"What else would it be?" I averted my gaze before meeting his full on.

"One can only imagine." He observed my shoes, my sweater, and my hair. "Red looks good on you. Even when it's your cheeks." The corners of his lips tugged with amusement. "And just so we're clear, I won't so much as blink about charging you with tampering if I find out that's what you were doing." He tilted his head back and stole a glance toward the parlor. "Think I'll go say good morning to Sister Alice."

Speechless, I only smiled. Well, I tried to anyway, but it felt like my face would crack. How did he know what I'd been doing? Was *he* the one who followed me and locked me in? To scare me away from any further involvement? A moment later, I found my voice and turned toward him.

"Noah?" He turned, hands in his pockets. "How long were you eavesdropping? And what did you hear exactly?"

"A detective never comments on an open investigation."

"Well, technically," I said, trailing off.

183

"Technically, as of first thing this morning, I'm officially an on-duty detective with the Spirit Lake Police Department."

I swallowed a lump in my throat. "Oh. So anything you may have heard…" I paused, carefully weighing my words.

"Anything I heard can be used against you." He winked.

I transferred my weight from one foot to the other. "Hm."

"Excuse me while I say a polite hello to Sister Alice." As I absently watched him, I saw my life swirling down the drain. "Andie Rose?"

My attention snapped back to the room. "Um-hm?"

"Just so you know, I heard nothing specific. Only the quiet murmur of voices."

I exhaled my relief. "You could have told me that to begin with. Not that I have anything to hide." *Right.*

"Of course not."

My fingers flew as I typed a text to Sister Alice—

—*he knows nothing so don't let him trick you into thinking he does.*—

I spun around and peeked around the corner to be sure she read it, then scurried away again.

Chapter 19

After Sister Alice left, I strolled toward Lily at the front desk. Guests wandered into the dining room for breakfast. Even Carmen and Bobby came down. His hand slid to her rear end as he leaned down close to whisper something in her ear. She reached for his as well. *Gag. Take it back to your room.* It was as if they'd forgotten the past forty-eight hours. Too bad I was about to remind them. I would have felt bad, but I wanted answers.

I trotted toward them. "Hey, guys. Carmen, got a minute?"

She held my gaze a moment, then looked up at Bobby when he placed his hand on her lower back.

"I'll get us a table facing the lake," he said.

When he was out of hearing range, I said, "Can we talk about last night?"

She tilted her head. "What do you mean?"

"I saw you going down the hallway and into your room after being outside."

She toyed with her ring and stayed silent. "I know you saw me, Carmen. And I heard you by the door when I said your name."

"How would you know I was outside?"

She thought I was stupid, or what? "Because with as toasty as I keep it in here, you wouldn't have had on a coat and hat if you'd been inside." Now toying with her ring *and* chewing on her lower lip, I said, "Relax. I'm not accusing you of anything." *Except I kind of was.*

"What happened to your hands?"

"I had a minor mishap."

"Oh."

"I'm curious why the mysterious disappearance last night."

She exhaled through pursed lips, looked away a moment, then down as she twisted her ring again. "Simon told me who Tootsie was seeing. I called him and we met up to talk."

Carmen and Wes? I hadn't seen that coming. So that meant Wes *had* bonded out. But on a murder charge? Was Carmen lying? And wait. Simon *knew* who it was? Had he only said he left town and instead waited for an opportune time to kill Wes?

"How did Simon find out who the man was?"

She shook her head. "I dunno."

"Did Bobby know you met with Wes?"

"Of course not." She cut a glance around the room. "Why do you think I didn't answer the door when you called my name?"

"That was pretty risky, wasn't it? Leaving for any length of time. I mean, the suites aren't huge."

"Bobby'd had a few drinks before he went to bed. I knew he'd be out for a while."

"Did he have a few drinks the night Tootsie was killed?" If boozing it up caused him to fall into a deep sleep, that would explain Carmen leaving with Simon. Or Wes. Sheesh. Who could keep up anymore?

She shrugged. "I don't know. I wasn't there."

I squinched my face. "What do you mean, you weren't there?"

"I'd been smoking with Tootsie and didn't want Bobby to smell it on me. She gave me her key when I left the hot tub, and I slept on the couch in her room."

I put a bandaged hand against my forehead "Carmen, why didn't you mention this before?"

She dropped her gaze. "I knew how it would look."

"It means you knew Tootsie didn't come back to the room that night."

Her head snapped back up. "Not true. When I got up about five and went to mine and Bobby's suite, I assumed she was in bed with Simon."

"Didn't Bobby wonder why you didn't come to bed until morning?"

"No, because I laid down on the sofa. I told him I didn't want to wake him up when I came up from the hot tub. Which isn't a lie."

Egads. I sighed. My head spun with the possibilities that could arise from this new information. "Did you tell Detective Griffin any of this?"

"No. You've got to promise me you won't say anything. It makes me look guilty."

I hesitated a moment as I pondered the gentlest way to ask the next question, eventually realizing there wasn't a gentle way to ask one if they killed someone.

"Are you? Guilty."

Her eyes glistened with unshed tears, and she swiped at them with the back of her hand. "No. Bobby is waiting for me. I have to go, Andie Rose."

"Carmen," I said quickly before she left.

"Yeah?"

"Where did you and Wes talk last night?"

"In his car."

"Here at the inn?"

She nodded slowly and left. I heaved a sigh. I was back at the starting line with my investigation. The more information I acquired, the more it muddied the waters.

After checking in with Lily, I decided helping Tony in the kitchen would be a welcome distraction. There was nothing like cooking or baking to take me to a place of serenity. Especially when I baked the specialty dog biscuits. We received sizable orders from businesses in town.

"Need help?" I asked Tony. "Aspen is out with Lily."

He glanced at my hands, then snickered. "Not unless you're planning to kill flies by batting at them. Of which there aren't any in mid-winter."

I puffed my cheeks and exhaled. "Guess I'll go call the doctor. And pop some more pills." He went still and blinked slowly, forcing me to clarify. "Acetaminophen. Geez."

"Andie Rose," Noah's voice said behind me as I began ascending the stairs. I waited for him to catch up. "Detective Griffin is on his way with the dog."

"Crap," I mumbled.

"What was that?" He cupped a hand behind his ear.

"I said nap. I'm tired, and I need a nap."

"You're welcome to come out there when he gets here. You'll have to stay outside, of course."

"Well, that sounds like a whopper of a good time," I said dryly. "But I'm hoping to get in to see the doctor this morning." I held up a damaged appendage. "Unfortunately, I'll have to pass."

"Don't worry. We'll keep you posted."

"I'm sure you will."

After closing the door to my suite behind me, I

leaned against it, letting my head fall forward. I lingered for a few moments, exhaling negative energy and inhaling positive energy. There was a light scratch on the door. I pushed myself away from it with my elbows, let Aspen in, and made the call.

****

Aspen trotted out the door after me from the doctor's office. I had a cast on my left hand for two tiny bone fractures and my right hand re-wrapped with an Ace bandage. With my addiction history, he agreed with me that narcotic pain meds weren't ideal, and he prescribed what I'd already been taking—over-the-counter extra strength pain reliever. Two remaining pills rattled on the bottom of the bottle just that morning when it fell out of the medicine chest. I headed down the sidewalk to the pharmacy, Aspen by my side.

Mary was kneeling on one knee, stocking shelves. When she saw me, she leaned her weight on one hand and grunted as she slowly pushed herself up.

"Goodness gracious. This getting old stuff isn't for sissies."

I held up my hands. "I'd give you a hand, but I don't seem to have one available."

She gasped. "What happened?"

"You should see the other person." I rolled my eyes. "Kidding. Long story. I just need some over-the-counter pain meds. The strongest you have."

She smiled warmly at Aspen. "I bet I can find something special for him, too."

Aspen's tail wagged as if he understood. She strolled to the isle with a few grocery items, tore open the cardboard from a four-pack of peanut butter, opened one of the mini containers, and set it on the floor in front of Aspen.

I grinned. "You'll be his best friend for life after that."

"Now for you." She walked to the next isle over that contained the pain relievers, grabbed a bottle off the shelf, and handed it to me. "Here. It's on the house."

"You'd better check with the owner about that," I teased.

She chuckled and waved her hand in dismissal. "He wouldn't dare say no. I know where he sleeps."

We laughed, and her husband said, "You two stop making fun of me when I'm too old to hear."

I glanced at the back of the store toward the pharmacy counter and waved at him. "Hey, Harry."

He closed a white bag and stapled a package insert and label over the top. "I hear you passed along the word about selling the store. Thank you kindly."

"The guy hasn't responded yet, but I'll let you know the minute I do."

"He already called me."

I raised my eyebrows in surprise. "Max called you?" Aspen trotted back to me, his tongue licking each side of his snout.

"Sure did. After we discussed some details, he said he's going to see if he could work his schedule around and come next week to check it out. Analyze things a bit. I suggested if he's planning to stay for a couple-a days, he oughta call the inn and reserve a room. With such short notice, you're probably all booked, I suppose." He tucked a prescription bottle into a bag and, once again, stapled the insert and label over the top.

My heart rate perked up at the thought of seeing Max. "This is the slowest part of the year, so we'll have at least one room available."

Mary patted my back. "All right then. Everything's worked out. I'll see you in two weeks for my next session."

After a brief hug of confirmation, I left, forgetting all about my pain, even though it was time for a pill.

As soon as I stepped outside Lakeview Pharmacy and the door closed behind me, I stood and inhaled deeply the fresh, brisk air. The temperatures were climbing from subzero to tolerable. Even enjoyable. Climbing *slowly*, but at least going in the right direction. Business was down at the inn, and while financially it wasn't ideal, given everything going on right now, it was just as well.

I scanned the sidewalk and on the other side of the street. People strolled on both sides, some with loop handled packages dangling from their arms while holding coffee or hot chocolate. The town's general population is fewer during January and February, but I'd never seen the streets empty. Today was no exception.

Christmas decorations remained outside most storefronts and on the vintage style three-head light poles that lined both sides of the street. The view was charming, and Max Winters was about to make it even better. I shook my head. My interest in Max's visit made me question my sanity. I'd only seen the guy a few times and didn't even know him.

I lingered in town a while longer to escape the debacle at the inn with Detective Griffin and now Detective Parker, too. Hoping to escape Wes's problems for the moment as well, I kept my eyes peeled for him so I could dodge him if I needed to.

A coffee date with myself sounded amazing. We had

two independent and uber popular coffee shops in town; Hallowed Grounds was conveniently across the street from the pharmacy, and Spirit Brew Coffee House sat next to Sweet Temptations Bakery. While both were remarkable, I hadn't quite recovered from an incident I'd had at Hallowed Grounds last fall. So Spirit Brew it was.

Lost in visions of a custard filled eclair and peppermint hot chocolate, I ran smack into Father Vincent as he emerged from the coffeehouse. And as had happened with Noah previously, Father Vincent's drink dripped down the front of my coat.

Father Vincent glanced at his cup on the ground, then at me. "Seems God didn't have coffee in mind for me today."

I stooped to pick up his cup, a bead of sweat on my brow despite the icy air. "Oh dear. This is so embarrassing, Father. Let me buy you a new one."

With a kind smile that crinkled the skin at the corners of his eyes, he placed his hands on my biceps. "Thank you, but no thank you." He noticed my hands, removed his from my biceps to hold mine gently. "Whatever happened?"

I sighed. "Long story."

He dropped his hands, stuffed them in his coat pocket, and smiled. "How's business?"

I bobbled my head from side to side. "So-so. The staff claims that's normal for this time of year. I remember Grandpop and Honey had more free time during these months, too."

His eyes warmed at the mention of my grandpop and Honey. "I sure miss them."

"I know," I said wistfully. "Everyone does. With the way things have been lately, I'm sure everyone wishes they were still running the inn instead of me." I focused my attention across the street, and down, anywhere except at Father Vincent's face.

"Hmm." He watched me a moment before continuing. "I heard about the unfortunate events of the past few days."

"Sister Alice?"

"Yes." He gently lifted one of my hands in his own and nodded toward it. "But apparently, she didn't tell me everything."

"I had a fight with a window. The window won."

He released my hand without breaking his gaze from mine. "I see." He finally looked away for a spell, giving me a break to recover from my emotional moment. When he turned back to me, he said, "The Lord's doors are always open, Andie Rose. I hope to see you sometime."

Desperate to change the subject, I said, "Are you sure you won't let me buy you a replacement coffee? I could drop it off at the church."

"No, thank you. But you two enjoy." He reached down and scratched Aspen's head.

I watched as he walked back toward St. Michael's, then turned toward Spirit Brew. As I reached to open the door, my phone rang. A glimpse at the display and I groaned. Detective Griffin. I waffled on whether or not to answer. When we hung up, I wished I'd have waffled on the side of *not*.

Chapter 20

On our way back to the inn, Aspen, the seat belt buckled securely around him, sat tall and proud in the front seat, stealing frequent glances my way. I wished I could be as oblivious to the turn of events as he was.

"This keeps going from bad to worse, Aspen," I said, keeping my eyes on the road. He whimpered a quiet acknowledgement.

When Aspen and I walked through the door of the inn, Detectives Griffin and Parker were waiting in the foyer. They both stood.

"Got a minute?" Detective Griffin asked.

"Does that mean I have a choice?" I forced a smile, then turned straight faced at his tightened jaw muscle. It was exactly the look on my father's face when he'd caught me sneaking in one time well past curfew. Like six hours past curfew. Well, okay, the *many* times he caught me sneaking in. Except with my father, I could wiggle my way out of it. Which frustrated my mother to no end. Getting out of it so easily with Detective Griffin, however, was unlikely. I sighed in resignation and prepared to receive whatever news they were about to dish. "Let's go to my office." It felt like I was in the principal's office, except we were in *mine*, and the principal hijacked it.

The three of us sat, following the seating chart from the last time we were in this room. A thin layer of dusty silence settled around us before Detective Griffin spoke.

"Funny thing happened." He leaned back in his chair and adjusted his belt.

"Oh?" I tried my best to appear innocent. I'd had plenty of practice with that in my younger years.

"Was pretty cold in the gardening shed."

"Why is that funny? It's not like it has great insulation."

"It happens when all the windows are fully open for some godforsaken reason in the middle of an insanely cold January." He cleared his throat. "Do you know how that might have happened?"

I shook my head, maintaining innocent, wide-eyed contact.

"No?"

"Nope."

Noah studied my hands, and I casually slipped them beneath the desk on my lap. "You sure? Maybe the window that caused your injuries was in the shed."

I struggled to think of the best way to phrase a response without incriminating anyone. "I didn't open the windows." Not exactly a lie since I opened *one*, singular, not plural, and that one closed before I left the shed.

"Well, I'm sure you'll be happy to know that the dog still picked up the scent," Detective Griffin said. "A few hours of open windows can't get rid of it that quickly. These dogs are smarter than that."

"Where is the dog? Aspen would love a playdate." I reached down and rubbed his head with the bandage on my right hand. "You would like that, huh, boy?"

"The officer took him back while we waited for you."

"Hmm." His gaze stayed on me. *Probably waiting for me to 'fess up to something.* I opened my mouth to speak, giving way to a satisfactory gleam in his eye. "Would now be a good time to tell you someone locked me in that shed last night?"

He drew his eyebrows together. "As concerning as that is, this tidbit of information could either work for or against your situation here. Or both. But tell me what happened."

"Aspen and I would have froze to death." *Way to play on his sympathies, Andie Rose.* I mentally patted myself on the back.

"How did you get out?"

"Frank saved us. He heard me screaming and pounding on the walls."

He chewed on his cheek as he appeared to contemplate the situation. Then he said, "I'll check into it. But I have two questions I'm dying to know the answers to."

I stared at him until I couldn't stand the silence anymore. "What are those?"

"First, what were you doing out in the shed last night when you, just a minute ago, acted insulted that I even suggested it. And, two, what was Frank doing out there after hours. During a brutal cold snap."

"I'msostupidmeandmybigmouth."

He turned his head a quarter turn, hand cupped behind his ear facing my way. "What was that?"

I licked my lips. "Umm…I said I'm sorry, my brain cells went south. For the winter. And my memory isn't what it used to be. You know—"

Amusement tugged at the corner of his mouth. "I'd probably stop digging now if I was you."

I caught my lower lip between my teeth. "Um, yeah—"

Noah shook his head, lips pressed together. "Yeah, I'd take the man's suggestion and stop."

Detective Griffin's cellphone rang. He pulled it from his pocket, peered at the caller ID, and stood. "If you'll excuse me for a minute, I need to take this."

He pulled the door closed behind him, leaving it ajar. I said to Noah, "Huh. Something more important than trying to get me to confess to something I didn't do."

Noah chuckled and shook his head slowly. "Except you kind of did. Confess to it."

I tugged my sleeves down. "The only thing I confessed to was getting locked in the shed. I would think finding out who left me to freeze to death would take priority over who opened stupid windows."

He sighed and smiled. "Well, I don't think you have anything to worry about with his priorities. Where you're concerned, that man is toast. I think he really *is* going to miss you."

I smiled warmly. "Yeah, I've become pretty fond of him myself. He's all bark and no bite."

He tucked his hands in his pockets, rocked up on his toes and back down, and jutted out his chin. "Not me. But rest assured, we will find out who locked you in. In the meantime, stay alert to what's going on around you. And stay out of where you're not supposed to be."

Detective Griffin came back into the room and tucked it into his pocket. He slumped in his chair and pursed his lips while he focused on the top of my desk. Finally, he said, "That was the ME. The official cause of death *was* drowning. With her intoxication level, she probably didn't even know what happened. Even if the marijuana contributed to her inability to function, we still can't prove where she got it from, so you and your crew are most likely off the hook." He leveled his gaze at me. "For the murder."

I stood abruptly, banging the cast on my hand on the bottom side of the desk. "Ouch!" I yelped, switching from foot to foot. Tears sprang to my eyes, and I closed them, muttering, "So all of this was for nothing." I opened my eyes to see I was the object of their amusement. "You can both wipe those silly little smirks off your faces. So much for chivalry."

Noah chuckled. "I was wondering what it would take to make you fess up to your crime. Now we know pain is the answer."

Realizing what I'd revealed at the mercy of pain, my cheeks grew hot with embarrassment. "I didn't open the windows. Not all of them."

Noah raised his eyebrows at the cast cradled close to my body with the other hand. "At least one."

I heaved a sigh and sat back down. "So my inn isn't in trouble?" Hoping to play on Detective Griffin's sympathies, I said, "Grandpop and Honey would be utterly heartbroken if anything happened to it."

He snorted, stood, and adjusted his belt once again. Noah stood as well, but neither turned for the door yet.

"Andie Rose," Detective Griffin finally said. "The inn, Mr. Flowers, and Ms. Carter are not out of the woods yet. Mr. Flowers had the grow operation in swing; Ms. Carter, a *minor*, mind you, got to it and knowingly served it to the public." My gut was an unhealthy marriage of joy and turmoil as I listened to him. "But" he put a finger up in the air, "I'm going to be busy solving this homicide before I leave." He put his finger back down. "So I don't have time to deal with this right now. It'll have to fall on Detective Parker. It should be his case anyway, since the specialty refreshments almost tanked his potential job offer with the department."

I turned my head slightly and said sheepishly, "Well, you *were* hired despite the laced refreshments anyway, right? So technically, it didn't cost you anything."

Noah tucked his hands in his pockets, fixed his eyes on me, and hesitated a minute. "It did. A whole lot of trouble." Just when my hopes began free falling, he added, "But since I got the job, I like to start with a clean slate."

I exhaled my relief and placed my pathetic, still aching hands on my chest. "Thank you, Detectives."

When they reached the door, Noah turned around. "But Andie Rose?"

"Yeah?"

"The next time, you won't be so lucky. Interfere with one of my investigations, and it won't turn out so well." He locked his gaze on mine. "Are we clear?"

"Noted."

When the door closed behind them, I snagged a minute to recover from the radical twist in the case, then plucked my phone from my desktop. "Come on, Aspen. This deserves another trip into town for a celebration." He stood and looked at me expectantly. I reached and rubbed his neck. "Yes, you can have a peanut butter ice cream treat. And how about a walk around Big Spirit Lake on this beautiful day?"

He pushed his nose in the air and howled in answer, his front paws performing a shuffle dance. I stooped and wrapped my arms around his neck. "You fix everything, Aspen." I opened the drawer where I kept his supplies (leashes, treats, etc) and pulled out his winter boots. He lay down, snout between his front paws. "Quit sulking. You know the wintertime drill." It wasn't so much the cold that affected him, but the sand and salt with which the town doused the sidewalks and trails, the granules sticking between his paw pads, causing him pain. Even so, he didn't like wearing them.

On the way to the foyer, we stopped in the kitchen to be sure Izzy showed up. Not only was she here, but I hardly recognized her. Her hair was smooth and in a sleek ponytail, her clothes were neat and fit nicely, and when I'd greeted her, she was friendlier and more sincere than ever. She thanked me profusely for the second chance. *Who was this kid?*

Tony cut me a glance and grinned. "Told ya."

Izzy gave him a quizzical look, but didn't ask.

But me? I stayed as straight faced and laced as I could. I didn't want to let her off *too* easily. Second chances were one thing, but a lesson learned was wisdom earned. For *everyone*.

I planned to tell Frank, though, because—well, because it was Frank. Yet, the niggling discomfort in the pit of my stomach every time I thought about getting locked in the shed gave me pause. I still couldn't fully trust him. Could I? He, Carmen, Simon, Jerry, Tina, and Wes all had the opportunity. But Frank and Carmen appeared the guiltiest as far as proximity. Although, if Carmen talked with Wes about Tootsie in his car at the inn last night as she'd claimed, he had been close by.

With the weight of the whole marijuana incident off my shoulders, I could spend my energy focusing on discovering Tootsie's murderer. And to shed some light on who wants me out of the way by locking me in the shed. Or worse. I shuddered. Was someone *that* peeved that I cut off their drug supply? Or was it because of my involvement in investigating Tootsie's murder? I still had so many unanswered questions.

When Aspen and I trotted out the door into the fresh air, I glanced up at the unusually bright cerulean sky. Winter skies in Minnesota were more often gray and overcast than not. But not today, no sirree. The largest icicles I'd ever seen hung from the eves on the corners of the building, clinging to the gutters. I made a mental note to ask Marcie to knock them down before someone walked underneath them. We didn't need another death. Although, given there were huge powder white snowbanks that lined the inn, it wasn't an emergency. Right now, the ice shimmered in the sun, and they looked glorious.

I called Sister Alice, greeting her with a sunny, "Hey there."

"What, did you win the lottery or something?"

"Pretty much." I gave her the scoop that the inn was out of harm's way. "That means I have more time and energy to find out who the murderer is."

"Well," she said, hemming and hawing. "I guess if you're going to do that, count me in."

I chuckled. "Can't keep out of it any more than I can, huh?"

"It's my duty to help keep the town safe."

I guffawed, and Aspen spun his head from enjoying the view out the windshield and toward me. "You tell yourself whatever you need to. I'm on my way into town for a coffee from Spirit Brew. Gonna take it with me on a walk around the lake with Aspen. Wanna come?"

"I have a house meeting with Sister Ida and Sister Eunice."

"Ew. Is this a good thing or a bad thing?"

"Let's just say I'd rather be having coffee and walking with you and the pup."

"A suggestion?"

"What's that?"

"Wear the most obnoxious frames you have. It'll take the focus off anything else."

"I'd say you're a bubble or two off-center of the level, but you might be on to something. Thanks for suggesting that."

I giggled. "Anything to help."

Chapter 21

When we disconnected, the impossibility of carrying my latte on the walk struck me. No way could I multitask by holding the cup with one lame hand and hanging onto Aspen's leash with the other. Aspen loved his expected treat of whipped cream, but if given the choice, he'd choose the lake, paws down. Boots or no boots. Besides, despite the brilliant sunshine, it was still cold. Warming up with a peppermint hot chocolate afterward would be perfect.

From the get-go, merciless gusts of wind blew across the lake. Aspen didn't seem to notice, but I shielded my face from the bite of the blowing snow. Still, the next hour flew by. Aspen terrorized critters, and I snuck frequent glances to where *the* fish house had been and processed possibility after possibility in my head. I wished I'd taken the time to write everything down on sticky notes and stick them up on my office wall. Standing back and studying them together as a whole was more productive than struggling to commit to memory mashed up pieces of information that got lost in the shuffle like a card in the deck. I was getting a headache from all the possible scenarios.

When we reached the car, I opened the passenger side door. Aspen hopped in and lifted a paw toward me.

"Sorry, my friend. The boots need to stay on a little longer. There's salt on the sidewalk by the coffee shop."

That earned what appeared to be an award-winning pout. "It will be worth it when you get your whipped cream treat." He put his foot back on the seat and let out a soft whine. "I knew you'd agree with me."

"Hey, Andie Rose."

Wes. I swept the empty lot—not a single other person in sight—then dashed into my car, slammed the door shut, and locked it at record speed. He jogged over toward me, and I rolled the window down a couple of inches.

"Roll your window down further so we can talk," he said.

Tilting my chin up toward the opening, I made a display of shivering. "I can hear you fine." I reached over and turned the heater on high.

He leaned over so his face was level with the window and rested a hand against the top of the car. "I got outta jail."

"I see that."

He stomped his feet and shoved his fists in his coat pockets. "It's freezing out here. Unlock the passenger door so I can get in."

I swallowed the lump in my throat, then tipped my head toward Aspen, who stared out the passenger side window. It was as if he refused to acknowledge Wes.

"Aspen would hate you forever if you booted him from *his* seat. Besides, we're in a hurry and don't have time to talk right now." Before rolling up my window, I said, "I left messages for a couple of attorneys, but none called back." My phone rang and I startled. Lakes News and Reviews. *Great*. I held a finger up at Wes and answered. Wes waited, fists shoved in his coat pockets, dancing from foot to foot to stay warm.

When I hung up, he said, "Well? Was that an attorney? Because I—"

"No. Lakes News and Reviews, asking a bunch of questions." They were always trying to catch a big story—to catch the big fish in a small town, so to speak—and it doesn't get any bigger than murder.

"Didn't sound like you answered much."

"Of course I didn't. I'm not stupid. I might be a slow learner, but I *do* learn."

"I got a hold of an attorney today, anyway. I meet with him first thing Monday morning."

"How did you bond out? I didn't think that was an option for a murder charge."

He narrowed an eye. "I thought you were in a hurry."

"We are."

"Since I use the fish house and the cabin all the time, it wasn't suspicious that my fingerprints were all over the place. Not enough evidence for probable cause and they couldn't hold me on suspicion alone."

I thought about last night's debacle in the gardening shed. "I heard you were at the inn last night."

He frowned. "Yeah. It was strange, though. Tootsie's new friend, Carmen, called me and asked if we could talk. She said she couldn't get away to drive into town, so I had to go there. So I did. I was curious why she wanted to talk and about how she got my number."

"Why didn't you just ask her on the phone?"

He lifted a shoulder and let it drop again. "Curiosity. And she specifically said *not on the phone*. Plus, I wanted to get a feel for whether she could have killed Tootsie."

"And? What was your conclusion?"

"Somethin's off with her, but I don't think she has it in her to murder someone. Been wrong before, though."

"Maybe she's in on it with someone else."

He appeared to think about that for a minute, then said, "Nah. I don't see it. If you ask me, I think it was Tootsie's jerk of a husband."

My eyebrows shot up. "You were the one having an affair with her, and you think *he's* the jerk? Wouldn't you be upset if you found out your wife was having an affair with another man?"

After a moment, he said, "I'd be more upset if she was having an affair with another woman. That'd be the ultimate insult to my masculinity."

My eyes popped wide as, yet another possibility hitched a ride on the rollercoaster that was my brain. *Tootsie and Carmen*? But why wouldn't Simon have been upset with Carmen, too? Instead, it seemed like they were quite chummy.

Lost in the conversation in my head, I rolled my window down all the way. "Wes, was Tootsie straight?"

He leaned over further, his arms resting on the bottom of my window, hands dangling inside the car. Instinctively, I jerked back toward Aspen. His eyes grew serious, and his shoulders rounded.

"You don't believe I didn't do it, do you? You think I'm guilty." He pushed himself up, one hand on his hip, the other running over the wool knit hat on his head. "That's why you won't let me in the car." He sighed and shook his head. "Andie Rose, I thought you knew me better than that."

I exhaled my exasperation. "I don't know who to trust anymore, Wes. Did you get out of your car last evening at the inn?"

"No."

"No?"

"No," he confirmed forcefully. "Carmen came out to the car. When we finished talking, she got out. I left. Simple as that."

"What time did she get to the car?"

He shook his head. "I don't remember."

"*About* what time? Can you at least just give me a timeframe?"

"Eight-ish? She said her husband was out cold, so she snuck out."

I stared through the windshield, vaguely aware of Aspen lying down on the seat next to me. "That's convenient."

"What is?"

I swiveled my head from the windshield to him. "That he passed out. I wonder if Carmen had a little something to do with that."

He lifted his eyebrows and tilted his head from side to side. "Probably slipped him something. She was pretty desperate to talk. Like I said—it was all really strange."

I absently reached over to pet Aspen. "Desperate people do desperate things. I need to go, Wes." I began buzzing my window up and struggled to shift my car into drive.

"Wait." he said, hand on my window. "Can I hitch a ride with you into town?"

I paused a minute. "How'd you get out here without a car?"

"Walked. Needed to clear my head. Doing anything I can so Monday doesn't seem so far away."

"Monday?"

"I see my attorney on Monday morning. I told you

that."

Keeping my own life straight during this mess was hard enough, much less keeping Wes's straight. "Yeah, you did. Sorry."

"Until then, I feel like a trapeze artist trying to walk a thin wire without a net."

I gave him a sardonic smile and tipped my head toward the back door. "I know all too well how that feels. Get in. But you'll have to hop in the back seat. Aspen already has shotgun."

I unlocked the door; he opened it and slid in. Aspen flung him some attitude of superiority from the front seat, then turned away in disinterest. When Wes's seatbelt clicked into place, I flinched. How dumb was I to have him behind me where I couldn't see? It was the most cliché attack in horror flicks. And I still wasn't totally convinced of Wes's innocence. Too many things pointed toward him. One glance at Aspen, my best buddy and sidekick, decided for me. No way was I going to ask him to move. Besides, it was a super short drive.

Nevertheless, I focused on my rearview mirror more than on the road in front of me. At one point, I had to swerve at the last minute to avoid annihilating a raccoon by a hair's breadth. Aspen gave me an *are-you-trying-to-kill-us-all* look, while Wes gave words to what Aspen couldn't.

"Sorry." Who knew driving while sober could be more dangerous than driving while intoxicated had been? Well, *almost* more. The dents and scratches I had gotten on my vehicles in those days—including the one I totaled—told a different story. And who knew I would have more interaction with the police now than back in those days?

I sighed as I pulled up in front of Spirit Brew Coffee House. Wes hadn't told me where he wanted to go, and I hadn't asked. "I hope this is good for you. I promised Aspen a treat, and me a little quiet time."

He rolled his eyes. "Yeah, I shoulda figured you were lying when you said you were in a hurry. Mind if I join you?"

Clearly, he didn't understand the meaning of *quiet time*. I glanced at his hopeful expression, exhaled, and acquiesced. If he was indeed innocent, I couldn't in good conscience leave him to flail about on his own, hurling him back to the drink. He didn't have a lot of time under his belt. And what he was going through could lead even an old-timer back to the bottle.

I sighed in resignation and climbed out of the car. "Come on." Aspen hopped across the seat toward my door. "I'll text Sister Alice and see if she's done with her house meeting so she can join us. If it's not quiet, it might as well be productive."

"As if I didn't feel unwanted before."

"Quit sulking and come on."

As luck would have it, Sister Alice had just finished and was all too happy to join us. Before she put her phone away, I quickly texted,

—*By the way—bring some stickies*—

—*Some what?????*— She responded.

—*Stickies*—

—*Have u lost ur ever loving mind? Sticky what?*—

—*Sticky notes. To write on*—

—*Well why didn't u say that to begin with?*—

I chuckled, got her order—black coffee, per her usual—and tucked my phone away.

St. Michael's Catholic Church was only two

business buildings away from Spirit Brew, so I hadn't even gotten to the front of the line yet when she arrived. I sent Wes to nab an open table in the back, away from the other tables. We didn't need anyone overhearing as we pieced together the puzzle of the murder.

"What took you so long?" But when I looked at her, I busted out laughing.

"What's so funny?" She stood beside me on one side, Aspen on the other.

"Those glasses." I hooted. She had cat-eye frames that included so many colors, it was as if she pulled them from a Crayola crayon box. Those gigantic boxes that all the cool kids had. I wasn't one of them. My dad, a bestselling thriller author, believed that using fewer crayons encouraged creativity and magic in art. "Did you get them just for Sister Ida?"

Sister Alice grinned. "You should have seen her face."

I snickered and stepped up to the counter to the waiting barista. Sister Alice surprised me when she changed her order to herbal peppermint tea. Wes requested the strongest black coffee they had. I think he was trying to emulate the coffee from the AA meetings so he could then, in essence, pretend he was in a meeting to help him through this mess he'd found himself in.

Aspen grasped the edge of the paper cup, containing an obscene amount of whipped cream, between his teeth and followed us to the table where he laid down. He clutched the cup between his front paws and dove in.

Sister Alice slipped a package of 3 x 5 notecards from her pocket and slapped them down in the center of the round table. "We didn't have *stickies*, as you call them, so notecards will have to do."

"They'll work just fine." She ripped the plastic from them, slid them in front of me, and Wes tossed me a pen. "Thank you," I said. "This will help keep *my* thoughts and *our* theories in order."

Chapter 22

After scrawling a single name on two of the notecards, I delegated the rest of the writing job to Sister Alice. She had two perfectly functioning hands.

I pushed them across the table. "Here. One name per notecard. We can lay them horizontally across the table and place any corresponding cards belonging to each name beneath it." I began naming everyone I could think of who had contact with Tootsie. "Carmen Perry, Bobby Perry, Tina Anson, Jerry Anson, Simon Timmons, Wes—"

"Why me?"

I swiveled my head toward him. "You seriously have to ask that?"

I glanced at the table nearest ours to find them staring our way. I waved at them, and they returned their attention to their own table.

Over Wes's continued attempt at dismissing his name from the lineup, she said, "Wes," as she wrote his name on the card and slipped it beside the others.

"We need some solid evidence to rule you out," I told him. "And there's a ton of evidence we need to refute."

He scowled. "Thanks for the vote of confidence."

I rolled my eyes and raised my hands, palms facing him. "Listen, Wes, you kind of got yourself into this mess, so you can help get yourself out of it. Own it instead of blaming me and Sister Alice."

Sister Alice raised her eyebrows and lowered her chin. "He wasn't blaming *Moi*." I leveled my gaze at her, and she reached into her pocketbook, removing a small white packet that she slid across the table to me. She said, "Someone's a little testy today. Here's some ibuprofen."

I looked at her, unable to contain a giggle. "It's hard to keep a straight face when I see your eyewear." She grinned and pushed them further on her nose with her pointer finger.

I tossed her my napkin. "Here. As always, your lenses are so smudged I don't know how you can see a thing."

She snatched the napkin. "Maybe that's intentional."

Wes appeared lost in thought and missed the entire exchange between Sister Alice and me. In fact, he hadn't even commented on her glasses.

He let out a long exhale and sat back heavily in his chair. "I know. You're right." Then he said to Sister Alice as if seeing her for the first time. "Groovy frames."

I struggled to suppress my amusement. Kicking Wes when he was down wasn't cool. I really felt for the guy. *If* he was innocent of the murder. We all make stupid choices, some just more than others, and having an affair with a married woman and murder were two *super* stupid choices. But then Sister Alice's words flooded back again, and I felt a pinprick of shame: *Don't judge other people because they sin differently than you do, Andie Rose.*

Unable to quell my amusement with Wes's comment any longer, I giggled, making a sound through my nose. "*Groovy*? I haven't heard that since—well, since my dad said it when I was in my teens, and he was trying to, and I quote, *connect with me*. It was embarrassing." I reached over and placed my bandaged paw on his arm and Wes startled, again unaware of anything other than his thoughts.

"At least your dad cared enough about you to *want* to connect. He took a swallow of his coffee.

I looked at him sideways. "How do you do that?"

He glanced at me over the rim of his cup. "Do what?"

"You're off in another world and yet you hear what's said in *this* world."

He stared off into nothingness again. "Women aren't the only ones who can multi-task."

I glanced at Sister Alice's eyeglasses for a dose of dopamine, *the happy hormone*, then focused back on the matter at hand—organizing information. The busy season at the inn loomed before me and I needed to destroy the dark cloud hanging above it. Starting in February through the summer months, the inn had only an occasional vacancy. Come the end of August, we had a waiting list. I was relieved we had a room open so Max could stay.

I straightened one of the name cards. "Sister Alice, add Joey Peterson's name on a card."

"The police have already ruled him out. Solid alibi."

"Forgive me if I'm not quite convinced." Sister Alice jotted his name and slid the card next to the others. "Wes, exactly how well did the two of you know each other. I assume pretty darn well if you're so friendly with his wi—ex-wife."

He glared at me. "So we're clear, I'm not *friendly* with his ex-wife. Me, her, and Joey grew up together."

"Sooo … I was right. You knew each other very well."

"We used to be drinking buddies."

Knowing what that meant, I screwed up my lips and took a deep breath. "Alrighty, then. Maybe not. What about the guy who supposedly busted in? Do you know him?"

He scratched his jaw and stared at me, at an unusual loss for words.

"What?"

"How would I know who that was, Andie Rose?"

I pressed my lips together, then said, "Mmm…you know a lot of other stuff no one else is privy to."

I stared through him, chewing on the inside of my cheek, as I thought for a moment. Drinking buddies frequently had a criminal record of some sort, no matter how minor. I wondered how to check into each of theirs.

"We need to find out the name of the guy. Maybe I can sweet talk either Detective Griffin or Noah to let me see their background check paperwork." The thought that it might have been Jerry haunted me.

Wes slowly shook his head, and Sister Alice scratched her head. "You're living in a disillusioned world."

"It doesn't hurt to try."

Sister Alice and I worked through several more cards, listing opportunity and motive for each name. Simon, as her husband, would have had ample opportunity. With Carmen inebriated and asleep on the loveseat, Tootsie could have come up to the room after the hot tub, and Simon could have taken her without Carmen even knowing about it. His motive was easy— the jilted husband, his wife having an affair with another man. There was Jerry, who had been the last to leave Tootsie that night. Had he made a move, she rejected him, and he got peeved? Was he the mystery man who called it in? As for Tina, had she seen something happen between Tootsie and Jerry, becoming the jilted wife?

"On Tina's card, make a note to check if she has any past domestic violence charges."

"Yeah, because Detective Griffin will hand that over to you, too," Sister Alice said wryly as she wrote the information.

"Hey Wes, do you think something could have happened between Tootsie and Jerry?"

He scowled and said in a derisive, emphatic tone, "What? No. No way."

"Okay, then." I patted his arm. "Maybe we should switch you to decaf, buddy."

He shook his head in disgust. "What's the point of coffee if you're not gonna get the buzz?"

"Heh, heh," Sister sniggered and shook her head. "Why indeed, Wesley."

All three of us chuckled, breaking the dismal mood that hovered over us.

I said to Sister Alice, "On a separate card, list each of their strange behaviors that make it seem like they're hiding something."

"Uffda." she said. "Maybe I should have grabbed more than one package of note cards."

I stared through her for a moment as I thought. "Okay, so Simon fled town without notice."

"To get the cremation services scheduled for his dead wife," Wes said. "That's hardly incriminating."

"That he did it so quickly and under the radar causes me to wonder. Did he really leave town? He supposedly knows you were Tootsie's lover. And why is he so quick to plan the cremation? Afraid something might surface?"

"The medical examiner already did the autopsy," Sister Alice added. "If there was something suspicious, they would've found it by now."

"What if he or she missed something that's evidence? And Simon wanted to destroy that *something*."

Sister Alice pondered this. "Possible, but not likely."

"Even if that's not the case, he still has the strongest motive. And we can't rule out anything, even if there's a whisper of possibility."

"Next is Joey." When no one said anything, I asked Wes. "Can you think of any motive—anything—he would have?"

"You're barking up the wrong tree, Andie. I already told you the police have already ruled him out. He has a solid alibi."

"And I already told you I was still planning to check him out anyway. Can you think of anything the police might have missed?"

He considered it, then shook his head. "Nope. Nothing at all for motive or opportunity. Like I told you before, he wasn't even in town."

"Not that you know of. Sister Alice, make a note to call the Raven Motel to see if he was there the night of the murder." I pointed to another card. "Next is Bobby."

"Opportunity and motive?" Sister Alice asked, pen at the ready.

"Opportunity is easy. He was at the inn, across the hall from the victim's room."

"And passed out in his own room," Wes reminded

me.

I narrowed my eyes and pressed my lips together, deep in thought. Finally, I said, "Yeah. He's super protective of Carmen, though, and he's protecting her from something. We just need to find out what that *something* is."

After a unanimous agreement, I inhaled deeply, then exhaled slowly.

"Okay, Sister Alice, next is Wes. Motive and opportunity."

Wes sat up and slapped a hand on the table. "There is absolutely nothing they can pin on me. I'm innocent."

I choked on the hot chocolate I'd just drank. "Right," I said. "We've already been through that. Okay, opportunity for Wes," I went on. "He was wide open since he and the victim planned to meet that very evening."

"But she didn't show." Wes's frustration was getting the better of him.

"Says you." I shot out my bandaged hand at his impending protest and leaned in. "I didn't say I don't believe you, Wes. Just that it looks suspicious." I watched Sister Alice write. "Add that his fingerprints were in the cabin and the fish house."

"I told you why that was, and the police couldn't even hold me on that."

"Again," I explained as compassionately as I could, "*we* know that, and the police may have let you go, but again, it looks suspicious. And as far as the argument that she didn't show, the police could argue that you were disgruntled at getting stood up. And you can't tell me the police will just forget about the prints. One shred of anything tangible and they'll pull it from temporary storage."

"This isn't fair." He slid down in his chair and crossed his arms in front of him.

Both Sister Alice and I glanced at him and spoke simultaneously.

"You're just figuring that out now?" I said.

"You got yourself into this mess you call unfair."

When Wes let up a little on sulking, I said, "Then there's Carmen. She was the last one to see Tootsie alive. The motive, however, escapes me. Did she and Simon have *a thing* going on? Maybe she's protecting him."

Sister Alice exhaled slowly, her glasses askew. I laughed and reached over to straighten them.

She blocked my reach with her forearm and pushed them up with her pointer finger. "Boundaries."

I glanced at Wes—he had once again zoned out to another planet.

"We need a few answers to clear up some things. Sister, jot down these questions. First, why did Frank install a deadbolt on that door in the shed? Could that have been the original murder scene? Also, I want to know if he's behind the incident of locking me in last night."

"Locked in where?" Wes said.

I glared at him. "Okay, you just need to stop that. It's freaking me out."

"Where did you get locked in?"

He seemed genuinely concerned, which led me to believe that it probably wasn't him behind that scheme. Carmen, on the other hand, I wasn't so sure about. "What time did Carmen leave your car last night?"

"'Bout eight-thirty—ish." He waffled his hand back and forth.

"You said that's the time she got there."

"It was."

I made a noise of frustration. "I asked what time she left."

He uttered something that sounded like, "I don't know."

"Approximately. How long did the two of you chat?"

"Twenty, twenty-five minutes maybe."

"Hmm. Theoretically, it could have been Carmen that locked me in."

"Locked you in where?" Wes said again.

I filled him in on the bare essentials of the event, then said to Sister Alice, "Regardless, write that down. I want to know why Frank installed a deadbolt *after* the plants were gone and the room cleaned out. And right before someone locked me in, leaving me to freeze to death."

She took a fresh note card, wrote *Questions* across the top, followed by *#1* and the question.

"Second, I want to know if Carmen heard something from the window that night. She heard me when I was out there, and I wasn't talking loudly. She has bat-hearing."

"Except she was in Tootsie and Simon's room on the opposite side of the hallway, not facing the back."

"Yeah, well, I want to ask anyway. Maybe she's not telling the truth and is trying to give Simon an alibi." As soon as I'd said the words, I gasped and shot up in my chair. "Holy wicked whiskey! That could be the missing piece that ties all of them together."

Chapter 23

Sister Alice looked at me quizzically.

"If Carmen assumes Simon did it, maybe she's protecting him. If Bobby assumes Carmen did it, it wouldn't be out of the question that's why he's protecting her. And the entire cycle leads back to Simon as the killer."

"That's a lot of *if*s and assumptions," Sister Alice said. "Don't go assuming and then fall on your face."

"*Somebody* heard *something* that night, and we have to find out who and what. Wes's freedom and the reputation of my inn depend on it." I stared hard at Wes.

He shook his head vehemently and put his hands up. "Why are you looking at me when I wasn't out there to hear anything? Far from it, since I was in town waiting for Tootsie to show up at the cabin. I heard nothin'."

I frowned. "No need to get defensive. I'm trying to help you. Your nerves are strung tighter than the shirts Jade wears. You've got to get a hold of yourself."

He pushed his coffee cup away and slouched back in his chair. "I know. But every time I'm reminded of how guilty I look, it freaks me out."

"Then help us find concrete proof other than you were in the cabin alone waiting for a dead woman."

He threw his hands up in the air. "That's all I got. Unless I lie."

"No one's going to lie," Sister Alice said. "We'll

just hurry and find the *real* killer. That's your best defense. Now Andie Rose, what makes you so sure someone had to have heard something? Other than Carmen heard you outside this morning."

"Because Bobby had cracked the window open for fresh air, and before he crashed, he heard Tootsie and Simon arguing."

"What were they arguing about?" Wes asked, suddenly more interested in our conversation.

"I have not a clue. He only said it didn't sound too innocent; Carmen said it was just a lover's spat." I rolled my eyes. "I can't believe I didn't ask him that. Guess I have a few things to learn about this detecting stuff." To Sister Alice, I said, "Jot that down on the list of questions—ask Carmen about the content of Simon and Tootsie's lovers' spat."

Sister Alice stopped writing and glanced at me. "You said Simon knew about the affair. You don't think that's cause enough?"

"But Bobby also said Tootsie didn't know he knew, and that Simon was trying to find out who it was. Which, by the way, Wes, don't get complacent about your surroundings. If Simon killed Tootsie and stuck around instead of leaving, like he said he was doing, you might be next."

He scoffed. "Well, good golly, thanks for that." He slapped his hand on the table again, startling not only Aspen, who snapped his head up, but also the people at the table over from ours. I guess they were part of the drama, whether or not they wanted to be. That neither of them attempted to move tables convinced me they did. "I feel so much better now, Andie."

I sighed and put my hand on his forearm. "Sorry,

Wes. I don't mean to be so hard on you. It's probably why I'm thirty and still single."

"And yet you're a relationship life coach," Sister Alice said. "The irony."

I laughed dryly. Sometimes, even when one didn't want to hear the truth, there's no point denying it. "Whatever. But regardless, Carmen admitted Simon said he knows who it was." We remained silent a moment until another thought struck me. "What if Simon thought it was Jerry and that's why Jerry didn't return either. Maybe he killed them both and Jerry's floating beneath the ice somewhere." I shuddered.

Wes leveled his gaze at me, and Sister Alice frowned.

"That's an ugly thought," she said.

Camping there for a minute before exhausting all the other ideas we came up with, I pawed the cards together. Sister Alice intervened in my pathetic attempt to keep them all on the table.

"Nah," I said. "Apparently Tina knew where he was if she left to pick him up. And she never returned without him, so it's safe to say he's alive and well. We just don't know if he's the murderer." My eyes sprang open wide. "Holy crap! Maybe there *was* something between Jerry and Tootsie and Tina killed them both. Maybe that's why she left so early with the excuse of picking up Jerry."

Sister Alice's eyes matched my own. "That, my friends, is a definite possibility."

"There was nothing between Jerry and Tootsie." Wes pressed his lips together and ran a hand over his face.

I sighed. "Oh, Wes. You need to take your head out of your—"

Sister Alice clamped her hand over my mouth. "Language."

I twisted my head away from her hand, snickered, and stood. We dropped our cups in the trash. "Wes, you gonna be okay?"

"I won't go drink, if that's what you're asking."

"If you want to, you're more than welcome to come hang out at the inn."

"No thanks. I hear the police frequent that place. And rumor has it you're chummy with the new detective."

I gently punched his arm, followed by an expletive at the pain that shot up to my elbow. I glanced quickly at Sister Alice and muttered, "Oops."

She smirked, then looked at Wes. "I'm trying to figure out how such a foul-mouthed ex-drunk could be kin of Honey."

I raised my eyebrows and folded my arms. "I'll have you know Honey and Grandpop were proud of me."

"Because you're so good at hiding what you don't want other people to see."

I scowled at her. "That's so rude."

"Yeah, it was," she conceded. "Especially since I just described most alcoholics."

When I pulled into the inn and unbuckled Aspen, he jumped over my lap and out the door before I could. Then I realized that with getting lost down the rabbit hole of trying to catch a killer—and who locked me in the gardening shed—I hadn't even taken him to go potty.

He ran for the nearest snowbank, relieving his overfilled bladder until I didn't think he was going to stop. When he finished, he trotted along the tree line of the driveway and sniffed, not stopping until he reached the alcove where Frank had parked his truck the night before and where—Wait a minute. If Frank's truck was there, Wes couldn't have parked there at the same time. One of them was lying. And since I'd seen Frank get in his truck to leave, that meant Wes was the untruthful one.

I jogged over and joined Aspen, searching the ground closely while carefully watching if Aspen caught a scent of anything that interested him. It wasn't unusual for a guest to park here when the small lot was full, patting down most of the snow with countless tire tracks. It was then I spotted the slight imprint of boots. I squatted beside them, and Aspen stood beside me, nose to the ground. The prints led from the inn but were too small for Frank. Maybe Wes' timeline was off, and he wasn't lying at all. He wasn't too certain. As much as I wanted to believe that, I couldn't shake the niggling suspicion of doubt. I visually followed the prints to where they disappeared into the woods and toward the backside of the gardening shed. By all appearances, Carmen had, indeed, visited the gardening shed last night.

****

After I walked through the door into the foyer, I fumbled my way out of my coat and scarf and hung them on the coat rack. Aspen trotted over to Jade, who reached down and kissed the top of his head. "Hey little buddy," she cooed.

"Do I get a kiss on the head, too?"

She smirked. "Not likely."

"Rude."

"Lily had to leave early," she said. "Also, thought you'd like to know that Bobby and Carmen checked out."

I stopped dead in my tracks and doubled back.

"What do you mean, they checked out?"

"They left," she said, as if simplifying it made a difference. "Said they were going home. Bobby had to work, and Carmen had to get home to the kids."

"Did they notify Detective Griffin or Noah?"

She shrugged. "I didn't ask. Why?"

I shook my head. "It's nothing." Jade didn't need to know any more than what was necessary. As I walked away, I wondered if I should let Noah know about their sudden departure, but then had an idea and pivoted back. "Hey, Jade?"

"Yeah?"

"The cleaners left before the Perrys, right?"

"Yep."

"Thanks." I trotted to the desk, snatched the master key ring, and hustled toward the stairs, taking two at a time, past the library, and down the hall. I wanted to search the Perry's vacated room before notifying Detective Griffin or Noah so they couldn't tell me not to. It wasn't considered interfering with any part of the investigation before that. *Right*? If they didn't know, neither could order me to stay away. I'd be sure not to touch or move anything. Easy peasy lemon squeezy. Besides, long ago, I'd learned it was better to ask for forgiveness than for permission.

With a quick glance over my shoulder, I let myself into the room and quietly closed the door behind me.

I did a quick once over of the suite, then got to work searching for anything that might give me a clue that incriminated Carmen. Except, I didn't for a minute think she'd done the dirty work; she could never have lifted Tootsie's body to take it anywhere. But that made it unlikely Tina could, either. I made a mental note to put that as her defense as well as Tina's. And yet Tina's innocence seemed less and less likely.

Then a thought popped into my head. Maybe after Jerry left the hot tub, Tootsie got Carmen, and they went into town together to continue partying. Carmen confessed she fell asleep on the sofa in the Timmons' suite before she went to her own room early in the morning. Bobby would protect her by covering for her, saying she was there all night; Simon would agree that she was in *his* suite, so he had an alibi. It was all making more and more sense. No matter how I spun things, it always came back to Simon.

But then I thought about Wes again. If Carmen wasn't in either room at all, but went with Tootsie into town to continue partying, could they have run into Wes? If Tina was the killer, could she have already killed Jerry by that point and met up with them? If not, did Carmen and Tootsie have a disagreement, Carmen did something to Tootsie, and Wes disposed of the body? Or perhaps Wes got upset if he saw Tootsie and Carmen, assuming Tootsie blew him off to party with Carmen. Tootsie's car never left the lot, but did Carmen's? And what about Tina and Jerry's car? I hadn't asked Tina, but Carmen said she hadn't left. But if someone was capable of murder, lying would come easy. I wished with all my might I'd kept the security cams installed.

I unlocked the window and slid it open a tiny bit, then crossed the short distance into the bedroom. The Birch room was the largest, more like a small apartment, but the Oak room, along with the Maple and Elm, were larger suites; each had a separate small sleeping space.

I stood there, listening carefully. The loud jeer of blue jays, followed by their whistling song, and several boisterous caws of crows, made it hard to hear much of anything else. I hoped the crows weren't an omen.

As if that wasn't creepy enough, the eerie sound of the ice cracking drew a chill, and I crossed my arms in front of me. Grandpop explained to me once that when ice on a lake changed temperature, it expanded or contracted, causing cracks. The sound from those cracks traveled over the sheet of ice that acted as a membrane of sorts. It was a sound that could unnerve even the strongest of people, and I wondered if the noise disturbed Noah. Coming from the south, I couldn't imagine he'd ever heard anything like it.

Voices rose from below. I crept toward the window and pressed my forehead to the frosty pane and peered down. A man in his robe was removing the cover from the hot tub while a woman in her robe transferred her weight from one slippered foot to the other as she eagerly waited. As soon as they removed the cover, both quickly shed their slippers and robes and jumped into the hot, steaming water. The smell of chlorine wafted up to the open window.

Aspen slid to a lying position, gave me a look that said, "I can't believe you're stooping to this level," and rolled onto his side. He closed his eyes as if not seeing me would make it not so. "Being a voyeur is awkward enough without your judgment, Aspen," I whispered to him. He lazily opened one eye and closed it again.

I listened anyway as they talked. I then realized that talking softly wouldn't allow one to hear another over the loud hum of the hot tub's motor. When the man said something—something I can't repeat here—about their upcoming plans for the night, she giggled as she nestled closer into him. My face flushed, and I crouched before

I quickly shut the window and crouched again. I stepped back before I stood. How embarrassing for guests to think they were staying at an inn with a perverted owner. Taking another step back, I began losing my balance and instinctively reached back to catch myself. I gasped and tears sprung to my eyes as a sharp, stabbing pain ripped through the fingers of my left hand. I buried my mouth in my elbow pit, silencing a yowl I couldn't stop. At the rate I was going, I'd be having a cast on *both* hands.

When it was safe to uncover my mouth, I inspected my hand and saw a diamond earring stud sticking out of the pad of my middle finger. "Appropriate," I muttered. I'd noticed this earring during the teatime that had begun the rollout of the whole disastrous mess of the past few days. The diamond glimmered with unusual rainbow colors. Wincing as I pulled it from my flesh, I sucked the blood from my finger—gross, I know—and studied the earring carefully, wondering if it was a crystal rather than a genuine diamond. I wished I could remember who was wearing them. Common sense said it was Tootsie, Carmen, or Tina. Since Carmen was a stay-at-home mom who catered to her family's needs, regardless of whether it was a diamond or a crystal, Tootsie or Tina seemed more likely the owner.

Not wanting to get chastised for interfering with an investigation by removing evidence—and eager to put this whole thing to bed—I put the earring on the end table before snatching it back and dropping it into my pocket. They'd find my blood or DNA on it. I mentally traveled back to that afternoon. Unfortunately, the pain in my hand overshadowed my memory.

As I searched through the rest of the small suite, the pain lessened, and my head cleared. I remembered someone wearing that earring but couldn't remember exactly who it was. I focused on that afternoon in question until I thought I'd wasted my last brain cell. I'd seen both Tootsie and Tina wearing them, but at different times. I couldn't imagine they'd be sharing earrings. Given that diamond studs were probably the most common, both were likely to have them. But even if that was true, why would it show up in Carmen's room? It made no sense.

The buzz I'd gotten from finding a clue to help solve the case evaporated when I found not a shred of anything else. I heaved a sigh and slumped onto the edge of the loveseat when I realized I hadn't searched between the cushions or underneath. I dropped to my knees and got down on my elbows to scan the narrow gap between the furniture and the floor. Nothing. Rising to my knees again, I studied the cushions carefully. Was it worth the risk of intense pain by using my hands to remove the cushions and yet again come up with nothing? I hemmed and hawed for a hot minute before standing. Detective Griffin or Noah could do it. One last glance around the suite and I went to the door, opened it, then turned around. Curiosity, a relentless bugger, dragged me back into the room.

Gently, I leaned over and investigated between the arm of the loveseat and one cushion, between the two cushions, and finally between the other arm and the cushion. Nothing. The door creaked open behind me, and I froze.

Chapter 24

"Well, looky here," Detective Griffin said, his voice low and rigid. "I can only imagine what you're doing."

I stood, one foot, then the other, turned toward him, and forced a smile. "Helping?" I said sheepishly.

"Helping with what, exactly?"

"I found an earring stuck into the carpet—which then stuck into my hand." I attempted to get it from my pocket but failed. Unlike dropping it in when I found it, I couldn't fit my hand to the bottom of the pocket.

"You seem to be in quite a predicament." He shook his head and growled. "Have one of the ladies get it out for you. And for God's sake, have her wear gloves. It's bad enough you contaminated the evidence. Again."

Embarrassment threatened to swallow me up. "Okay."

"I'm almost afraid to ask this question, but what were you doing on the floor? And *why*," he said, forcefully, "do you insist on getting in my way?"

"It's not like I wanted to stick my hand with an earring," I said defensively. "I'm not a masochist. How did you know they left, anyway?"

"When I couldn't reach either of them, I called the front desk gal. The bigger question is, why didn't *you* tell me? Or tell Noah, for God's sake."

"Because I just found out myself. And I didn't want to keep him from dinner. Izzy made stuffed butternut squash."

He inhaled deeply, his chest expanding. He let it out slowly. "How thoughtful. You're gonna be the death of that man after I leave."

I made a face. "I hope not. We've had enough death around here." He made it clear he wasn't about to share information, so I said, "I'll go get Noah." Maybe he would be more forthcoming.

"I'm already here," Noah said from around the corner of the doorway. "That I'm not surprised you got here before us again scares me."

Detective Griffin snickered. "Fast learner." He looked at me. "Scram."

I sighed. "Okay. But you have to admit, I found some pretty sound evidence."

"Evidence that we would have found, and that you contaminated before we could get to it."

"Oops."

"That's why we ask the public to stay away from an investigation," Noah said. "And right now, you're the public."

I started to speak then pressed my lips together and turned to leave when a syringe off to the side of the door and stuck into a rug seized my attention. "What's—"

Detective Griffin was by the syringe in a heartbeat, his arm straight out, blocking me from getting closer. "Go!"

I put both hands up and sidestepped toward the door. "Yep. I'm going. But so you know, the earring I found belongs to either Tootsie or Tina." Their expressions begged for an explanation, but I was hesitant in expounding on the situation in case I inadvertently backed myself in a corner again.

"How do you know that?" Noah finally asked.

Fast forwarding scenarios in my head on possible repercussions, I found it safe to say, "I remember both wearing them. Not at the same time, of course. Tootsie at teatime that afternoon, and Tina a different time. I can't remember exactly." Their expressions begged for further explanation, but learning a valuable lesson, I kept my mouth shut.

Detective Griffin said, "*Both* of them?"

"It's not surprising if they both had their own pair. I'd guess diamond studs are one of the most common. The interesting piece is that I found it in Carmen's room." I pointed to the syringe, still unmoved. "And then there's that."

Noah said, "Yes, don't you worry. We'll handle *that*."

I turned again to leave.

"Hey, Andie Rose?" he said.

"Yeah?"

"Thanks. That helps."

I grinned. "See how much better it is when we work together?" Detective Griffin tugged at his mustache and Noah drew his eyebrows together over eyes that hypnotized me momentarily. "Okay, I'm going now."

The door yawned closed on its own behind me. Draft or ghost? "Lady Lucy," I whispered.

I stopped by a window and drank in the evening's darkened clear sky dotted with stars. It was hard to believe the space beneath such beautiful darkness could hold even darker secrets.

Before going back downstairs, I stopped in at my suite to nurse my emotional wounds and snag some time to think uninterrupted.

233

When I opened the door, shadows danced on the walls in the moonlight and compelled me to duck. Feeling like a fool, I gently kicked the door shut behind me and locked it before retrieving the notecards from the brainstorming session with Sister Alice and Wes. I wondered, again, whether it was a smart move to include Wes in on that session, but then reminded myself that since he'd gotten himself into this mess, he could help get himself out of it. Taking responsibility is a huge part of sobriety. I just hoped his hands were clean of the entire ordeal and we hadn't instead given him a means of escape.

Lying the notecards out on my bed in the appropriate columns, I stepped back and studied them. I was missing something huge that was right in front of me. Even though I could feel it, it seemed out of reach.

Moving a few of the notecards around, I scrutinized them again. Still nothing. I wrote some additional thoughts on a few more cards and placed them accordingly, my handwriting more like chicken scratch or a doctor's handwriting on a prescription pad. Once more I drew back to scrutinize them, crossed my arms in front of me, then lifted them behind my head. The only thing that popped up were more questions; questions I hoped a few phone calls could answer. The first to Frank.

I punched in his number, and he promptly answered. "Good evening, Miss Andie."

"Hi, Frank. Got a minute?"

"I was just about to call my daughter, but I can take a minute for you, um-hm."

My heart grew heavy. "So you're going to move in with her, then?"

"I can't expect you to give me a raise just so I can

pay my bills, Miss Andie. 'Specially not after the trouble and bother I got you into."

"I trust you would do nothing like that again, Frank." When he didn't reply, I pleaded, "Will you at least hold off on making a final decision until we've talked face-to-face?"

He hesitated, then said reluctantly, "I guess that's the least I could do, um-hm."

"Thank you, Frank." I was just about to hang up when I remembered the reason I'd called to begin with. "Before you go—" I paused a minute, partly afraid of both the answer I didn't want to hear and for an answer I did. "I have a question." He remained quiet. "The new deadbolt on the door to the back room of the gardening shed, why did you—"

"I know where this is going, Miss Andie. I didn't—"

My heart fell at the attempt to lie. "Frank, I know it was you."

"I'm not denying that I put a deadbolt on there, Miss Andie."

"Then why did you say you didn't? Please, Frank. All I'm asking is that you're truthful with me."

"I always am and always have been, um-hm." His tone let me know I'd hurt his feelings. "I started to say I didn't want young Izzy to get in there again because I was goin' to use it for storin' chemicals like worm cutter, bug killer, paint and thinner, and such. You know how some a those kids like to huff paint. It's dangerous."

I heaved a sigh and sank down onto the edge of my bed. What a heel I'd been. After apologizing profusely for jumping to conclusions and seeking his forgiveness, we hung up. But not without a trace of strain that lingered between us.

Taking a few minutes to regroup, I stared out at the dazzling evening sky and took a few deep breaths. Then I called Simon. Not surprisingly, it rolled into voicemail. While his message played, I scrambled to decide whether to leave a voicemail or try calling back later. He'd probably ignore calls from my area code, regardless. If I left a message asking him to call me as soon as possible, at least there was a snowball's chance he would get it.

Next, I called Tina. Taken aback that it rolled to voicemail with room to leave one, I began speaking when she answered. "Hallo?"

"Tina, it's Andie Rose from the Spirit Lake Inn."

"Hi, Andie Rose. We're almost there. We—"

"Wait! Jerry's with you?"

"Of course he is. Why wouldn't he be?"

I couldn't decide if I was relieved or disappointed, or simply more confused. "Where was he?"

"What do you mean where was he?"

I scratched my head. "You checked out early to pick him up. Is he okay?"

She laughed. "Oh, boy. How things get so blown out of proportion. Of course. There's nothing to worry about."

Again, I scratched my head, then my neck. "Okay, then. But I've been trying to call you and your voicemail box was full."

"Again, no mystery. I just needed to empty it." I imagined her rolling her eyes with irritation. "Anywho, the reason for your call?"

"Just making sure Jerry was okay is all." *And alive.*

"Rest assured, he's fine. You can see for yourself in just a few seconds. As I was saying, I lost an earring there. I can't seem to find it anywhere."

Playing it totally cool, I said, "An earring?"

"Yes. It used to be my grandmother's. I must have left it in our room."

More like in Carmen's room. Unless… Oh, shoot. More questions popped up in my head. Every time when I thought I'd finally solved the murder.

"The police have the earring, Tina. "They've been trying to get a hold of you, too."

"What are you talking about, Andie Rose? Why would they have my earring? And why would they want to talk to me about it?"

"Did you leave behind anything else?" I asked.

"Like what?" There was a subtle change in her voice, of what I couldn't decipher.

"Maybe a syringe?"

"I'm diabetic and could have dropped a needle, I suppose. Why? Surely that's not a crime."

Finding it in someone else's room might be.

When I kept quiet, she cleared her throat. "Just come out and ask your question."

Here goes nothin'. "Did something happen between Jerry and Tootsie?"

"What?" she screeched. "Are you crazy?"

"I only ask, because on the night Jerry didn't come back, Tootsie didn't return either."

She scoffed. "I'm confused, Andie Rose. How does Tootsie failing to return involve us? Jerry is right here. With me. And did whoever found Tootsie ask her? What did she say?"

I took a deep breath. "Nothing. She was murdered."

Tina gasped. "What does my earring have to do with this? And why do the police want to talk with me and

Jerry?"

I knew I was walking on thin ice with information here. If I said too much, I could blow the investigation. If I didn't say enough, I wouldn't get *any* information.

Hers and Jerry's voices were muffled as they spoke back and forth with one another. I tilted my head back, wishing I had an uninjured hand with which to massage the taut muscles in my neck.

Finally, Tina came back on the line, sparing me the impossible decision of how much to say, "You know what, Andie Rose? This is ridiculous, and we don't have time for this. Tell the police they can cross us off their suspect list. We have absolutely no idea what happened to Tootsie. We're turning around and going back home. If they want to talk with me or Jerry, they can come to us. And the earring? Mail the darn thing." The line went dead.

"That wasn't suspicious at all," I said into the empty room. And I didn't believe for a minute that they were going back home.

I stared at the phone while contemplating the next best step, then turned to run and notify Detective Griffin and Noah. Forgetting Aspen was in back of me, I toppled over him. My head cracked on something hard, and the room spun around me as I lay on the floor, trying to get a grip on what happened. Aspen's nose touched mine, then his tongue lapped my cheek. I groaned and, forgetting about the cast, flung my hand to my head and wailed in pain. That was the last thing I remembered.

I awoke to a knock on my door, followed by a male's voice.

"Andie Rose, are you home?"

Aspen, sitting beside me, barked, sending pain

shooting through my head.

The man rapped on the door again, and said louder, "Andie Rose, are you in there?"

Confused and still trying to reorient myself, I opened my mouth but couldn't utter a word. Memory returned, bringing embarrassment at my clumsiness. I ran my tongue over my lips. "I'm here," I croaked. Aspen, my phone under his paw, barked again, and I pressed my eyes closed.

"She must have left the dog in the room."

"Maybe she's downstairs," another man said. The sound of footsteps retreated from my room and down the hallway.

When my head began clearing from the fog and the pain, I sat up gingerly and grimaced at the throbbing in my hip and tailbone. I stretched them gently. Miraculously, I hadn't landed on my hands. Who knew owning the inn would be so dangerous for my health?

Aspen nudged his nose against my arm and leaned into me again, as if hoisting me to a standing position. I snatched up my phone and popped some ibuprofen, wishing for a brandy chaser about now. I handed Aspen a special peanut butter dog biscuit. Okay, what had I been doing? I knew it was something critical, but … I recalled the voices at the door. Detective Griffin and Noah. And then it all came back at neck-breaking speed.

I made for the door, this time paying attention, Aspen right on my heels. He'd long since devoured his treat—the only thing, other than whipped cream, he ate with any gusto. Holding onto the handrail as I descended the steps, I strode up to the front desk, where Izzy was talking with Jade.

"Did either of you see Detective Griffin and Noah

come by here?"

Izzy said, "They left a few minutes ago." She got starry eyed. "That hunk of a man, Noah, went with Griffin to check out a lead.

"Tina and Jerry Anson," I exclaimed.

Jade frowned. "They left a long time ago. You already knew that."

"I know. I need to catch Detective Griffin."

From behind me, Izzy said, "Don't catch Mr. Hottie. He's mine."

As I snagged my coat from the rack by the door, I heard Jade scoff. "He's decades too old for you." Followed by, "Ouch. I can't believe you smacked me, ya little twerp."

Once outside, I swept the grounds for any sign of them. Detective Griffin's car wasn't there, but Noah's was still in the lot. I snagged my phone from my pocket and tapped the speed dial number assigned to Griffin when I saw a few missed calls from Sister Alice. I'd call her back, but not until I got a hold of Griffin or Noah first.

When it rolled into voicemail, I said, "Detective Griffin, call me. It's urgent." Right before I disconnected, I said, "Oh. It's Andie Rose." *As if he wouldn't know, dummy.*

I wondered whether Noah hitched a ride with him to wherever they were going, which I figured was most likely the case, or if they split up, Noah investigating something here at the inn. I called Noah and heard a faint ringing in the frosty night air toward the gardening shed, followed by silence.

"Come on, Aspen." I said as I scurried in that direction.

****

Sister Alice was in the rectory celebrating Father Vincent's birthday with him, Sister Ida, and Sister Eunice who made a special celebratory meal for him. His favorite—German bratwurst with sauerkraut, potato dumplings, and Black Forest gateau for dessert. She'd even gotten a growler of Rothaus' Pils Tannen Zäpfle, his favorite German beer, of which Father Vincent was most appreciative.

"I wish I could have seen the expression on the man's face when you bought this," Sister Alice told her as she set it on the table with cooled goblets. Sister Ida surprised her by accepting a goblet.

"Don't be so surprised, Alice," Sister Ida said. "I'm not a complete stick in the mud."

Uffda! *From your lips to God's ears.*

They celebrated all of their birthdays and holidays with meals at this old, oblong, dark wood table. Mostly, this old wood has heard polite conversations. But there had been a time or two that Sister Ida hadn't been there, when the conversation was livelier. That's when this old table heard laughter. Sure, they all loved Sister Ida, but she couldn't possibly be more different from the rest of them. Each worked to respect her no-nonsense, stern nature, except Sister Alice usually failed.

Sister Alice poured sparkling apple juice in her own goblet, they raised their glasses, and Sister Ida, as the house moderator, gave the toast. A dry one at that. Sister Alice closed her eyes for a moment. When Sister Ida was done, Sister Alice stood to make a toast as well. Instead, Sister Ida said, "Here! Here!" and glasses clinked together, closing her window to liven it up.

Sister Eunice took a gulp of beer and with a sputter,

it sprayed all over Sister Ida. Everyone sat stock still, in shock, including Sister Ida.

"Ack!" Sister Eunice said, breaking the tension. "This is terrible."

As if in slow motion, Sister Ida reached for her napkin and began blotting her face with it. Finally she said, "You might have taken a small sip until you know whether you like it." Her tone was taut.

Sister Alice held her breath and glanced at Father Vincent who appeared stunned as well, then back to Sister Ida.

"Well, I've never tasted beer before, only wine. I didn't think it would taste like skunk."

"And how would you know what skunk tastes like?" Sister Ida said, brushing the front of her blouse with a new napkin.

Like swivel head dolls, Father Vincent and Sister Alice turned from one to the other until Sister Ida's resolve cracked. A smile began to form, her shoulders shook slightly, until unable to contain it any longer, she doubled over in laughter. Sister Eunice gawked at her as if she'd lost her mind, Father Vincent and Sister Alice wide-eyed and quiet. Until Sister Alice laughed with Sister Ida, followed by the other two. With tears in her eyes and holding her side, Sister Ida finally regained her composure. The rest followed, bubbles of laughter unable to be contained, continuing.

Sister Ida said, "I haven't laughed that hard since someone asked the paper to print an article they sent. The headline read, "Local Business Cuts Staff in Half." She laughed again at the memory.

Sister Alice stared at her and said, "I'm kinda scared right now. Who are you?" She was indeed witnessing a whole new side of Sister Ida. Proof one never really knows anyone through and through.

"Relax, Alice" she said. "You'd see this side more often if you weren't so busy avoiding me."

Father Vincent quieted a snort, and Sister Alice glanced at him.

Sister Eunice, apparently still mulling over the headline, said, "Was that supposed to be a modern-day take on King Solomon's suggestion of gleaning out the true mother of the child two women claimed as their own?"

Sister Ida, Sister Alice, and Father Vincent all swiveled their heads to stare at her.

"For the love, please tell me you're joking," Sister Alice said.

Sister Eunice raised her shoulders and let them drop. "What?"

"Eunice," Sister Ida said, back to her serious self, "it was a misspelling of a grievous nature. It was supposed to say, "Local Business Cuts Staff *by* Half.""

Sister Alice's phone rang, and she glanced at the display.

"Hi Andie. Can I call—" She heard Aspen bark on the other end of the line. "Andie Rose?"

Aspen barked again and she heard shuffling in the background. Sister Alice ended the call, blotted her mouth with her napkin, and set it on top of her dessert before she rose.

"Who was that?" Sister Ida asked.

"Aspen."

"Who?" Father Vincent said, clearly puzzled.

"Andie Rose's dog, Aspen. She needs my help."

Sister Eunice chuckled. "You didn't even drink any

beer and you're hearing dogs talk to you?"

"Something's wrong. I can feel it."

Getting Father Vincent's permission to use his car, Sister Alice made her apologies and quickly left.

****

As we followed the trampled snow toward the shed, the lake groaned, and a squirrel barked its annoyance at our intrusion.

When I reached the shed, Noah was lying in the snow as if he'd fallen backward to make a snow angel. Until I got up closer and used my phone's flashlight app to see his eyes were closed and a trace of blood seeped scarlet into the otherwise dove-white snow beneath his head.

"Noah." I said into the night as I stooped beside him. "What happened?"

From the corner of my eye, I caught movement. Instinctively, I stood and whirled around, face to face with Bobby, menacingly holding one of the monster-sized icicles from the inn's eve in his gloved hand.

I took slow steps backward. If I turned and ran, I'd be going straight into the woods. Not exactly a viable option if I wanted to live. The only way I could get back to the inn was if I passed Bobby, and I didn't see that happening without a fight.

"What did you do to Noah?" I asked, sidestepping as discreetly as I could.

He clucked his tongue as he shook his head slowly. "He won't know what hit him. Or rather, *who*. And since you'll be the one left here with him, even though you'll be dead, he'll think it was you." He held up the icicle. "The perfect crime. Leaves no trace. No fingerprints, nothing. I'm finding wintertime in Spirit Lake to be quite opportunistic. A hole in the ice, icicles—"

"*You* killed Tootsie." He walked slowly toward me as I took small diagonal steps. The progress was infinitesimal, but at least I was moving in the right direction, giving me a chance, no matter how small. Conversations from the past few days played in my head like a movie reel. "You didn't hear about Tootsie's affair from Simon at all. You heard her from the window that night when she told Carmen in the hot tub." But then I remembered the order in which they'd supposedly all left the hot tub that night. "But how could she have told Carmen when Jerry was still in the hot tub when Carmen left. Did she admit it in front of him, too?"

"He didn't say anything so he was probably in using the can. Not all of us men are animals and go in the water."

I shuddered at the thought and vowed not to use a public hot tub until I could scrub that from my brain. "So, you conveniently elaborated on a story to make the police focus on Simon. But why did you care what Tootsie was doing? It had nothing to do with you."

His lips curled as he sneered. "Oh, but it did. Carmen was happy and fulfilled as a wife and mother. She's never wanted anything else. Me and the kids were enough for her and depend on her."

Still sidestepping, I worked to keep him talking while I did. "So *you*, not necessarily Carmen, was happy with the way things were."

"You're wrong. Carmen's whole life is me and our kids. Tootsie was convincing my wife that there's much more to life than just staying home with her husband and kids. Can you believe it?" He snorted contemptuously. "And then she said the affair spiced up the sex life with her husband and suggested that Carmen try it. That it livens up the marital bed." He shuddered. "What a sinful disregard and disrespect for marriage."

In one action, Bobby glanced toward Noah, and Aspen sprung toward Bobby. He gripped Bobby's pant leg between his teeth. With Bobby distracted, I grabbed the small window of opportunity, and darted past him. Free of Aspen, he reached out an arm and grabbed me, yanking me backward into him, one arm around my neck, the other holding the icicle above his head. As he sliced it downward, I reached up with my cast hand and deflected the blow. Part of the icicle shot off into the darkness. As he reached up to hammer it down once again, Aspen barked and lunged at him again, while I smashed my cast back into Bobby's face. The sound of bone crunching turned my stomach. Bobby's grip around my shoulders loosened as he cursed a few choice words, giving me the precise opportunity I needed to twist away from him.

With Bobby occupied staunching the flow of blood from his nose, and in apparent shock, I dropped to my knees beside Noah and checked for a pulse as I called 911.

The 911 operator answered just as Aspen barked, and from my peripheral, I saw Bobby lift his hands high above his head, clutching the broken, but still deadly, icicle. As he hauled it down, I flinched and held up a forearm, waiting for the inevitable strike.

"Hi-YAH!" I opened an eye as Bobby spun around in time to catch Sister Alice with a shovel held above her head with both hands. She whacked it across his arms, and he cried out with impressive expletives. He dropped to his knees.

In shock myself, and perhaps disoriented, thanks to my self-inflicted head injury, I struggled with the pieces of the evolving scene.

Sister Alice, feet planted apart, held the shovel over Bobby, ready to come down on him.

"Don't dare to even so much as blink," she warned him, which scared even me.

I knew nothing about the life of a sister, but I was pretty sure murder wasn't allowed. Disconnecting from the 911 operator, I asked Sister Alice, "How did you know to come out here?"

Keeping vigilant watch on Bobby, she said, "Aspen."

Hearing his name, he trotted toward her, planting himself beside her.

I squished my eyebrows together. "Aspen? Have you been nippin' at the bottle?"

Her eyes widened as she cut a glance at me and back to her subject. "Right? I wouldn't have believed it either. And you should have seen Sister Ida give me the *what for* without a single word. I think she's getting ready to have me committed to an asylum. When I got here to check things out, I followed Aspen's barking and to where the foul language led. This time from someone other than you. And here I am. Let's call it divine intervention."

"Let's call it what it is, Aspen's a genius."

Movement behind Sister Alice caused a surge of adrenaline, and I sprang forward. Sister Alice's jaw dropped as I lunged toward her.

"Watch out," I yelled. She and Aspen both ducked, and I flew right over the top of them and into a shocked Carmen. My cast, once again, connected with bone. As painful as this break was, getting more so by the minute, it was also turning out to be quite the convenience.

Carmen cried out, causing Bobby to stir, which, in turn, led Sister Alice to lift the shovel above him once more. I sucked in a breath in anticipation of what she would do. Aspen left her side and strolled toward me. He licked my neck, his tongue hot on my cold skin.

The only sounds in the woods were Bobby and Carmen's groans. The squirrel had even scampered somewhere far away, probably deciding humans were far more dangerous than dogs.

Sirens came along and pierced the silence along with my throbbing head. Noah stirred and slowly pushed himself up. "Mother of Mary, what happened?"

Sister Alice snickered. "What d'ya know. Another Catholic in your life, Grasshopper."

"Funny," I said to her. Then to Noah, "I saved your ass, that's what happened. You owe me."

Chapter 25

Sudden bright light and the smell of banana bread and coffee pried open my eyes. I squinted at the glaring sunlight streaming through the open curtains.

"Good afternoon, sunshine."

I glanced through slits in my eyelids at Sister Alice as she leaned against the door frame. She sported yellow frames today, along with a yellow sweater and the usual crucifix draped around her neck. It took me a minute to get my bearings straight, and I sat up too quickly, getting lightheaded. Aspen was curled up next to me on the bed.

"What time is it?" I asked, still groggy.

"Twelve-oh-five."

I gasped. "My alarm."

"Guess you forgot to set it with all the commotion."

I blinked and shook my head slowly. "It's scheduled to go off automatically at the same time every morning."

"Oh. Well, I might have turned it off last night before I left."

I squinched my face. "Why would you do that? I have an inn to run."

"Don't get your knickers in a twist. I've taken care of Aspen, and the inn is running smoothly. Everything is golden."

I lay back against my pillows again. "My arm is throbbing."

"I'm not surprised. You broke some bones with that

thing last night."

My thoughts wandered back to the night before, remembering all that had gone down. It was one in the morning by the time I got back to the inn from a visit to the emergency room. Noah received treatment for a concussion and three stitches in his cheek, released with the appropriate instructions. None of which he'd probably follow since it required him to take it easy. Not unlike me, I guess.

Bobby had a few cuts, a deep one on his forearm— I guess it's allowable for sisters to assault people for the right reason—and both he and Carmen received treatment for broken noses. Nothing that couldn't heal in a jail cell. I had to get my hand recast, this time up to my elbow; the already-injured bones had shifted, causing more damage up into my wrist.

"I thought casts protected broken bones," I'd said to the doctor as he delivered the news to me.

"They do," he'd said grimly. "But they're not intended for battle."

Still, I figured I'd gotten off reasonably lucky compared to the rest.

"Bobby," I finally said, staring past Sister Alice. "One of the few who didn't have a motive that I knew of." I looked at her. "Have you talked to Wes?"

"He'll be out later."

"I'll take that as a yes." I closed my eyes and groaned. "Guess I owe him an apology."

"He understands how it appeared and admits his stupidity. He said no more married women, that he's going to try for you. But he's not Catholic, so I vote for the handsome new detective."

"Oh, good Lord," I mumbled and closed my eyes

again, resting my right arm over my eyes.

"Detective Griffin is stopping by this afternoon. He's rather impressed with how you helped Noah."

I lowered my arm a tad and peered at Sister Alice. "Correction: I didn't *help* him. I *saved* him."

She chuckled. "I brought you up a piece of banana bread and a cup of coffee. Thought you could use it."

"Just one piece and one cup? How about the full pan and the whole pot?"

She pinched her nose. "Take a shower. I'll be downstairs waiting. Detective Griffin will be here at two. He and Noah both want to talk with you before Noah heads for home."

It felt like an entire month's worth of life happened in the brief span of the few hours that I slept.

She made for the door, and I said, "Sister Alice?" She turned back toward me. "Thank you. For everything."

"Father Vincent recommended I take a leave of absence, so I have enough time to watch over you."

"He did not."

"Nah, he didn't. Now hurry up."

I got up and locked the door behind her. I had to make one important phone call before I showered. Izzy.

****

By one o'clock, I had showered and slipped into a hoodie and yoga pants. My damp hair hung loose past my shoulders. For the first time in probably ever, I hadn't even attempted to apply eyeliner and mascara.

I sauntered downstairs, where Detective Griffin and Noah relaxed in front of the fireplace in the parlor with a cup of tea.

"Good afternoon, gentlemen." I sat on one of the

wingback chairs.

"Well, if it isn't Sleeping Beauty," Detective Griffin said.

I grinned. "Where's Sister Alice?"

"Had to run to the church for a minute. Said she'd be right back. We'll fill you in on everything once you're both in here."

As if on cue, she waltzed through the door, slipped out of her coat, and tossed it over the back of a chair. She strolled to the fireplace and warmed her hands.

"We're waiting for you to sit down," I said.

She turned toward us. "Why? Something else happen?"

"Why would you ask that?"

She tucked her chin, her eyebrows raised. "Come again?"

"I'm impatiently waiting to get the last details of the case." I looked at the two detectives.

"Who was it that found Tootsie's body and called it in? I couldn't find a solid answer for that."

"Because you're not a trained detective," Noah said.

"So tell me who it was."

Both detectives glanced at each other and then down at the floor. "We found the burner phone in a snow drift along the shoreline. Wiped clean."

"So you didn't discover who it was either?" I raised my eyebrows at Noah. "What happened to being a *trained detective*?"

"We're still determined to find out who it was. He may not have been the murderer, but he still committed a crime."

I rolled my eyes and ran my hand over my face. "*Oy vey*. You won't admit it, but you're going to need my help, Detective Parker."

"Oh, godfrey!" Detective Griffin laughed. "I'm so glad I'm done with this town."

I winked at him and smiled. "No you're not. Can you tell me what the deal was with Carmen? She was guilty as sin in every respect. All arrows pointed to her."

"Poor woman," Noah said as he sat back and crossed one leg over the other, ankle resting on his knee. "She got caught up in something much bigger than she was equipped to handle."

"Such as?" I asked.

Detective Griffin said, "She thought Bobby had something to do with it and was trying to protect him. She's so dependent on him I think she's scared to death to live without him. And as far as the thing you thought Carmen had with Simon, she was protecting him as well. She felt guilty that Bobby placed the blame on an innocent man."

"But Carmen's footprints leading into the woods toward the gardening shed?"

Detective Griffin heaved a sigh. "We don't have an answer for that. Bobby insists it was him who locked you in because you wouldn't stop investigating and let the police zero in on Simon. But I'm not sure I buy that. He's probably protecting Carmen. Either way, both deny unlocking it."

I asked the obvious. "Did you ask Carmen?"

"Hadn't even thought of that," Detective Griffin scoffed. "Of course I did. But she said she wasn't there. We'll never know. And if she did, we'll never know why. But Bobby, supporting husband that he is, coached her into letting him take the fall since he was already going down, anyway."

Thank you, Lady Lucy. I smiled, sat back in the chair and stared into the fire.

"Think of it this way," Sister Alice said. "You got back at her by popping her in the nose."

Detective Griffin said, "Always the one to find the silver lining."

We chuckled before silence settled around us for a moment.

"So Simon never told Bobby about Tootsie's affair. He overheard it when she told Carmen about it and elaborated on details to plant the focus on Simon."

"Yep," Noah said. "A real stand-up guy. Carmen really did crash that night in the Timmons' room, so Bobby was completely free to do what he wanted to."

"What was the deal with Jerry?" I asked. "Where was he and why was Tina acting so weird about it?"

Detective Griffin coughed and popped a cough drop in his mouth. "Apparently he called an Uber to take him into town." He made air quotes and said, "Passed out in a bar."

"But that wasn't exactly the truth," Noah chipped in. "Not exactly anyway."

I gave him a questioning look. "Meaning?"

"He passed out with a woman in her car. Tina was trying to cover for him."

I grimaced. "Why?"

"She said she threatened him within an inch of his life if she ever caught him doing something so stupid again. Said she wasn't about to have her reputation destroyed by his foolishness."

I shook my head slowly. "Nice. See why I'm single?"

"Don't paint all of us with the same brush," Noah

said.

Sister Alice grinned. "Especially the Catholic ones."

I laughed and stared into the fire again, absorbing it all. Aspen sprawled lazily in front of the fire. "How did I totally miss so much?"

"We already told you, because you're not a trained detective," Griffin said. "Yet another reason to leave the investigating to the police."

I narrowed my eyes at him. "As I recall, you didn't catch on either."

Noah chuckled, and another moment of thoughtful silence settled before, as usual, Sister Alice lightened things up.

"Grasshopper, who'd a thought we'd have so much police contact years after."

"After what?" Noah asked, unaware of Sister Alice's background.

"Pshaw. I'm not Andie Rose's sponsor because I have a flawless background."

Noah's jaw dropped. "You?"

"We didn't know each other back then," I said. "She was close to Grandpop and Honey. I only officially met her when I moved here."

"And Spirit Lake has never been the same."

His tone was gruff, but I could see a smile lurking.

"I remember once when I was in a bar somewhere—"

"Once," Sister Alice said with a snort.

I grinned. "Yeah. I guess back then I was *always* in a bar *somewhere*—" All three of them laughed. "The police were at the table right next to me. They weren't in uniform, but I knew they were police." I giggled at the absurdity of it. "I swear they were just waiting for me to leave. So I ordered soda all night, making sure they knew it. Eventually they got bored and left."

"If they weren't in uniform," Detective Griffin said, "did you ever think they were just out having a drink? We like to kick back with a drink now and again, too. We're human."

"Back then, the entire world was about me. Don't take that away."

Izzy peered around the corner at me, and, struggling to keep a straight face, I waved her in. "Gentlemen," I said as she approached with a tray, "I've arranged for a celebratory treat." Izzy uncovered the tray, producing a mouthwatering display of white chocolate chip blondies. The two men blanched. "Detective Griffin, there are some without nuts, so you can enjoy them as well."

Still speechless, his attention bounced from me to Izzy, until he growled, "Is this a joke?" Unable to contain it any longer, I laughed. Noah, unsure of how to respond, looked tentatively at Detective Griffin, then at us and let out a belly laugh that would make a baby envious.

Detective Griffin waved away at the tray. "Think I'll pass."

I said, "Noah, do you have something you'd like to say to me?"

His forehead crinkled. "Not that I know of. Like what?"

"Like *Thank you, Andie Rose, for saving my butt*."

His eyes twinkled. "You wouldn't have had to save my butt if your staff hadn't started the ball rolling with laced bars."

I cocked my head to the side. "Fair enough."

"There's something you can do for me to make up for it, though. I need a place to stay for a couple of weeks until I find a place to live."

I thought about Max Winters' upcoming reservation. "Starting when?"

"Tomorrow."

A weird feeling I couldn't describe settled in my stomach. "Hmm." I pondered the idea, and the weird feeling intensified. "I think we can make that happen."

A word about the author…

Rhonda is a retired paralegal and victim witness specialist, an exercise enthusiast, avid reader, lover of words, and coffee and dark chocolate connoisseur. She is the author of The Inheritance, a contemporary women's fiction novel; seven books in the Melanie Hogan cozy mystery series; and Finding Abby and Abby's Redemption, a romantic suspense duology. She is also an indie author consultant and was awarded the 2022 Master of Literary Arts Award from the Brighton Chamber in Colorado. She can be found at her online home at www.rhondablackhurst.com.